TREASURE COAST
Discovery

EMERALD BAY
BOOK 5

LEIGH DUNCAN

Treasure Coast Discovery
Emerald Bay, Book #5

Copyright ©2024 by Leigh D. Duncan

Digital ISBN: 978-1-944258-55-9
Print ISBN: 978-1-944258-54-2
Gardenia Street Publishing

Published in the United States of America

Welcome to Emerald Bay!

After a lifetime of running the finest inn in Emerald Bay, Margaret Clayton has to make a decision...sell the Dane Crown Inn to a stranger or put her hopes for the future in her family's hands. For most people, the choice would be simple. But nothing about her family is simple...especially not with her daughter and four nieces whose help Margaret needs now more than ever.

The five cousins know the inn as well as Margaret does. As young girls and teenagers, they spent every summer keeping the cottages and suites spotless, and enjoying the gorgeous beach as a tight knit family. Thirty years later, though, these five women have complicated, important, distant, and utterly packed lives. The last thing any of them can do is drop everything and save the inn. But, when it comes to family, the last thing is sometimes the *only* thing.

As the once-close cousins come together on the glorious shores of Florida's Treasure Coast, they learn that some things never change, but others can never be the same. And the only thing that matters is family which, like the Dane Crown Inn, is forever.

TREASURE COAST DISCOVERY

To get the most enjoyment from the Emerald Bay series, start with *Treasure Coast Homecoming* and read the books in order.

One

Belle

Belle's breath stalled in her chest as she stared up at the figure that loomed over her in the doorway of the little cottage behind the Dane Crown Inn. Over the last few months, she'd grown closer to Jason than to any man she'd ever known. He had, in fact, come to mean more to her than she'd thought any man ever could. She cared for him so much that, recently, she'd gone so far as to put a name to the feeling.

Love.

There. She'd said it. She was in love with Jason Dennis.

It didn't matter that she'd only whispered the words to herself in the privacy of the bedroom that had been hers ever since her mom brought her home from the hospital as a newborn. Her insides shimmied whenever she was around Jason. They could talk on the phone for hours about everything and nothing at all. She could—and did—go to him for advice, trusting that he'd give his honest opinion without expecting her to blindly follow it. She loved him—not because he carried the power to make or break a singer's career with the flick of a finger but despite it.

Until five minutes ago, she'd thought he felt the same way about her. After all, didn't his expression soften whenever he looked at her? Hadn't he mentioned plans for a future that included her? Didn't he call her each night just to hear how her day had gone? He'd even flown to Florida to meet her family and spend the weekend with her, hadn't he?

He had indeed.

But that was before. Before she'd opened the door of her makeshift studio and found him standing on the welcome mat. Before he'd stood in front of her, his body stiff and unyielding, his face an unreadable mask. Before she'd spotted her name on the cover of the latest edition of *Variety* Jason held in a clenched fist.

Was this the end of them?

"May I see that?" Belle extended her hand, palm open and expectant.

Jason handed the magazine over without saying a word.

Belle flipped pages until she found the article she dreaded reading. She scanned it quickly, her stomach sinking lower with every word. Just as she'd predicted soon after her career as a pop singer tanked, the entertainment industry's premier news source had featured her in a where-are-they-now article. Usually, those were reserved for aging rock stars or actors whose careers had long-since faded. In this case, however, *Variety* hadn't waited. Barely six months had passed since Noble Records had pulled the plug on her unreleased album and canceled her nationwide promotion tour.

After years at the top of the charts, Belle Dane has turned her attention in an altogether different direction. Word on the street has it that the former pop star is planning a return to her roots in gospel music with a newly formed band, The Emeralds. Whether she'll be any more successful in this endeavor than in her single, ill-fated foray into country music remains to be seen.

Unable to read any further, Belle closed the magazine. So much for her hope that she and Daclan could play a couple of gigs before they drew too much media attention. The article would put the paparazzi on alert. She wouldn't be at all surprised to see at least one—or as many as a dozen—reporters show up for the inaugural appearance of The Emeralds at the ribbon-cutting ceremony for Sunshine Villa, the long-awaited community center at the heart of Sunshine Village.

"So it's true?" Jason growled. "You've launched a whole new career without letting me know? We talk practically every day, and you didn't consider such a monumental move worth mentioning?"

"I didn't think I needed your permission," Belle said, feeling her own temper flare. She might love Jason, might actually be *in* love with him, but how she handled her career was her business, not his. Still, she hadn't intended to keep her plans a secret. At least, not now that she'd finally reached a decision. "I was going to tell you. Next week, when you came down for a visit. I'd planned to tell you all about it then."

Jason's shoulders rounded, defeat replacing the anger that had seemed to radiate from him in waves. "I thought I meant more to you than that. I thought…"

"You do," Belle rushed to reassure him. "You mean everything to me. I tried to bring it up the last time you were here. When we were in the game room, while we were playing Scrabble. But

4

then you got sick and…" Her voice trailed off. The terrible case of food poisoning had struck Jason hard and fast, ruining their plans for spending a quiet weekend together.

"It's been weeks since then," he pointed out. "You could have mentioned it at any point."

"This isn't the kind of thing I wanted to tell you over the phone." It hadn't helped that Jason had spent the last ten days in Europe on business. Between the time change and his busy schedule, their communications had been limited to recorded messages and a few brief snatches of conversation.

"Instead, you let me be blindsided by an article in *Variety*?" A note of incredulous disbelief framed his words. "Do you have any idea how many calls I've gotten about this? It's ignited a media firestorm. Everyone wants to know who The Emeralds are, who's representing them, which house they've signed with."

Belle sucked in a breath. "That's ridiculous. We haven't even played our first gig yet."

"So it *is* true."

"Why don't you come inside." Opening the door wider, she stepped aside. There was too much at stake—their relationship, her fledgling new career, his position at the head of Noble Records—to risk having this conversation where guests or employees of the Dane Crown Inn could overhear. When Jason hesitated, she added, "I need to take care of something first, but then I'll tell you everything. I promise. You want something to drink? Coffee? Tea?"

"Nothing, thanks." He lumbered into the living room of the small cottage, stopping on the mat just inside the door long enough to take in the electric piano in one corner, the array of mics clustered around two tall stools, a sound board off to one side.

Belle took a quick peek out the door. Relieved when she didn't spot Daclan or Jen on the pavered path that wound from the main house to the cottages, she hurriedly typed a text postponing their practice session. Once her cell phone whistled that the message was on its way, she took two bottles of water from the small fridge in the kitchenette and joined Jason on the couch.

"Nice setup." He tipped his unopened bottle toward the pair of mics. "Just two of you in the band?"

Belle nodded. "And Jen to run the sound board. Daclan's on guitar. I handle the vocals."

"Naturally." His eyes narrowed the tiniest bit. "Who's this Daclan?"

Was that a hint of jealousy she heard in Jason's voice?

Belle fought the laughter that bubbled up from her midsection despite the seriousness of the situation. Jason had no reason whatsoever to feel threatened by Daclan. Why, she was old enough to be the boy's mother.

"Relax," she soothed. "He's a friend of Caitlyn's. She heard him playing in the church praise band and convinced me to listen to him. The boy has talent. Tons of it. He's a little raw yet, but I'm working on that."

"Talented, huh?" Jason fired a barrage of questions. "What's his style? Does he play anything besides guitar? Can he sing?"

She could almost see the wheels turning in Jason's head. The man was always on the lookout for the next new shining star. She held up a hand. "Wait a minute. The kid doesn't even have his driver's license yet. He needs to grow a bit—as a musician and a person—before you sign him to a contract. Let me work with him for a while."

"I lo—" Jason laughed. "I like that you knew exactly where I was headed. Okay. The boy is off-limits. I'll leave him in your capable hands. You'll let me know when—and if—things change."

Belle traced an *X* over her chest. "Cross my heart," she said, happy to know that at least

Jason valued her opinion about the young player. She, perhaps more than he, understood the pressure that came hand-in-hand with every recording contract. It exerted itself in a thousand different ways, from the need to meet the record label's expectations right down to the hopes and dreams of the other members of the band. Like a mother hen protected its chick, she wanted to shield Daclan from that stress for as long as possible. Or, at least, until he was ready to handle it.

Beside her, Jason leaned forward. With his elbows resting on his knees, he twisted the top off the bottle of water Belle had handed him. His earlier statement to the contrary, he drank deeply. Replacing the cap on the bottle, he pointed to the magazine Belle had discarded on the coffee table. "You want to tell me what that's all about?"

"More than anything," she answered truthfully. The question was, once he heard her story, would the choices she'd made destroy any hope they had of building a future together?

"Take your time." Jason scanned the room. "I'm not going anywhere. Are you?"

"No, but…" Hoping to calm her racing heart, she took a steadying breath. When that didn't work, she took a couple more.

"Belle?" Jason prompted when several minutes had passed and she hadn't said anything.

"I, um, I'm not quite sure where to begin."

"You could start with that." He tapped the banner on the magazine cover. "Gospel music?"

"Yes and no." Like a lot of entertainment journalists, the writer of the *Variety* article had barely scratched the surface of their topic. "I'd say we're more eclectic. Yes, we sing some gospel, but we aren't limited to that. I'd call it more Christian music."

"It's an easy line to blur." Jason nodded. "Some sources say gospel is a subset of the Christian music genre. Others separate the two."

"Exactly." Why was she surprised that Jason understood the differences and similarities as well, or better than, she did? He hadn't climbed to the top of the music industry without developing an in-depth knowledge of all aspects of the subject. Belle shifted toward him, tucking one foot under her while she let her other leg dangle off the edge of the couch.

"I still don't understand why you didn't just tell me," Jason said with a touch of grumpiness.

Okay, she couldn't blame Jason for being upset with her. She should have confided in him. If for no other reason than because of his position as the head of Noble Records.

"You're right," she said. "I should have told you sooner. It's just that, well..." Her voice faltered. The decision to follow her heart had been a deeply personal one. One she hadn't discussed in depth with anyone. Oh, she'd hit the highlights with her cousins. And her mom knew a bit more of the story. The two of them had talked about her struggles, but even then, Belle had focused more on the difficulties she'd faced in making a decision. Not the options she was trying to choose from.

Jason, on the other hand, deserved more. Didn't he? He, of all the people in the world, was the one she wanted to know the whole truth. Even if he walked away from her after hearing it.

She took another breath. "I had a hard time accepting this was the direction I was supposed to go," she confessed. When surprise shone in the steely glint Jason focused on her, she refused to sugarcoat the truth. "You have to admit, there's not a huge upside to singing in churches on Sundays or at potluck dinners on Wednesday nights or at the occasional camp revival. The first few years, The Emeralds—the article got that part right. That's what we're calling ourselves," she explained. "If we're lucky, The Emeralds will make enough to pay for gas and meals. I'm certainly never going to be able to afford the lifestyle I had before."

"Is that important to you?" Jason asked evenly. "The luxury apartment? The fancy cars? The expensive artwork?"

She could lie, she told herself. She could say none of those things meant anything to her, but that wouldn't be the truth. Not really. And he needed to know the whole truth about her. Even if it painted her in a very dim light.

"For a long time, I thought it was." She wasn't particularly proud of that fact, but she wasn't going to lie. "Not because I loved the designer dresses or the fancy jewelry or hobnobbing with the rich and powerful. Mostly, I thought all the trappings of success were proof that I'd made the most of the talents I'd been given."

"And now?"

"I'm still a work in progress where that's concerned," she admitted. "You might say I've had a change of heart. I think when all is said and done, no one's going to look to see if you have piles of gold and silver lying around. I think it's all going to boil down to whether or not you followed your heart and did good works."

"And by going into Christian music, you're following your heart."

"Yes." With more conviction, she added, "Yes. I am." Almost unable to breathe, she waited for his reaction.

At last, Jason nodded. "I can see this working out for you. The author of the article got something else right—you are returning to your roots. Didn't you tell me once that you'd grown up singing hymns while you and your cousins did the dishes?"

Belle blinked. "You remember that?" she whispered, incredulous.

A wistful smile formed on Jason's lips. "You say that as if I could forget anything about you."

The comment ignited a fire in her midsection. Warmth spread outward in waves.

Maybe there was a chance for them after all.

The thought had barely formed when Jason's expression soured. He cleared his throat.

"Since we seem to be telling all our secrets, I have my own confession to make."

At the serious note Jason's voice struck, she straightened. "Oh?"

"I've been worried about you."

"About me? Whatever for?" Belle thought quickly, trying to dredge up something she might have said or done that would give Jason cause for concern. Sure, the last few months hadn't been the easiest time of her life. But she thought she'd done a pretty good job of staying positive and upbeat despite losing everything she'd accumulated throughout a long and successful career, as well as the impending sale of the only home she had left.

"I was beginning to think you wouldn't be able to move on. That you'd get stuck." He must have noticed her confusion, because he said, "Think about it for a minute. I bet you can name a dozen performers who've spent some time in the limelight, but then they lose their edge or they lose touch with their audience. Whatever the reason, instead of moving on, they stagnate. They stop trying anything new. They're content to live off the laurels of their glory days. They sing the same old songs to smaller and smaller audiences until, eventually, they fade out of sight."

Horrified, Belle pressed a hand over her heart. "There but for the grace of the good Lord go I," she whispered. What Jason had described sounded like a fate worse than death, and yet she could have easily joined the ranks of the has-beens who eked out a living making nightly appearances in smoky cocktail lounges. "And that's how you thought I'd end up?"

"Not me," Jason corrected. "I've always had higher hopes for you. But it's been six months

13

since Nashville, and as far as I knew, you hadn't even started to explore other options." He held a thumb and forefinger about a half-inch apart. "I was starting to get a wee bit concerned."

"That's sweet of you," Belle said, thankful that she'd chosen a different path. "Now that I know which direction I'm headed, though, you don't have to worry about me anymore."

"That's kind of like telling the waves to stop washing ashore, don't you think? It's only right to worry about someone when you care deeply about them, isn't it?" Reaching for her hand, Jason hooked his little finger around hers.

"I suppose so," Belle said softly, her heart swelling. "I—I've never felt this way about anyone else," she admitted while she stared down at Jason's much larger finger wrapped around her own. On the verge of telling this man how much she loved him, she stopped herself from saying the words out loud. Sensing Jason hadn't said all he'd come to Emerald Bay to say, she sighed when he lifted her hand to his mouth and pressed a kiss onto her fingertips.

He sucked in a deep breath and expelled it forcefully as he untangled their fingers. "I get why you didn't want to discuss this new direction until you were sure it was the right move for you. But if we have strong feelings for one another, once you made the decision, once you were committed, why on earth didn't you loop me in?"

"You have every right to ask that question, but whew! You have no idea how fast everything came together. It was like one of those puzzle boxes, the kind that are so hard to open. You struggle with it for what seems like forever. Then, you move one piece and all of a sudden, everything falls into place. One day, I was wrestling with what I was supposed to do with the rest of my life. That evening, I sang at the church potluck, and suddenly, it was like someone had turned on the lights. Everything became crystal-clear. All my doubts, all my fears—swept away." Just thinking about that night still gave her chill bumps.

"I've had a moment or two like that. It's the best feeling in the world," Jason said softly.

"So true." Belle shook her head, still amazed at how quickly all the pieces had come together. "As we were sitting around the firepit after church that night, Kim and the others asked me what was going on. I'd barely gotten the words out of my mouth before Nat was designing a new website and planning press releases. Within days, Caitlyn was dragging some poor kid with a guitar home to meet me. Two weeks after that, my new website had gone live, and we'd discovered my cousin Jen was a whiz on the sound board—who knew?"

"Whoa. That was fast. No wonder you didn't call. You've been awfully busy."

"Some days, I haven't known whether I was coming or going." Belle shook her head. "I was expecting a slow roll—a couple of special appearances at services over the next couple of months, maybe some busking up in St. Augustine. Boy, was I wrong. Nat is a natural at this stuff—she's lined up five gigs for us already." She hesitated, her plans for the afternoon rushing back. "As a matter of fact, I'm supposed to be in a practice session with Daclan and Jen right now. We've been asked to perform at the opening of a new fifty-five-plus community in Vero on Saturday."

"Tomorrow, you mean?" Jason looked surprised. "I guess that means I'll be here for it, then."

Belle felt her jaw drop. "You're staying?" she asked, unable to wrap her mind around the idea.

"If you have a room available."

She grinned as that warm feeling in the pit of her stomach came rushing back. "Reservations have picked up, but I think we can find something for you. After all, I hear you're friends with the owner's daughter."

Jason's smile spread easily across his face, all trace of his previous pique erased. "Is that so? Just friends?"

"Very, very good friends." Belle's heart swelled.

But when Jason's head dipped toward hers, she placed a restraining palm on his chest. She inclined her head toward the clatter of footsteps on the pavered walkway outside. Just as she'd suspected, Daclan and Jen unceremoniously entered the cottage seconds later.

"Why the dela—" Jen's voice cut off midsentence. Understanding dawned in her eyes. "Oh! Hey, Jason! When did you get here?"

A wry smile on his face, Jason squeezed Belle's hand. "Later," he mouthed before standing with an easy grace. "I haven't been here long. Sorry for interfering with your practice. Belle and I had a few things to, uh, discuss."

"No problem." Jen waved a dismissive hand. "Kim baked cookies and needed a couple of taste-testers. We were only too happy to oblige. Isn't that right, Daclan?"

"Yes, ma'am. They were good." The teen lowered a battered guitar case to the floor.

Jason's eyes riveted on the boy. "You must be the young man I've been hearing so much about." Crossing the small living room in three long strides, Jason extended a hand. "I'm Jason Dennis. And you're Daclan…?"

"Daclan Medford, sir. Nice to meet you." The lanky teen shook hands with Jason.

"Jason's a big mucky-muck at Noble Records," Jen said as she took her place at the sound board.

Daclan, who'd dropped into a crouch while he flipped the latches on his guitar case, looked up. "You are?"

Belle tried not to wince at her cousin's announcement. Not that she intended to keep Jason's position a secret from her young protégé. But she'd hoped they could get through at least one practice without putting any added pressure on him.

Jason held up both hands. "That's my day job. Today, I'm here simply as a friend of Belle's. Would you mind if I stayed for your practice? I'd like to listen to her sing."

If the thought of performing before one of the most powerful men in the recording industry gave Daclan any qualms, the boy hid it well. "It's fine with me as long as it's okay with Belle."

Belle nodded. "I'd like Jason to stay." She couldn't very well ask the man to leave after he'd come all this way, could she? Besides, she wouldn't mind getting his take on their sound, either.

From her spot at the sound board, Jen twisted a knob. High-pitched feedback from the mics squealed through the room. "Let's get started, folks," she said. "Time's a wastin'."

"Yeah. I got youth group tonight." Daclan lifted a vintage Martin from the guitar case. After slipping a leather strap over his head, he plucked on the strings and adjusted the tuning until deep-throated melodic notes filled the air.

"Sweet guitar," Jason said, eyeing the instrument with a well-informed eye. "D-18?"

"Yeah." Daclan ran a hand over the wood's aged patina. "It was my grandfather's. My dad doesn't play. After Grandpa died, no one was using it, so my dad said I could have it."

"Mind if I take a look?"

Daclan turned to Belle, his expression questioning.

Belle shot Jason a puzzled look but nodded. "Sure."

In a move Belle could only describe as reverent, Jason grasped the neck of the guitar, slipped the strap over his neck and plucked a few strings. Apparently satisfied with the tuning, he sank onto one of the stools in the center of the room and fingerpicked the opening bars of "Never Going Back Again."

Mesmerized by the way his fingers plucked

the guitar strings in perfectly timed rhythm, Belle stared. "I thought you said you just played in a garage band," she said accusingly when he finished. Over dinner at Georgio's, Jason had insisted he didn't have what it took to make it professionally. Yet he'd handled the song's difficult riffs and complicated fingerpicking as well as Fleetwood Mac's Lindsey Buckingham.

"I believe I said that wasn't the life I wanted." He slipped off the strap and, with apparent reluctance, handed the instrument back to Daclan. When he did, Jason's gaze fell on the guitar case that was little more than cardboard held together by duct tape. His face paled. "You probably ought to get a better one of those," he told the boy.

"Don't have the money right now," the kid answered. He shot a mischievous look at Belle. "Maybe when you and me hit the big time," he said with a grin.

"Which we won't do if we don't practice. We have a lot of ground to cover if we're going to be ready for tomorrow."

"I'm ready." Daclan moved to his usual spot behind one of the mics.

Maybe she should have worried about her own reaction to having Jason in the room rather than Daclan's, she thought when the boy seemed completely at ease. Motioning their tall guest into a seat on the couch, Belle tried to ignore her own nervous shiver. Once she started reviewing the music they'd selected for The Emeralds' first-ever performance, however, her jitters faded. Soon, she and Daclan were hard at work, running through the collection of hymns and familiar numbers, repeating each song until they had it down pat.

She frowned when the boy's timing felt rushed on the last number in their set. "Slow it down. This one's supposed to have a sense of the majestic," she coached when he finished the hymn with a flurry of notes. "Let's take it from the top."

They repeated the song twice more. Rather than improving, though, Daclan's timing got worse with every pass. Feeling frustrated, Belle ran a hand through her hair. Should she strike the hymn from their list? On the verge of doing exactly that, she reminded herself that final rehearsals were always a bit rough.

"Tell you what," she said at last. "Play this one tonight before you go to bed and again in the morning. Let me know tomorrow whether you think we should skip it." Hiding her hands behind her back, she crossed her fingers. She'd hate to drop the song from their repertoire, but the decision needed to be Daclan's.

"Yes, ma'am." The teenager crossed to the case he'd left open on the floor. Stuffing the guitar inside, he flipped the latches, grabbed the case by the handle and turned toward the door. "I gotta run if I'm going to make it to youth group on time."

Belle smiled. She could hardly fault the boy for wanting to spend time with people his own age. "Be here at nine tomorrow to help load the van." Though she and Jen could probably handle the amp, sound board and mics on their own, loading and unloading the equipment was a rite of passage for a young musician. "Make sure you eat a good breakfast," she said just before her guitarist could dash out the door.

"Will do!"

At her station behind the sound board, Jen began checking equipment and coiling wires.

"You were right about him." Jason stared into the space the young player had vacated seconds earlier. "He's extremely talented. Did you say he's self-taught?"

"Yes and no." In the weeks since the afternoon that Caitlyn had all but kidnapped the boy and brought him home from school with her, Belle had gleaned a good bit about Daclan's background. "His grandfather played in a folk group that made the rounds of music festivals and camps here in Florida." She smiled as a memory of those days came rushing back. "They let me sing with them a couple of times before I left for Juilliard." Stepping onto a stage made up of a half dozen wooden pallets arranged beneath a white canopy had been one of the highlights of her youth.

"I guess that explains your interest in the boy," Jason observed.

"I do like to pay it forward," Belle admitted. "And I needed a guitar player. Daclan's the best I'm going to find around here. He says his grandfather started teaching him how to play the guitar when he was three, but Art passed on when Daclan was twelve. Everything he's learned since then, he's gotten from YouTube videos."

"Kudos to his grandfather. He made sure the kid had all the basic skills."

"And he left him that guitar." Belle teased, "I saw you eyeing it."

Jason didn't bother denying his interest. "It's a classic. I know people who'd give their eyeteeth for one like it."

"For that old thing?" She paused. Musical instruments weren't really her thing, though she owned several. "I suppose he shouldn't haul it around on the back of his bicycle," she suggested.

"In that case?" Jason groaned audibly. "Let's put it this way—Daclan could afford to pay his way through college on what he'd get for that guitar."

"Yeah, but he has a sentimental attachment to it, since it belonged to his grandfather. I don't think he'd ever part with it."

"As well he shouldn't. But maybe, just maybe, he could protect it better. That case..." Jason shook his head. "If Daclan wrecks his bike, he'll be picking up that guitar in pieces."

"I hate to interrupt, but everything's ready to go for the morning," Jen called on her way to the door.

Belle swung toward her cousin. Sure enough, while she and Jason had been talking, Jen had packed the mics, stacked the miles of cords they'd need to take with them tomorrow and gathered the mic stands and other equipment in one spot. "I would have helped," she protested.

"You had other things on your mind. Besides, it's my job, isn't it?"

Belle started to argue that she'd never intended for Jen—or anyone else—to do all the work but, seeing as the task was already complete, she simply mouthed her thanks.

"I'm going to head back to the main house and check on a room for Jason." Turning to him, Jen said, "I'm pretty sure Ruby's vacant. It's on the ground floor and has its own separate entrance. Would that be all right?"

"I don't want to put you to any trouble," Jason demurred.

"No trouble at all. It's an inn. Finding rooms for people is what we do." With that, Jen slipped out the door, which closed with a soft *snick* behind her.

Belle took a deep breath, inhaling Jason's spicy, male scent. She tipped her head to find a bemused smile on his face. One look at the warmth in his gray eyes and she no longer remembered what they'd been talking about. "Where were we?" she asked tentatively.

Jason closed the gap between them. "I believe, before Jen and Daclan arrived, I was planning to kiss you."

"You were?" Belle ran the tip of her tongue over her lips in anticipation just before Jason's lips met hers, and for a while, nothing else mattered.

The final notes of the last hymn faded. A hush fell over Sunshine Villa's roomy meeting hall. The quiet stretched for a full measure before the crowd seated in rows of folding chairs surged to its feet. A deafening applause filled the room.

Tears welled in Belle's eyes. The first performance of The Emeralds hadn't just gone well; it had been near perfection. Jen had handled the sound board like a natural. Daclan had positively nailed that last number, along with all the songs that led up to it. As for herself, it didn't matter whether hundreds or thousands had gathered for the performance. Of all the many times she'd walked on stage, she'd never been more absolutely certain she was doing the right thing than she'd been today.

After sending up a quick prayer of thanks, she pressed both hands over her heart while she flashed her signature smile at the audience. For good measure, she blew kisses at the family members, friends and neighbors who'd streamed into the community center, prompting the surprised staff to break out more chairs than they'd anticipated. When the noise died down, she motioned to Daclan, who bowed low over his guitar in response to a round of applause. More clapping erupted when Belle pointed to her cousin.

Belle spoke into the mic. "Thank you all for coming out this afternoon. And a special thanks to Sunshine Village, our hosts today." She looked to her right, where the beaming sales manager waited just beyond the curtains. "Now I'll turn the stage over to Nancy Aldridge, who'd like to say a few words about Vero Beach's newest fifty-five-and-over residential community."

Heading for the wings, Belle paused long enough to give a warm hug to the woman who'd taken a chance on an unknown band. Surprised not to see Daclan at her side when she and Nancy parted, she glanced around for the boy. The nod she'd sent the teen had been his signal to leave the stage. Instead of following her, though, he remained rooted to the spot behind his mic, his guitar clutched in his hands while he stared at the audience like a deer caught in the headlights of an oncoming car. Belle smiled inwardly. She knew that look, that feeling. Crossing to him, she linked arms with the teen and nudged him toward the exit with just enough force to break the spell that held him in place.

"Did I do okay, Belle?" the boy asked once they'd made it as far as the library they'd turned into a temporary green room.

Belle wrapped her arms around the teen and

squeezed tightly. "Better than okay," she assured him. "You were awesome." Which was not to say there was no room for improvement. However, any criticism—constructive or otherwise—would wait for another day, another time.

Nat poked her head into the room. "Are you up for speaking with the reporters? There's a half dozen of them out here."

"Tell them I'll meet them under the portico in five minutes," Belle directed. She twisted the cap off a bottle of water and guzzled half of it in one gulp. She and Daclan had agreed that she'd handle the press for the time being. Later, when he had a wee bit more experience, she'd ease him into the fine art of fielding questions that could be downright intrusive.

Her smile, which she'd thought couldn't stretch any further, widened when Jason walked into the room with a veritable phalanx of family members trailing in his wake.

"Belle! Daclan! Superb job. Fantastic!" Jason declared. He flung his arms wide and swept Belle into a tight embrace. When he let go, he lingered at her side, his arm a warm and welcome weight around her waist.

"Did you like it, Mama?" Belle asked when her mother emerged from the group of well-wishers.

One hand still grasping her cane, Margaret swiped at her cheeks, where tears had left tracks through her face powder. "It was wonderful, honey. The best ever."

The praise sent a bright burst of reassurance through Belle as they exchanged tender hugs.

After that, everyone seemed to speak at once. Kim and Craig, Amy and Max, Diane and Caitlyn crowded forward, each offering their own congratulations to the band's trio. Spotting Daclan's mother among the well-wishers, Belle took special pains to thank the woman for "lending" her son to the group. Before she knew it, though, it was time to meet with the reporters.

"We'll load the equipment while you're gone," Jen said. She'd already commandeered Max and Craig as her helpers.

"I'll walk you out," Jason said, his firm manner a clear indication that he wouldn't take *no* for an answer.

"I'd like that," Belle admitted. After a hectic breakfast and the ensuing chaos of loading the van, followed by two intense hours of preparing to walk out on stage without her usual entourage of stylists and makeup artists to help her get ready, Belle hadn't managed to spend a minute alone with Jason all day. A couple of quiet minutes in the corridor wasn't much, but she'd take it.

"I'll come, too, Aunt Belle. I want to get some pictures for the website." Nat brandished a camera.

What could she say? She couldn't very well deny Nat's request. Still, she'd been looking forward to those few stolen moments alone with Jason. Especially since Kim had unwittingly wrecked their plans to sneak off to Waldo's last night when she'd pulled out all the stops for a family dinner. All had been forgiven, though, when Kim had served dessert—an outstanding tiramisu that Jason had declared the best he'd ever eaten.

Perhaps sensing her mood, Jason leaned close as they stepped into the corridor with Nat on their heels. "Let me take you to dinner before we head back to the inn," he whispered.

"That sounds awesome!" Nat gushed before Belle had a chance to answer. "I'll let the others know."

If Jason hadn't had his arm around her, Belle might not have noticed the slight hesitation in his step. "Um, hold on," she said, struggling not to laugh out loud. Nat's ears might look normal, but the girl had the hearing acuity of a bat.

"Nah! It's all good." Jason surprised her by

overruling her objection. "Go ahead and invite them all, Nat," he said over his shoulder. "Daclan's folks, too. It's not every day someone launches a new career. It ought to be celebrated. There's no better way to do that than with family…and friends." His grip on Belle's waist tightened briefly.

She scoured Jason's face, searching for any sign that he'd experienced the same sharp pang of disappointment she'd felt now that their quiet dinner for two had turned into a family event. Spotting nothing but anticipation in his gray eyes, she thought the man just might qualify for sainthood. She peered up at him. "Want to try Waldo's again?"

"The third time's the charm," Jason answered, referring to their two previous attempts, which had been foiled, first by food poisoning and then by last night's family dinner. His hand fell from her waist as they reached a set of smoked-glass doors. Beyond it, a small cluster of men and women milled about.

"I'll watch from here," Jason announced.

Belle understood perfectly. Appearing in public with the head of Noble Records at her side would shift the focus. At best, the reporters would clamor to know whether The Emeralds had signed with the recording company. At worst, Jason's presence would stir the kind of stories that regularly appeared in the gossip rags. They might have professed strong feelings for one another, but neither of them was ready to go public with their relationship.

"Wish me luck." She crossed her fingers and stepped outside as Jason held the door for her and Nat. The movement caught the attention of the reporters who surged toward her, each one trying to outshout the others.

Belle, an old hand at dealing with the press, hushed them. "One at a time, people," she admonished. Taking a lesson out of the playbook used by the press secretary in the Oval Office, she pointed to the first reporter who caught her eye. "The lady in the red dress."

"Dawn Hastings. *Miami Herald*," the woman said, identifying herself and setting the tone for all the others. "Excellent performance this afternoon. This is quite a change from pop, though. With all the many types of music to choose from, what led you to focus on Christian music?"

Fifteen minutes later, Belle had singled out each reporter at least once and handled their questions with an easy grace that came from years of experience. Making sure Nat got what she needed for the website, Belle willingly posed for pictures with those who requested them before she brought the session to a close.

"That went great, Aunt Belle." Nat recorded follow-up notes using an app on her cell phone. "I'll get us a table at Waldo's." She checked the time. "In an hour?"

"That ought to work." The restaurant was only a short drive from the retirement community.

"Alone at last," Jason murmured when the young woman sped off to get a head count. The heated look in his eyes told her how much he'd been looking forward to having her all to himself.

"For about two seconds," Belle warned. Her family and Daclan's would stream out of the library momentarily.

Jason chuckled. "Sounds like we'll have to take extreme measures if we're ever going to spend any time alone together. Want to join me for a run on the beach tomorrow morning?"

"You'd think that would work, wouldn't you?" Letting her eyelids flutter closed, she pictured her and Jason, standing at the water's edge, the sun just beginning to peek over the horizon. She could almost hear the whisper of the waves washing ashore, the cries of the terns and gulls searching for their breakfast, the casual greeting of the Treasure Seekers, members of a club that scoured the beach with metal detectors after each high tide.

The very pleasant daydream came to an abrupt stop, squealing like a record needle being dragged across vinyl. Jason wasn't the only one who enjoyed his morning exercise. She shook her head.

"I run every morning, too," she said. "With Kim. Though they're walkers, Diane and Nat usually tag along. Sometimes a guest or two will join us." There'd be fewer people left at the inn than there would be on the beach.

The crow's feet around Jason's eyes deepened as his laughter filled the corridor. "I guess this is my life now that I'm involved with a celebrity." He shifted closer. "I like it. Though I will have to learn to take advantage of every opportunity, no matter how short." Leaning down, he brushed kisses across the bridge of her nose, stopping only when the door to the library popped open and her family began to stream into the corridor.

As the group headed for the parking lot, Jason grumbled when his cell phone buzzed insistently. Pulling the device out of his pocket, he gave it a quick glance. "Shoot," he said, frustration creasing his brow. "This can't wait. It might take a few minutes." His gaze shifted between his rental car and the inn's van, which Jen and her volunteers had just finished loading. "I hate to ask, but would you mind if I meet you at the restaurant?"

Belle stared up at the concerned expression on Jason's face. Did he really think she'd begrudge him however long it took to answer a text after all the time he'd devoted to her this weekend? She aimed her best, sweetest smile at the man. "I'll save a place for you," she assured him before she signaled Jen that she'd be riding in the van after all.

Sixty minutes later, Belle took in the faces of the family and friends who sat around hastily shoved-together tables in the restaurant that had survived countless hurricanes despite looking like something that had been slapped together willy-nilly. Overhead, Tiffany-style lamps hung from the restaurant's painted tin ceiling. The work of local artists—some talented, some not— dotted rough, cedar-paneled walls. An eclectic mix of items rumored to be part of the infamous Waldo Sexton's personal collection gathered dust on shelves above tall, stained-glass windows. Belle relished the feeling of contentment that came from being surrounded by people she loved—and who loved her—in a place that was nearly as familiar as the Dane Crown Inn.

Now, if only Jason would join the party.

She ran her hand along the back of the empty chair beside her. Jason and his rental car hadn't followed their van out of the Sunshine Village parking lot. A good forty-five minutes had passed since they'd been shown to a side room where a waitress wearing a bright green T-shirt had handed out menus and taken drink orders. When he hadn't shown up by the time they ordered appetizers, she'd begun to worry in earnest. Fighting to distract herself, she leaned toward her mother. "Have you decided what you want to order, Mama?"

"I do love the fried green tomatoes here." Margaret fiddled with the straw she'd stuck in a glass of sweet iced tea. "And I've always liked their coleslaw. What are you getting?"

"The stuffed shrimp, I think." In her rush to get to the venue on time, she'd skimped on breakfast. Stuffed with coconut and cheese, the fried shellfish was a sure cure for her hungry tummy.

"Maybe I'll have some of that, too." Lowering her menu, Margaret raised the very question Belle had been trying her best not to ask. "Where's Jason?"

"I'm not sure," she admitted. "He should have been here by now."

Sucking in a breath, she ran down a few possibilities that didn't involve a blowout on the highway or his car going off the road and into a ditch. Had he gotten lost? That seemed unlikely, not in an age where directions were only as far away as the nearest cell phone, and she knew for a fact that Jason had his. It was more likely that the text he'd received involved some crisis at work and had taken longer to resolve than he'd expected. An artist who needed some extra hand-holding. Or an agent who absolutely insisted on renegotiating a sticky contract on a Saturday afternoon.

"No worries." Margaret pointed. "Here he comes."

"What?" Belle asked when her mother's voice derailed her train of thought. She straightened, her gaze following her mom's finger. Sure enough, looking better than any man had a right to, Jason trailed a young woman into the room.

"Is he one of your party?" A steely glint in the hostess's eyes announced to one and all that she wouldn't hesitate to have Security toss the interloper out of the restaurant.

"We were about to give up on him, but yes, he's one of ours." Belle patted the seat beside her.

"Sorry for the delay, everyone. I hope I didn't

hold you up." Looking properly abashed, Jason squeezed in between Belle and Craig.

"Nah, man." Craig scooted his chair to the side to give Jason a bit more room. "We were just about to order." The mayor inclined his head toward the waitress who'd just stepped into the room, her pen poised over an old-fashioned order pad.

"What's good?" Directing the question to Belle, Jason scanned the menu in front of him.

"You can't go wrong with any of the seafood dishes." Belle was so relieved to see him, she barely registered the floral scent that clung to him, reminding her of the inn's rose bushes. "If you'd like, we can share the fish dip as an appetizer." The delicious house-made spread was not to be missed. Although, mindful of the kisses she hoped would come later, she planned to skip the mounds of jalapeños and chopped onions that came with it.

They'd barely placed their orders before servers arrived with their starters. Laughter and conversation soon flowed throughout the room as the group munched on fried mozzarella, conch fritters and the curiously named dolphin fingers, which were actually strips of fried mahi. Jason pronounced the dip "excellent," and Belle smiled to herself when she noticed that neither one of them piled onions on top of their crackers.

She and Jason were halfway through their entrees when Belle heard Kim ask Tom Medford how plans were coming for the Spring Fling.

Daclan's father polished off the last of his fish and chips before, wiping his fingers on his napkin, he said, "Wonderful. This is going to be our best Spring Fling ever." He looked to Craig for confirmation.

"Sounds like it, Tom. You've had some great ideas." Craig dredged a piece of romaine through the dressing he'd asked to have served on the side of his Ceasar salad. "If everything goes according to plan, don't be surprised if we ask you to run it again next year."

Tom's chest swelled visibly. "It's been a community effort. Definitely not a one-man show." His gaze honed in on Kim. "Was it your suggestion to sell tickets for the food and beverage trucks?" At Kim's nod, he continued. "Good idea. The money we'll raise will pay for all the extra costs of having a dance that night."

"Glad I could help," Kim said.

With a speculative gleam in his eyes, Tom next turned to Belle. "Now, if we could just find a headliner. Someone who'd really draw a crowd."

Crammed side-by-side together as they were, Belle felt Jason stiffen. She placed a restraining hand on his forearm. Letting her grip telegraph her intentions to take care of the matter on her own, she met Tom's gaze. Before she had a chance to speak, though, Craig intervened.

"Tom," Craig said, the word loaded with mayoral disapproval. "The Emeralds already have a slot with the other bands during the Fling." Local groups were invited to perform throughout the day. "I don't think…"

Not to be deterred, Tom ignored him and aimed a beaming smile straight at Belle. "What do you say, Belle? Won't you do a favor for your hometown? People would come from miles around to hear you sing 'Jimmy, Jimmy, Oh.'"

"I'm tempted. Seriously, I am." She wasn't lying. It had been a while since someone had begged her to perform her old songs in public. And, heaven help her, just being asked set butterflies loose in her stomach. But she had a new focus, and she had to be true to it. "I'm just not into the pop scene anymore. And I doubt if anybody at the Spring Fling will want to dance to 'Amazing Grace,'" she said, softening her refusal with a sympathetic expression.

Though she'd braced for a rebuttal, she had to give Tom credit when the man immediately shrugged his shoulders and grinned. "I hope you won't blame me for trying, but I had to ask."

"Not at all," Belle said smoothly, glad she'd been able to put the issue to bed so easily. Especially since Daclan had been staring at his empty plate ever since the start of the conversation.

Totally relaxed now, Jason lifted a fry from the plastic basket that had arrived brimming with fish tacos and a generous helping of crispy steak fries. He cleared his throat. "What exactly is the Spring Fling?"

Sensing his cue, Craig provided the answer. "It's mostly a craft fair. We hold it every year to raise money for the town's operating expenses. This year, we have—what? Over two hundred vendors?" He looked to Tom, who nodded.

"Sounds like fun. I'll have to put it in my calendar." Jason bumped Belle's elbow with his own. "That is, if you know somewhere I can stay."

Belle fought down a moment's hesitation. Rooms were at a premium the weekend of the Fling. As a result, all of the inn's suites had been reserved months ago. But if Jason wanted to make another trip to Emerald Bay, she'd find a place for him. Why, she'd even bunk in with her mom and give him her room if need be. "I think that can be arranged," she assured him.

She would have said more, but the clear tone

of a knife striking a glass rang through the room. Belle's gaze landed on Diane, who still held her butter knife poised above the rim of her glass of tea.

"Da-de-dah-dah-de-dah!" Diane gave her best trumpet call. When she had everyone's attention, she announced, "I'd like you all to be the first to know that we just heard from the coach. Caitlyn made the varsity team at Emerald Bay High!"

"Squeeee!" Amy shouted. "Go, Pirates!"

Congratulations erupted as those gathered at the table praised the girl's hard work and raised toasts to a successful season. From there, conversations ebbed and flowed until, all too soon, the dishes had been cleared, the bills paid, and they were emerging from the restaurant into the bright sunshine, where Jason motioned for Daclan to accompany him and Belle to his car.

"I'm not sure I'll see you again this week-end," he told the boy while they strode past parked vehicles. "And I want to give you something before I leave. Before you ask, I've already cleared this with your folks." A click of the key fob popped the trunk of Jason's rental car. Reaching into the darkened depths, he pulled out a hard-shelled guitar case.

"Sheesh! You got me a guitar case? That's drip!"

Belle tried not to laugh at the teenager's expression by recalling how her parents had cringed whenever her younger self had referred to something as *cool.*

"There's more. Look inside," Jason urged.

Anticipation filling his face, the boy flipped the latches of the case open like a kid opening a Christmas present. Confusion swam in his eyes when he spotted a shiny new D-18 nestled in the padded green lining. "But...I already got a guitar," he said slowly.

"Yes, you do. And it's a *very* valuable instrument." Jason's voice slowed to emphasize the point. "I don't think your dad realized quite how valuable when he gave it to you."

"I shouldn't use it?" Conflicting emotions played across Daclan's face.

"You definitely should. Especially whenever you're on stage. But the rest of the time—for practices, or when you're just noodling around at home—use this one. And it might be a good idea to keep your grandfather's guitar in this." Jason bent low and rapped his knuckles on the molded plastic. "That case will protect it from just about anything."

"Yes, sir," Daclan said, looking like a boy who'd just won the grand prize at the dart booth at the county fair. He lifted the new instrument and played a few chords. The strings hummed to life. "Sweet," he whispered, seconds before his face fell. "But I can't accept it. It's too expensive."

To Belle's shock and, from the look on his face, to Jason's as well, Daclan returned the guitar to the case and sat back on his haunches. As if he couldn't help it, the boy stroked his fingers over the curved case that fit the guitar perfectly.

Belle felt her heart melt for her young protégé. She'd known quite a few musicians who'd never even consider refusing such a gift. But Daclan was clearly torn between wanting the new guitar and doing the right thing. She stepped back, determined to let Jason handle the situation.

To his credit, Jason's head bobbed. "I get it. You're right to be careful. You're a talented young artist, and if you want it badly enough, you have a great future ahead of you. Lots of people—agents, managers, other record labels— they're all going to want a piece of you. But this is just a gift. Plain and simple."

"No strings," Daclan asked solemnly. "You swear?"

Jason held out his hands, his palms empty. "No strings. I swear."

Belle watched Daclan's gaze flick from Jason

to her. Though she wanted to reassure the boy that Jason was as honest and upright as they came, she remained silent. This was his decision to make. She wouldn't interfere.

Daclan wavered a moment longer before, exhaling a huge breath, he grasped the handle of the case and stood. "I can't thank you enough, Mr. Dennis," he said. "It'd be years before I could afford to buy a guitar like this on my own. I'll put this one to good use."

"I'm sure you will." Jason clapped the boy on the back.

Daclan danced on the balls of his feet. "Can I go show this to my parents?"

"You do that," Jason said. "I'll see you next time I'm down this way."

"I'll see you at practice Monday. Four thirty," Belle chimed as the boy loped off in the direction of his parents' car.

"That was awfully nice of you," Belle said when she'd slipped into the passenger seat of Jason's rental. *Beyond nice*, she corrected silently. The guitar itself was worth several thousand dollars.

"Please. All I did was make a phone call. You know Noble Records has a warehouse full of instruments and equipment, just for people like Daclan." Jason lifted one shoulder in a noncommittal shrug as he snapped his seat belt in place and started the car. "I can't think of a more deserving kid. Besides, I just couldn't stand it if anything happened to that old guitar."

Belle had to agree. Before she'd gone to bed last night, she'd looked up the cost of vintage D-18s. The price tag had been shockingly high.

"Where to next?" Jason asked as he backed out of their parking space.

"The inn," she directed, while she deliberately shoved all thoughts of music, her young guitarist and her family aside. She thought a long walk along one of the trails that wound through the inn's twenty acres was exactly what they both needed. If she had anything to say about it—and she would—they'd take that walk by themselves.

Two

Jen

"You have a better handle on all this computer stuff than I ever did." In the tiny office beneath the staircase, Margaret gave Jen an admiring glance. "Of course, I should expect as much. You young people grew up with computers. Not so long ago, I had to keep track of reservations, cancellations and room assignments in a register."

The fact that her aunt considered her a "young person" made laughter rumble in Jen's chest. After forty-seven years on this earth, she'd long since outgrown her youth. Why, she was middle-aged at best and, at worst, on the downhill slide. Sure, she knew her way around a keyboard, but the computer didn't know the inn's history nearly as well as her aunt.

"You kept a lot of it in your head, too." Jen tapped an index finger to her skull. "I could never have kept everything straight like you did. My memory's never been that good." She relied on daily printouts to tell her who was staying in which suite and how long they'd be there.

"Poppycock," Margaret fussed. "You're just as smart as I am. It's all a matter of practice. I bet you never mixed up the drink orders when you were waitressing, did you?"

"Um, no," Jen admitted. "My bosses would have fired me on the spot if I delivered shots of pricey Patron to a table that had ordered a round of Coors."

"Right. And at Waldo's the other day, didn't you separate the bills for everyone?" Their waitress had been so overwhelmed at the prospect of dividing the check for a party of fifteen that Jen had taken on the task.

"Well, yeah." Not that it had done a fat lot of good. She'd no sooner figured out who owed what than Jason had announced he'd put the entire tab on his expense account.

"Since you've been helping me with reservations, you haven't shown a guest to the wrong room yet, have you?"

"Ah, there's where you're wrong. I kind of did. That's actually why I'm here." She'd made a beeline for her Aunt Margaret after Mr. Harrison had chewed her out over the type of candy she'd left in his room. "How am I supposed to keep track of special requests and the like? Mr. Harrison was not happy about the chocolate I left on his pillow when I did his turn-down service last night. Apparently, that was a big no-no."

"Harrison," Margaret mused. "Rob Harrison. He and his wife, Gloria, are in Jasper, right? They're from somewhere in the Midwest. Champaign, Illinois, I think. Which is odd, since he doesn't like chocolate or champagne."

"How on earth do you know that stuff?" Jen blurted as wonder filled her head and her lips parted. She only wished she'd be half as sharp as Margaret when she reached eighty.

"Well, I don't. Not entirely." Margaret's brows arrowed down in the middle. "I write it all down when they check in."

"You do?" Jen didn't bother trying to hide her surprise. She'd been helping her aunt with the hostess duties for weeks. In all that time, why hadn't she heard about this?

"I used to jot notes in the margins of the ledger," Margaret explained as if that was something Jen should already know. "But I stopped when Diane moved all our records to the computer." She gave the machine a sour look.

"There was something so satisfying about writing in that register. It was almost like a journal."

Jen recalled the thick leather binder that used to sit, front and center, in the middle of the desk. Where was it now, she wondered.

"I still have to make some notes. The computer doesn't keep track of special requests or allergies or the like, so I jot those down on three-by-five cards. They're all right here." With an age-spotted hand, Margaret pulled a small plastic box off a nearby shelf. She flipped open the lid to reveal hand-lettered dividers, one for each suite. "This one is for the Harrisons," she said, pulling out the card from behind the tab labeled *Jasper*.

Jen took the stiff paper and read Margaret's spidery script. Apparently, the couple had three grown children and six grandchildren. In addition to Mr. Harrison's aversion to chocolate and champagne, they'd also requested extra pillows.

"This is great information." Jen tapped the edge of the card against her knee. The more she learned about the hostess duties at the inn, the more it seemed there was to learn. "What do you do with these after they check out?"

"I stick them in this box." Margaret pulled a

long narrow tray from a different shelf. "Everything gets filed by last name. Then, if someone comes back to stay with us again, we already know their likes and dislikes." Resting the tray on her lap, she heaved a sigh that carried a note of sadness. "I've been meaning to go back through the register and transfer that information to the cards, but there's always something more important to do."

Jen frowned. "How long ago did Diane set up the computer system?"

Margaret thought for a moment while she idly thumbed through the card catalog. "It must have been six or seven years ago."

"I wouldn't give the ledger another thought, then," Jen said. When Margaret looked at her questioningly, she added, "A lot can change in seven years. People move. Their preferences change." She'd even heard of people who developed allergies later in life. "Besides, if they haven't stayed with us in all that time, chances are they won't be back."

"Now why didn't I think of that?" Margaret wondered aloud. Her blue eyes watered, and at first, Jen worried that she'd upset her aunt. But Margaret only cackled softly. "Child, you don't have any idea how big a weight you've taken off my shoulders."

Jen's glance flitted from the tray of cards to the computer screen and back again. "I have an idea that might make things easier on all of us, Aunt Margaret. What if we have Nat add a space for special requests to the form people fill out when they register online? Then, when we print our daily reports, it'll have that information on it." Not only would having that kind of data stored in the computer prevent another run-in with the likes of Mr. Harrison, it would benefit all their guests. And wasn't that the whole point—to make everyone's stay at the Dane Crown Inn as carefree as possible?

"No more three-by-five cards?" Margaret asked, sounding wistful as she returned the tray to its spot on the shelf. "Do you think she could?"

"The only way to find out is to ask her." Jen reached for her cell phone.

"Now?" Margaret's gaze strayed to the box of cards. "Don't we want to think about it for a while?"

"Don't worry," Jen soothed. Change was hard. She should know. Her mom had moved around so much, she'd woken each morning without a clue as to where she'd be when she went to sleep that night. It was only after her mom died and Aunt Margaret gave her and Kim a permanent home that she'd gotten her first real taste of stability. "We're not going to rush into anything. Let's find out if it's even possible to add more to the form. It may not be. If it is, we'll consider all the pluses and minuses before we do anything."

She selected Nat's number from the Favorites list on her phone. When her niece didn't answer, she left a message asking the younger woman to join them in the office when she had a chance.

Margaret fidgeted with the card file. Jen stilled her aunt's hand by placing her own atop it. Eager to put her aunt's mind at ease, she said, "I have something else to show you. I'm pretty sure you're going to like it." Turning to the computer, she pressed a few keys. The screen blinked. A second later, the calendar of future bookings popped into view.

"We're booked solid the week of the Spring Fling," Margaret said with a cursory glance. "We usually are."

"Yes, but look at all the others." Jen pointed to weeks where most of the rooms in the inn had been spoken for. "I compared these bookings to the ones a year ago. In March and April and May, reservations have doubled from last year."

"Really?" Squinting, Margaret peered closer. "Well, I'll be."

The uptick in occupancy was good news, but

there was more. Jen brought up the report she'd prepared before her unfortunate run-in with Mr. Harrison. A tapping sound at the open door prevented her from showing it to her aunt.

"Sorry I kept you waiting, Aunt Jen. I was lying out on the balcony, getting my daily dose of Vitamin D. I got here as fast as I could." The straps of her bathing suit peeking out from beneath a loose cover-up, Nat stepped into the room, bringing the scent of sunblock and salty ocean air with her.

"Your timing is actually perfect, sweetheart. Drag a chair in from the other room and join us."

While Nat rushed off to do as she'd been asked, Jen squelched a stab of envy. *Oh, to be young again*, she thought. *To be young and know what we know now*, she corrected. As teens, she and Kim and their cousins had slathered each other in baby oil and baked in the sun for hours, turning over to their other side only when they were burned to a crisp. Today, wrinkles testified to the sheer folly of those actions. She reached for the bottle of lotion on the desk and rubbed a dab into her hands and arms. By the time she finished, Nat perched on the edge of her chair in the tiny office.

"I was just showing Aunt Margaret how much business has improved." Jen pointed to the screen. "We're up sixty percent over last year's bookings. Most of those reservations came in after you revamped the website." Her niece's degree in graphic design had certainly come in handy.

"A healthy online presence is vital for business these days." Nat nodded her approval at the report. She pointed to an old photograph of the inn mounted on the wall. "Wait till the painters are finished and we replace the pictures of the inn's exterior on the website." For the past three weeks, workmen had been scurrying up and down scaffolding. They'd almost finished giving the inn a fresh coat of white paint with sky-blue trim. "We'll see another bump then for sure."

"If this keeps up, the inn will be operating in the black in no time." Jen snapped her fingers. Expecting Margaret to be pleased, she studied her aunt's reaction.

"Oh, my." Margaret fanned herself with one hand. "I knew things had picked up a bit, but I had no idea…" Her voice trailed off. "We've been losing money for so long, I don't quite know what to think about all this."

Jen leaned forward and clasped her aunt's hands, momentarily taken aback by how cold they felt. She swallowed and forced herself to go on. "That was the point of doing the renovation, though, wasn't it?" she asked. "To get the inn in the best possible shape so we can find a buyer for it?"

"You'll be able to move into that nice Emerald Oaks. You won't have to work so hard." Nat stared at Aunt Margaret.

"Yes, that's the plan, isn't it?"

Jen felt her aunt tremble. Concern shot through her when tears formed in Margaret's eyes. Relinquishing her grasp on the older woman's hands, she pushed away from the computer.

"You know what?" she asked, directing the question at her aunt. "All this talk about numbers and reservations has made me thirsty. I'm going to fix a cup of tea. Anyone else want some?"

"I could use a glass of water," Nat said. "It was warm on my balcony."

Margaret hastily dabbed at her eyes. "I think a cup of tea sounds perfect. There's something else I've been meaning to talk to you about anyway. Something that has nothing to do with the inn."

What else did her Aunt Margaret have on her mind, Jen wondered as she slid her chair under the desk. Turning to see if the older woman needed help getting up, she was just in time to see her aunt fix the computer with a look that said she wasn't exactly pleased with the results of all their hard work. In fact, if Jen wanted to label her aunt's expression like one of the cards in Margaret's little box, she'd call it downright baleful.

"I'm surprised Kim isn't bustling around in here." Scouring the spotless kitchen with a searching gaze, Margaret took her usual spot at the large table.

"She's at the store." Nat read from the blackboard mounted on the wall nearest the exit. Running a successful catering business required her mom to stick to a firm schedule that included shopping on Mondays and prepping on Tuesdays. The rest of the week, the inn filled with delicious aromas as Kim bustled about cooking the homemade, heat-and-serve meals she'd deliver to her growing list of subscribers on Fridays.

"I hope she remembers to get extra napkins. We're nearly out." Margaret added a spoonful of sugar to the cup of tea Jen had set in front of her.

Jen blew a cooling breath across the surface of

her own steaming mug. "If you asked her to get them, she won't forget," she assured her aunt. Her sister lived and breathed by her lists. She wouldn't dream of leaving the grocery store without crossing off every single item.

"I'm just saying, we're down to a handful." Margaret released a thready breath while she stirred her tea in rapid strokes.

It wasn't like Aunt Margaret to complain. Jen eyed the twin spots of color high on the older woman's pale cheeks. Clearly, something besides the state of the inn was bothering her. "What is it, Aunt Margaret? What'd you want to talk to us about?"

Margaret's spoon rattled onto the saucer. When she looked up from her cup, she spoke in a faltering voice. "I'm concerned about Scott and Fern and this new baby."

Jen felt her heart clench. Did her aunt know something she hadn't shared with the rest of them?

Stay calm, she cautioned. Catching Nat's eye, she did her best to telegraph the same unspoken message to her niece. But she'd never qualify as the next Uri Geller, she decided when her niece's reaction was anything but calm.

"Oh, no!" Nat cried out. "Is something wrong with the baby?"

"Wrong?" Margaret peered at her grand-daughter. "No. Nothing's wrong with the baby, dear. Or Fern. At least, I don't think so. Have you heard anything?" The lines that wreathed her face deepened as her concern shifted to worry. She pinned Jen with a hard stare.

"It's a perfectly normal pregnancy, as far as I know." Jen hurried to reassure both women. "Fern's considered high-risk because of her age." She turned to Nat. "She's thirty-six, so they're taking extra precautions." She held up her hands, palms facing the others. "But, according to Diane, there was nothing out of the ordinary at her last checkup." And as Scott's sister, Diane would be one of the first to know.

"Well, that's a relief." Margaret sipped her tea.

Nat's head tilted inquisitively. "Why are you worried, Aunt Margaret? If not about the baby?"

"It's just that everybody's got their own problems to deal with—Belle's in a dither. After those reporters showed up at the ribbon-cutting ceremony in Vero Beach on Saturday, her phone's been ringing nonstop. Amy's got her hands full with the expansion of Sweet Cakes. Diane's busy running Caitlyn back and forth to school and practices…when she isn't fighting with Tim."

Margaret silenced Nat's protest with a pointed glance. "I might be old, but I'm not blind. I know a troubled marriage when I see one."

After Nat answered with a meek, "Yes, ma'am," and chugged her water, Margaret continued. "As for Kim, well, Royal Meals is off to a good start, but she's swamped. Don't get me wrong—it's all good. And I couldn't be happier for them. I'm just afraid we're not making enough fuss about this new baby." She took a gingersnap from the plate of cookies Jen had placed on the table between them and broke it in half.

"It's early for a baby shower, isn't it," Jen asked softly. "Besides, this their third child. Won't they have everything they need already?"

Margaret tsked. "You can never have enough onesies or blankets or diapers."

"I'll have to take your word on that," Jen replied. She'd been too afraid she'd turn out as footloose and carefree as her own mother to ever consider having a baby of her own. A fact she'd been perfectly up-front about with her first husband. Not that the man had listened. When he'd announced that it was time for them to settle down and start raising kids, she'd reminded him that children had never been part of the bargain. And that was the end of that. Before the ink on their divorce decree was even dry, he'd found himself a new wife, one who gave him the kids he'd wanted more than he wanted Jen.

"Ooooh, I have a thought." Ice clinked in Nat's glass as she tipped it back and forth. "We should throw a gender reveal party."

"You mean with colored balloons or a cake with a pink or blue filling?" Jen cringed inwardly. She'd seen enough of those on the blooper reels to know the so-called reveal could go terribly wrong.

"Yes, but ours would be fun. Maybe an Easter egg hunt?" Nat asked hopefully.

Margaret shook her head. "Fern should find out the sex of the baby at her next checkup. Easter isn't until the end of March. That's too long to keep such a big secret. But I do like your idea, Nat. Jen, why don't you check with Fern and set a date. I'd recommend having it on a Sunday afternoon. That's usually our quiet time, since most of our guests check out on Sunday mornings. Once Fern agrees, you two can plan the party." She wagged a finger between Jen and Nat.

"Us?" Jen felt her eyes widen in surprise.

"Of course," Margaret said evenly. "You and

Nat have the most free time on your hands. The others are too busy."

Free time? Trying not to laugh out loud, Jen drained the rest of her tea. Ever since she'd arrived in Emerald Bay, she'd been running from pillar to post, trying to earn her keep. Lately, she'd been shouldering more and more of her aunt's responsibilities as hostess of the inn. A job she thoroughly enjoyed, even when guests like Rob Harrison gave her a hard time. As if that didn't keep her busy enough, she also served as Kim's sous-chef, ran the sound board for Belle and The Emeralds, and handled the deliveries for Sweet Cakes three days each week. She certainly didn't spend days on end twiddling her thumbs.

Before she had a chance to object, though, Nat spoke for both of them without so much as a glance in Jen's direction. "We'd be glad to handle the party, Aunt Margaret. That's what family's all about, after all."

"Good. Then it's settled." Placing both her palms flat on the table, Aunt Margaret pushed herself to her feet. "I'll leave everything to you. It's time for my nap."

Jen looked on in amazement as her aunt hobbled toward the family suite. She, who knew next to nothing about babies, was going to plan a gender reveal party. How had she let herself get roped into that?

"Fern and I had a long talk." Jen sank into the buttery soft leather of her favorite overstuffed chair in the library.

"Did she say yes?" Fresh from the shower, her short blond curls framing her face, Nat sat cross-legged on the love seat in baggy sweats and socks. She'd balanced an open laptop on her knees.

Jen nodded. "Aunt Margaret was right. Fern was starting to feel a little, um, how'd she put it? Overlooked?" Jen had felt so bad for the younger woman that she'd nearly cried when Fern admitted feeling left out. "When I told her we wanted to host a gender reveal party for her and Scott and the girls, she was practically over the moon." To tell the truth, the expectant mother's excitement had been so infectious, it had completely erased all of her own reservations about getting involved.

"That's awesome, Aunt Jen. Did she pick a date?" Nat held her fingers poised over the keys.

"Yep. On the afternoon of the first Sunday in March."

Nat's fingers made a tapping sound as she entered the date. "Whoa. That just gives us two weeks. We won't be able to mail the invitations. We'll have to use e-vites. We'd better order the cake right away. Do you think a full sheet cake will be enough? Should we ask Mom to handle the catering? Or should we hire someone else?"

"Hold on. Let me tell you everything Fern said before we get in over our heads."

Nat's hands fell away from her computer. "I'm all ears."

Not exactly. A pair of expressive blue eyes were definitely her niece's best feature, and right now, Nat's were focused directly on her. Jen smiled.

"Fern wants us to limit the invitations to family and a few very close friends. She mentioned Craig and Max specifically. Jason, too, if he's in town, I guess. Maybe Daclan, but that's it. No one else."

"No friends from church? Or anyone from town? What about her parents?" Nat's lower lip stuck out just the tiniest bit, giving her the look of a petulant child.

"Don't be upset. Fern's mom and dad thought they'd better get a vacation in before they're pressed into babysitting duty. They're on a six-week jaunt across the country. As for the others, Fern had a pretty good reason for not wanting a lot of people at the reveal. If we expand the guest list, she'll feel obligated to include the people from Scott's office. The last thing your Uncle Scott would want is for a client to overhear his staff and co-workers standing around the water cooler discussing his wife's pregnancy." The high-powered attorney was very protective of his family's privacy.

"Well." Nat bounced lightly on the cushions of the love seat. "I can understand that. I hated having my co-workers all up in my business when I was working in an office."

"So we should plan on fifteen or sixteen guests total."

"That will definitely make things simpler. I'll put us down for a quarter sheet cake." Nat typed rapidly. Looking up, she said, "We can decide on the decorations after we pick a theme. Pinterest has tons of great ideas."

Theme? Isn't "find out the sex of the baby" good enough?

Apparently not, because when Nat flipped her computer around, the screen displayed at least a dozen different party ideas. She pointed to one on the upper right.

"A team party might be nice," Nat suggested. "We could tell everyone to wear pink or blue, depending on whether they're Team Boy or Team Girl. For games, we could play tug-o'-war or duck, duck, goose."

Jen shifted uneasily in the leather chair. Her nieces, Isabella and Sophie, would love it. Her sister and her cousins, not so much. Middle-aged women chasing one another around in a circle sounded like a fantastic recipe for broken legs and sprained ankles.

Trying to let Nat down easy, she said, "I think I can speak for most of us when I say my tug-o'-war days ended in my twenties. You're not going to get me on one end of a rope unless there's copious amounts of beer involved…and I don't think that's the right environment for a party with children."

Apparently imagining her drunken aunts racing around the yard, Nat giggled. "Okay. Not a team party." She pointed to the next image. "What about a taco party? We could set up a taco bar, hire a mariachi band, and stuff a piñata with either pink or blue confetti for the reveal."

"I do love tacos." Jen patted her tummy. "But a mariachi band might be over-the-top, don't you think?"

Not to be deterred, Nat moved on. "This one

is cute. Princes and Princesses. What do you think?"

Jen nearly groaned. What was next—teddy bears and unicorns? The ideas felt too generic, too humdrum.

"What if we came up with a theme that hit a little closer to home?" she asked. "Maybe something that involves Emerald Bay? Or the Treasure Coast?"

Nat's face scrunched. "I've never understood why they call this the Treasure Coast. There aren't any gold mines around here, are there?"

Jen had heard the story of the Spanish fleet that sank off the coast in 1715 so often that it struck her as odd that Nat didn't know it. She skimmed over the story for her niece. "The ships were loaded with treasure—gold and jewels—for the king. A vast fortune. A hurricane sank most of the ships just off the coast. Most of the crew and passengers died. The few who made it to shore had to survive attacks by hostile natives and pirates. Salvage operations—past and present—have recovered a lot of the loot, but an emerald or a gold doubloon will still wash ashore every once in a while."

"That's why you used to go on treasure hunts when you were children. My mom told me about those. They make a lot more sense now."

Jen nodded. "We had this old map someone had drawn. And a tricorne hat. Sometimes we dressed up like pirates." Some of her fondest memories involved traipsing through the tall seagrass with her cousins.

Nat fell silent for a moment. "I've got it!" She closed her laptop with a snap. "We'll have a treasure hunt, and we'll all dress up like pirates! We'll get glass gems, the kind they sell to put in the bottom of a vase. Pink and blue ones. We'll bury them in different locations, and then we'll draw maps to each spot. When we've all found our treasure, we'll sort the beads into pink and blue piles and weigh them on one of those old-fashioned apothecary scales. The heaviest, or most, beads will indicate the gender. We'll have that taco bar—tacos are Spanish, aren't they? And ask Amy to decorate a cake with a pirate ship and a beach."

Jen blinked. Had that idea sprung, fully formed, into Nat's head? Whether it had or not, they were on to something. She traded high fives with her niece.

Nat opened her laptop again, and they set to work. Within an hour, they'd decided on every detail of the gender reveal party, right down to the pink and blue "gems" scattered on the beachy cake.

At last, Jen sat back, her half of a long list of things to do resting on the end table beside her. "I can't believe we put all this together in such a short time," she told Nat. "You're very good at this kind of thing."

"Planning's easy," Nat said with a grin. "The tough part is getting everything done over the next two weeks. You know, with all our *free* time."

As they both laughed, Jen shook her head, glad to hear her niece had shared her reaction to their Aunt Margaret's assumption that the two of them sat around all day with nothing to do. What with serving as Belle's personal assistant, plus all the time she'd spent building websites for Belle and Royal Meals, not to mention revamping the inn's, Nat was just as busy as Jen was. Maybe more so.

She stood, her list in her hand. "I guess we'd better get cracking. I'll call Amy and order the cake."

Nat scrambled to her feet. "I heard Mom in the kitchen a bit ago. I'll talk to her about the food." They'd settled on tacos, even though the dish had originated in Mexico rather than Spain.

"Let's meet again tomorrow to work on the maps," Jen said as she headed upstairs to her room. "We'll need to find some good hiding places and identify some landmarks." It was a pity they couldn't use the original map as a pattern, but it had long since disappeared.

"So that everyone finds their treasure." Nat nodded.

"Right," Jen agreed, though the real treasure, the best treasure of all, would be Fern and Scott's baby.

Three

Diane

With the score at two-one, Caitlyn rushed the ball that hurtled toward the net. Sliding across the grass feet first, she made contact at the last possible second. The game ball bounced off her foot and rolled to a stop midfield, where a player from the opposing team gave it a desperate kick. The ball sailed out of bounds. Whistles blew, signaling the end of the game and dashing Sebastian High's hopes for a tie. Grass stains smeared across her shorts and bright yellow goalkeeper's jersey, Caitlyn accepted a hand up off the turf from one of her teammates. Along with the other girls in their green-and-white uniforms, she rushed to the sidelines, where players and coaches alike slung their arms around one another for a victory dance.

From her perch in the metal bleachers where she'd watched numerous football games beneath the glow of stadium lights during her own four years at Emerald Bay High, Diane yelled until her throat felt raw. She wasn't alone. The stands vibrated as family members, friends and students drummed their feet. The air filled with happy cheers.

"What's happening? Is it over? Did they win?" Bundled against the chill in a warm blanket, Margaret had followed the black-and-white ball in its travels up and down the field with more interest than understanding.

"Yes, ma'am," Diane said happily. "Caitlyn kept the other team from scoring, and Emerald Bay won." She pointed. On the field, the home team had lined up to exchange the traditional handshakes with the visitors.

"I hate that Belle and Jen had to miss Caitlyn's first game." Margaret pulled the blanket tighter around her shoulders as the stands began to empty. The Emeralds were on the road, headed to Ocala, where they'd perform during a weekend church revival.

"Exciting game." Kim stepped down from the row behind Diane.

"She's an excellent player. Is she thinking about playing in college?" Craig joined Kim on the broad walkway that led to the stairs.

"That's the hope." An athletic scholarship to a four-year, Division 1 school had long been Caitlyn's dream. A dream Diane supported…as long as her daughter kept her grades up and stayed out of trouble. She scanned the field.

Caitlyn had finished shaking the opposing team's hands and was walking back to the sidelines.

Was she limping?

Diane searched the bleachers until her gaze landed on Tim, who'd chosen to sit across the aisle and two rows up from the rest of the family. Unlike the majority of the students and parents who were hurrying to get on with the rest of their Friday night plans, Tim remained seated, his eyes glued on their daughter. It felt like forever before he turned toward her.

She's okay, he mouthed, answering her unspoken question.

Diane exhaled the breath she hadn't known she was holding. She looked up to find Amy staring down at her. "Huh?" she asked, vaguely aware that her sister had asked a question.

"I wanted to know if we're all going to Brother's." A trip to the ice-cream parlor after every winning game was a high school tradition.

"Of course." Diane gathered her purse and

stood. "A win like that deserves celebrating, doesn't it? How about you, Aunt Margaret? Would you like a banana split?"

"Oh, no. That's too rich for me." Her head peeking out of her blanket, Margaret paused. "I wouldn't mind a small hot fudge sundae, though."

"With three cherries on top?" Amy teased. According to her aunt, no sundae was complete without extra cherries.

Reaching for her cane, Margaret stood. "Right."

"Why don't you ride with us?" Amy hooked arms with her aunt. "Diane needs to wait for Caitlyn. If we hurry, we can get seats."

"I don't know about hurrying, but I wouldn't mind going someplace warm." Discarding the blanket on the bench, Margaret emerged from her cocoon.

"I'll bring up the car." Max jingled the keys in his pocket. When Amy nodded, he plunged into the throng of departing spectators.

"We'll be along as soon as we can," Diane said to Amy and her aunt's departing backs. Each coach had their own post-game routines. Some dismissed the players immediately, saving their praise and criticism to dole out at the next practice. Others preferred to talk to their players while the memory of the game was still fresh.

"What's that all about, I wonder," Tim said, materializing at Diane's elbow once the rest of her family had moved out of sight. He aimed his chin toward the field where the coach had pulled Caitlyn aside for a one-on-one chat.

"You don't think she was upset about that final play, do you?" Diane studied the woman who was undeniably in their daughter's face.

"I don't see how she could be. It won the game." Tim hummed a barely audible bar of "Anything You Can Do (I Can Do Better)" before he said, "I guess we'd better get down there and see what's going on."

Tim took the blanket Diane had folded and tossed it over his shoulder. Following her lead, he trailed a half step behind her down the ramp. Together, they crossed the hard-packed dirt strip where cheerleaders showed off their moves on Friday nights during football season. Without discussing it, they chose a spot midway between two groups of other parents who displayed varying degrees of patience while they waited for the coach to dismiss the team.

"I forgot how much I missed all this," Diane said softly as she watched a couple of youngsters chase a soccer ball around the field. Drinking in the smell of fresh-cut grass, the lingering scent of popcorn that wafted from the now-closed concession stand, it hit her that more than four months had passed since she and Tim had waited to take Caitlyn home after a soccer match.

"I've missed it, too. And I know it's all my fault. I should never..." Tim took a breath. "This is all on me." He struck his chest with a closed fist. "I hope you can forgive me one day."

"I did that long ago." How did he not know this, she wondered. Hadn't she told him she'd forgiven him at Christmas? And again the night they'd gone to dinner at Fog Horn's?

Tim shook his head, disbelief apparent in the wide-eyed gaze he focused on her. "If you truly forgave me, you'd come home. We'd be a family again. Caitlyn would be back at Plant High, where she belongs."

Frustration clogged Diane's throat. Through gritted teeth, she managed to growl, "One thing has absolutely nothing to do with the other."

As much as Tim wished it to be otherwise, the coach at Plant High was never, ever going to let their daughter play soccer on her team again. The teachers and staff at the school had decided Caitlyn was trouble with a capital *T* and would always be watching the girl, ready to throw the book at her for the tiniest infraction of the rules. Diane knew she could bet her last dollar on that...and win. All of which made it impossible to return to Tampa and pick up their lives there where they'd left off.

"Mom! Dad!" Dragging her gear bag behind her, Caitlyn loped across the field toward them.

Diane's head jerked. She'd gotten so wrapped up in the discussion with Tim that she'd nearly overlooked the real reason she was standing in the middle of a high school athletic field. Stuffing their marital problems into a box she'd reopen at a better time, on a better day, she spread her arms wide. "Great game." She wrapped her daughter in a hug. "You were amazing out there!"

"Good game, kiddo," Tim said when it was his turn. "You nailed that final block. That slide was a thing of pure beauty."

"Coach liked it, too," Caitlyn gushed. "She said I showed talent and teamwork. She said as long as I keep playing like I did tonight, she'll start me as goalkeeper."

"Caitlyn, that's wonderful!" Diane's chest swelled with a potent mix of happiness and pride. This, she thought, this was what her daughter deserved. After all the hard work and effort she'd put into becoming the best soccer player possible, the teen was finally getting the praise and recognition she deserved. "I'm so proud of you!"

She glanced at Tim, expecting his reaction to

echo hers. Instead, the man stood stock-still, a positively stricken expression on his face. It took only a second for her to understand why. While the coach's words had elated their daughter, they'd also obliterated his last hope of Caitlyn ever returning to Plant High. Giving him a minute to come to grips with this new reality, she focused on her youngest.

"How about the rest of the team? Was coach happy with the way they played, too?"

Caitlyn nodded. "All but Stacey. She was the goalkeeper last season. She was giving everybody a hard time tonight. Coach moved her to sweeper. She was mad 'cause she missed the block on that last play."

"Ouch." Diane felt a pinprick of sympathy for the other girl. Changing to a new position wasn't easy at the high school level.

Caitlyn peered up at her, sweat still glistening on her face. "Mom, the team's going to Brother's for ice cream. Can we go?"

"Of course." Diane didn't bother telling Caitlyn the rest of the family were already on their way to the shop on Main Street.

A slight frown creased Caitlyn's brow. "Can—can Dad come, too?"

"Of course." She and Tim might have their share of problems, but tonight they'd both celebrate their daughter's success. She prodded her still-silent husband with an elbow. "Tim. You'll come with us for ice cream, won't you?"

Like someone waking from a dream, Tim shook himself. His trademark grin filled his face. "Of course. Wouldn't miss it. Where are we headed?"

"Why don't you ride with us? I'll drop you back at the school to get your car afterwards." As long as Tim was taking it on the chin tonight, she had something to show him. Something he'd like about as much as the fact that their daughter had found a new home at Emerald Bay High.

Blocks away from the turquoise building decorated with oversize sugar cones on either side of a pair of hot pink doors, Diane finally spotted a parking spot. She eased her car to the curb. Seat belts zinged into their holders, doors opened, and in no time, she and Tim and Caitlyn took their places at the back of a line that snaked out of the ice cream shop and past the vacant pharmacy next door.

"Whoa. Big crowd. It's going to take forever for our turn," Tim commented.

Diane peered ahead to the doors just as a

group of four walked inside. "The line will move faster than you'd think. And it's worth the wait. They make their own ice cream using a secret family recipe." Oscar Brother had opened the ice cream shop in the mid-Seventies. When he retired, he passed the business on to his twin sons. From the looks of things, Brother's had continued to thrive.

"Uh-oh. Don't look." Caitlyn shrank against Tim as distant car doors slammed and footsteps sounded on the sidewalk behind them.

"What's up?" Tim's head swiveled.

"Dad, I said, 'Don't look.'" Caitlyn, who had exchanged her cleats for zories in the car, stomped one foot. "That's Stacey."

"Stacey, the other goalkeeper?" Diane caught the reflection of three people in the plate glass of the empty storefront.

"Yeah. She doesn't like me. Can I go find the rest of the team? Or Aunt Amy?" Caitlyn pressed her palms together, her fingers intertwined. "Please?"

"It never pays to run away from your enemies," her father intoned.

Diane lowered her voice. "You're going to be on the same team for the next season, possibly the next several seasons. You should try and make friends with her."

"Pfft." Caitlyn blew a raspberry. "Fat lot of good that'll do."

"What did I hear you say?" Diane's eyebrows rose.

"Nothing. Sorry." Immediately contrite, the teen hung her head.

Within seconds, a compactly built brunette and her parents joined the line. Diane waited until they'd all moved another step or two toward the entrance of the ice cream shop before she turned to greet the new arrivals.

"Hi," she said forcing a cheery tone into her voice. "We're Caitlyn's parents. I'm Diane." She pressed a hand to her chest before pointing at Tim. "And he's Tim."

"Oh. You're the new people." The words fell from the other woman's mouth with all the warmth of ice cubes taken straight out of the freezer.

Diane stiffened at the rebuff. An awkward silence descended, broken only by the sound of passing cars and the voices of people up ahead in line. Her eyes widened when Caitlyn spoke.

"That, um, that nutmeg you pulled off right before Sebastian's final drive was neat, Stacey."

Stacey's mom had the manners of a mule. Apparently, though, she'd taught her daughter better, because the girl murmured a quick thanks. Showing a bit of her father's tenacity, Caitlyn pressed the point.

"I don't think I'd ever have the guts to pass the ball between their forward's legs the way you did. Where'd you learn that move?"

A flicker of pride shone in Stacey's eyes. "My mom taught me. She played goalie for Florida."

"Go, Gators." Stacey's dad supplied the response that was expected whenever someone mentioned the state university in Gainesville.

"Nice!" Diane let her admiration show. Not only did the school have one of the best women's soccer teams in the nation, it was also known for its academic excellence.

"I sure would like it if you'd teach me that move sometime," Caitlyn said.

Stacey lifted her head to her mom as if asking permission. At her mom's grudging nod, she said, "Okay. But you have to show me how you did that slide. That was a pretty good kick."

Caitlyn scuffed her flip-flops against the sidewalk. "Aw. I was lucky. It could have gone either way. But yeah, sure. Maybe next practice, we could work on them together."

"Yeah." Stacey's gaze shifted toward the ice cream shop. "Um, the rest of the team is hanging out on the patio. I was gonna head over there. You wanna come?"

"Sure." Caitlyn's gaze shifted to her parents. "That's okay, isn't it?"

"Of course." Diane answered for both of them. "But what about your ice cream?"

"No worries," Stacey interrupted. "The winning team gets free sundaes. They'll bring 'em to us once the crush thins out."

The all-important matter of dessert settled, Caitlyn joined her teammate as they headed toward the other side of the building, where a large open patio offered outside seating.

As the girls hurried off, Tim extended his hand toward Stacey's father. "Tim Keenan. This is my wife, Diane. Her family owns the Dane Crown Inn."

"A pleasure. Ron and Ellie Cuthbert." The men exchanged firm handshakes.

Ellie's demeanor thawed noticeably. "I hear you've been giving the inn a bit of a makeover. I'll have to swing by sometime and check it out. You know how it is when you live in Florida— someone's always coming to visit. We'd love to put them up at the inn instead of one of the hotels out by the interstate."

"Stop by anytime," Diane encouraged. "The painters should finish with the exterior next week." Paint and landscaping were the last items on what had started out as a very lengthy list.

Once Ellie's initial iciness had melted, the conversation proceeded smoothly. Diane was pleasantly surprised to learn that she and Ellie shared some interests in common. Both were working moms. They each had two children— Ellie's oldest, Glory, was married with a baby due in the spring. Tim was pleased to discover that Ron enjoyed golf, and the two men made plans to play a round together the next time Tim was in town.

"What brought you back to Emerald Bay?" Ellie asked when they'd finally neared the entrance.

Without glancing at Tim, Diane said, "My aunt broke her arm a couple of months ago and needed help. Once I was here, I realized how much I'd missed living in Emerald Bay." There was so much more to it than that, but she had no interest in airing the problems in her marriage with someone she'd just met.

At the door, Tim grasped the handle and held it while Diane and the Cuthberts stepped inside. A quick glance around told Diane the shop had seen quite a few changes since the last time she'd been here. The checkered linoleum floor of her youth had been replaced with gleaming tile. Sturdy tables wore fresh coats of white paint that paired well with metal chairs in the same turquoise as the exterior of the shop. Best of all, gone were the old-fashioned display cases filled with sad-looking five-gallon tubs. In their place, drop lights shone down on oblong trays that held mounds of ice cream with names like Parrot Head, Choco Orange and Bay-Limer. Her mouth watered.

"Stacey's going home with friends, so we're getting ours to go," Ellie said when they neared the counter, where no less than six teens hustled to take and fill orders. "But give me your digits, and I'll touch base in a day or two. We have several team events lined up for the season. You should know about them."

Vaguely aware that Tim and Ron were busy setting up a golf date, Diane quickly provided her number and email address. By the time Ellie had typed her info into her phone, one of the clerks was summoning them to the counter.

"Welcome to Brother's. What can I get for you?" asked a young man who sported a beige baseball cap with the name of the shop embroidered in a greenish blue.

"I'll have two scoops in a sugar cone. Rum Raisin and…" She scanned the many choices. "Is Parrot Head a strawberry?"

The boy grabbed the scoop from the rum raisin bin and began dipping a generous helping.

"Yes, ma'am. But if strawberry is your thing, I recommend the Berry Bliss. It's one of our most popular flavors."

"Sounds good to me," Diane said. She nodded goodbye to the Cuthberts, who'd selected tubs of prepackaged ice cream from a walk-up cooler and were already headed for the door.

Taking her towering cone from the young man, she waited while Tim settled their bill. She scanned the dining area that overflowed with parents and teens. At last, she spotted Amy and the others clustered around two tables at the back of the room.

"Why do I feel like a kid who just barely managed to pass his final exams?" Tim asked as they threaded their way through the crowded room.

"I think because we did." Diane licked a drip of rum raisin that ran down the outside of her cone. "Thanks to Caitlyn," she added as her heart swelled with pride in her daughter for the second time that night.

All in all, the evening had been a huge success. Caitlyn had literally saved the game with that final block. Equally as important, she'd broken the ice with Stacey and her family. Tim had found a potential new friend in Ron before spending a pleasant hour chatting with her family. They'd even had ice cream, a rare treat for her health-conscious husband.

Would there ever be a better time to tell him about the house?

Not anytime soon, Diane admitted. If she didn't take advantage of this opportunity, it might be ages before another chance this good came along again. By then, the house might not be available any longer and she'd have missed her chance.

Crumpling her napkin into a ball, she pitched it into the trash can on her way out of the ice cream shop, which had started to empty.

"Amy," she said, pulling her sister aside. "I need a favor."

"Shoot."

"Can you and Max drop Caitlyn off at the house? I'd ask Kim to take her, but she already has a car full." Plus, after playing her heart out on the soccer field, her daughter needed a shower in the worst way. She couldn't expect her Aunt Margaret or Nat to let the girl squeeze in between them, not even for the short drive to the inn.

"Not a problem." Amy glanced at Max, who nodded. "We were going there anyway. Aunt Margaret asked Max to fix a leak in her bathroom sink."

"Tonight?" Diane's eyebrows rose.

"Between his regular customers and work on the storefront, he hasn't done much work around the inn lately." Ever since she and Deborah had put money down on an old flower shop in Sebastian, Max had been spending all his spare time planning how to convert the space into a smaller version of Sweet Cakes. Amy eyed Tim, who lingered nearby. "You two want some alone time?" She enclosed the final two words in air quotes.

"Not the kind you're thinking." Diane's long-awaited severance package from Ybor City Accountants had finally arrived earlier this week. Once she'd verified that the amount was correct down to the last penny, her first task had been to pay the inn's insurance premiums out of the funds. With that accomplished, she had enough left over to make her own dreams a reality. "I feel like I ought to let Tim see the Wallaby property before I put an offer in on it."

Amy whistled low and slow. "That's not going to be an easy conversation."

"Tell me something I don't already know." In truth, Diane dreaded the upcoming talk. To say Tim hadn't reacted well to the idea of starting her own accounting firm would be putting it mildly. Why, the man had stopped speaking to her for three full weeks after she'd told him she wanted to open her business in Emerald Bay. She could hardly expect him to do cartwheels when she told him she wanted to buy a house here. "Which is why I don't want Caitlyn to come with us."

"You don't need to worry about her. Aunty Amy has her." Amy grinned.

"Thanks. This means a lot to me." Diane clung to her big sister for several long seconds. The simple task of giving her daughter a ride home might not seem like such a big deal to Amy, but it sure felt like one to her. After all, she'd lived on the other side of the state for the past twenty-five years. Separated from their families, she and Tim had learned to rely on themselves for practically everything—from raising their children to building their careers.

Here in Emerald Bay, though, things were different. *Better*. Hadn't the entire family turned out for Caitlyn's first game? Didn't they all celebrate birthdays and anniversaries together? Or pitch in as a group whenever there was work to do? In their free time, they liked nothing more than spending time together. Was it any wonder she'd decided to make Emerald Bay her permanent home?

"Hey. You're not getting all maudlin on me, are you?" From anyone else, the words might sound harsh or critical, but Amy's voice was light and teasing.

"No." Diane wiped her eyes despite her protest. "Just wanted to say thanks." Inhaling deeply, she squared her shoulders while she searched for the best way to break the news to her husband that she was never moving back to Tampa.

"Do you need something from the store?" Tim asked when she pulled into an overgrown parking lot in front of a T-shaped building constructed of concrete blocks. He stared through the windshield at the rusted sign that listed to one side over a nondescript entrance. "Mr. Wallaby's Grocery? Is it still open? This place looks closed up tighter than a drum."

"Come on," Diane said without answering his questions. "I want to show you something." Gravel crunched beneath her shoes as she stepped from her vehicle.

This far from the beach, the ocean provided a soothing background noise that ran counterpart to her hammering heart. Moving toward the building, she avoided the weeds that grew tall in the cracks of the concrete. In the darkness, a dim bulb over the entrance bathed the area in a pool of yellow light. Taking the key the Realtor had given her from her pants pocket, she slipped it into the lock. The front door opened with a rusty squeal. Inside, the air smelled of dust mingled with the slightest trace of something rotten. She flipped a wall switch, and overhead lights shone down on bare shelves that lined two walls. Between them, an empty display rack ran the length of what had once been a store.

"It doesn't look like much now, but thirty years ago, this place was bustling," she explained to Tim, who hovered at her elbow. "Amy and I used to come here at least once a week. We'd save up our allowance or the money we earned when we worked at the inn and we'd treat ourselves to a soda. Mr. and Mrs. Wallaby—they were the owners—they were the nicest people."

"You're not thinking of going into the

grocery business, are you?" Doubt laced Tim's words. "'Cause it'd be hard to compete with the big chain stores."

"I can't quite see myself as a grocer, can you? C'mon." She moved forward. "You need to see the rest."

Waving outstretched arms in front of her to keep from running face-first into a spiderweb, she picked her way around clumps of dirt and a few discarded boxes. Behind the counter, a rickety chair with a missing leg had been propped against the wall. Peering at it, she nearly lost her footing when a wave of nostalgia swept over her. How often had she seen Mr. Wallaby sitting in that very spot, dispensing advice to whoever would listen? And how often had she and Amy pretended to hang on his every word with the sure and certain knowledge that Mr. Wallaby would dole out Red Vines when he finally ran out of things to say?

"Lord, bless that man," she whispered, the taste of the fruity licorice dancing like a ghost across her tongue.

Clearing her throat, she opened the door that led to the rear of the building. From the store, she stepped straight into the living quarters. The cramped space that had served as the Wallabys' main room looked disappointingly smaller than she remembered it. Beyond it stood a kitchen that cried out to be updated. Two bedrooms, each with its own bath, stood on either side of the *T*-shaped space.

Tim dutifully followed her from room to room without commenting while she pointed out the home's admittedly few features. When she'd finished, he stood in the center of the empty living room, his arms crossed over his chest. His gaze centered on a water stain on the popcorn ceiling, he asked, "Why are we here? What is this all about, Diane?"

Time for the moment of truth.

Now that it had arrived, her nerves faltered. Hating the uncertainty that crept into her voice, she asked, "Remember how I told you I wanted to open my own accounting firm the night we ate at Fog Horn's?"

"How could I forget?" he snapped. As if he regretted the tone, Tim's voice immediately softened. "It's practically all I've thought about."

Diane waved her hand through the stale air. "I was thinking this might be the place." Scanning a spot on the wall where the paint had peeled away and exposed the concrete beneath it, she swallowed. "It would need some work. I'd convert part of the old grocery store into office space and turn the rest into another bedroom…for Nick." Their son was in his junior year at Virginia Tech. "The kitchen would have to be gutted, of course…"

"Of course." Tim eyed the tired avocado-green appliances, relics from the Seventies.

"The bathrooms need updating, but the yard's big enough to put in a soccer goal."

"You're serious?" Tim slowly rotated to give the room a second look. "You want to buy *this* place?"

"I'm thinking about it." *She was still thinking about it, wasn't she?* Though she'd run the comps—such as they were—and examined the numbers, she'd held off, not certain why she wanted Tim's approval but unable to move forward until she had it.

As if he'd had the wind knocked out of him, her husband doubled over. He braced his hands on his knees the way Diane had seen him do countless times when he reached the end of a long run.

"Are you all right?" she asked.

"It's been a night of surprises, that's all." He straightened. "Can we talk outside? The smell in here is…rank."

"It's probably the rugs." Wondering if they were original to the house, she added *Replace the carpets* to a growing list of changes she'd need to make before the house was habitable again.

She followed Tim out, shutting off lights and closing doors, making sure she left the place exactly as she'd found it. Once they were back in the car with the windows rolled down, she turned to him. She felt certain she already knew his opinion, but she needed him to say the words.

"Okay, let's hear it." She braced herself. "I already know you hate the idea."

"I wouldn't go that far, no. But I think you've underestimated how difficult it would be to move into this particular place." He ticked items off on his fingers. "New kitchen. New bathrooms. New carpets throughout. Remodel the old store to make an office and—what? A family room? Maybe another bedroom? All that will run a hundred *K*, easy. That's assuming the roof, plumbing and electrical are in good shape, which, from the look of the walls and ceiling, I seriously doubt." He took a breath. "But that's not the biggest problem."

Diane's chest tightened. He was right about the expense. She'd known that fixing up the place would take a pretty penny. Maybe not quite as much as Tim's off-the-cuff estimate, but her figures were in the same ballpark. "Which is?"

"It's too small. The whole house—store included—has less square footage than our kitchen and family room."

For an instant, Diane saw herself standing in their spacious kitchen in Tampa, the ingredients for chicken tacos spread out on the immense island, her family gathered around the table by the bay window. The idyllic image faded into memory. Those days were past, she reminded herself.

Resolved to move forward, not backward, she insisted, "Caitlyn and I don't need that much space. Since we've been in Emerald Bay, we've managed fine with just two rooms." Though, truth be told, sharing a bathroom with her teenage daughter had been challenging, to say the least.

"You say that, but you have the run of the entire inn and the grounds."

Tim had a point, she admitted. The Wallaby property wasn't much bigger than the tiny cottage she and Caitlyn had lived in while workmen refinished the floors in the main house. Their cabin had been...tight. They'd both gotten a little testy.

"I'm not saying *no*," Tim said, pressing the issue. "I just don't want you to rush into anything and then regret it later. It'd be better for you to take your time. Wait for the right place."

Diane eyed her husband. Though he'd given her sound advice, she couldn't shake the feeling that he'd find fault with whatever house she showed him. Even if it was the Taj Mahal. But was she reading more into the situation than it warranted? She took a steadying breath. Somewhere nearby, orange trees were coming into bloom. The air carried the faintest trace of blossoms and salt.

"Are you sure you wouldn't reject *any* house I find here?" she challenged.

Tim tapped his knuckles to his chest. "Ouch. That hurts."

"You have to admit, you haven't exactly been keen on the idea of me staying on in Emerald Bay permanently." She couldn't really blame him for wanting her to move back to Tampa, but that wasn't in the cards...for her or for their daughter.

"I'll admit I didn't take the news well when you originally brought it up. But I've had time to think about it since then. Time to see how important this is to you. And..." Tim's breath stuttered. "And how good it's been for Caitlyn to be here. That all struck home tonight when the coach practically guaranteed Cat a place in the starting lineup. I meant it when I said tonight

97

had been a night of surprises. That was a big one."

"And the others?" she prodded.

"I can't get over how well-adjusted our daughter has become. How confident she is. The old Cat was too shy, too wrapped up in what Marty or Sara thought—Marty in particular—to reach out to Stacey like she did tonight."

"You're absolutely right," Diane said, giving Tim his due. Marty had always been the leader of the threesome, with Caitlyn and Sara following along with whatever the bossy girl said. If she ever needed proof, Diane only had to look as far as the party that had upended her daughter's life. While Caitlyn bore her own share of the blame, it had been Marty's idea to invite their dates over while she and Tim weren't home. One thing had led to another—as it often did with teens—and before anyone could so much as blink, Caitlyn had been kicked off the soccer team, drawn a ten-day suspension from school, and lost her best friends.

"I was so worried about her," she admitted. "We both know adults who haul out some childhood trauma and wave it like a banner whenever they fail at something. It becomes their excuse for everything that goes wrong in their lives. I was afraid Caitlyn would become one of those people."

"You're not still afraid of that happening, are you?" In the faint light, concern threaded itself across Tim's features.

"Not as much." She took a breath. It was important for him to understand why she'd brought their daughter to Emerald Bay. "I think a lot of the credit goes to Amy and Aunt Margaret and my cousins. They were the role models our daughter needed. They showered her with love and support. They encouraged her to overcome her problems."

"We owe them so much," Tim whispered. "I just wish I had been here. I *should* have been here."

True, but piling more blame on his shoulders made as much sense as flogging a dead horse. Refusing to do that, she continued. "Since we've been here, Caitlyn has studied hard in her home school classes, made new and better friends, and she absolutely didn't let up on soccer. As a result, she's stronger now than she was before."

Tim's gaze turned speculative. "It's not just Caitlyn, though. You've changed."

"I've lost weight." Diane ran a hand over her jeans. Thanks to a new diet and exercise regimen, she'd shrunk two sizes since moving to Emerald Bay.

"You look…great. Healthier. It's more than

that, though." Tim seemed to struggle with what he wanted to say. "When we talked at Fog Horn's, I overlooked something—you're more at ease, more content than you've been since, well, in forever."

Diane thought her current emotional state was largely due to getting out from under the stress of working for Jeff Thomlinson. She hadn't realized how awful her boss was until she'd walked away from her job at Ybor City Accountants.

But Tim wasn't finished. "Now, when you talk about working with small business owners, your eyes light up. How could I ever take that away from the woman I love? More to the point, why would I want to?" He gazed at her, his eyes pleading. "I'm sorry, so, so sorry for ever hurting you. If you'll let me, I'll spend the rest of my life making it up to you."

Though Tim had said nearly the same thing at Christmas, this time she saw the depth of his sincerity in his eyes. She felt the brokenness of his heart. She heard the deep contrition in his voice.

And the final kernel of doubt inside her melted.

"I love you, too, Tim." Her voice cracked. She'd waited months for the chance to say those simple words. To mean them with all her heart.

Tears glistened in Tim's eyes as his arms slipped around her. Her own tears mingled with his when they kissed. A soft sigh sifted through her as the feeling of being exactly where she belonged spread through her chest.

Letting their kisses serve as a seal and a promise of other things still to come, they pulled apart. For a few minutes, they sat, Diane resting her head on Tim's shoulder, simply enjoying the familiar feel of being in one another's arms again.

The feeling of contentment came to an abrupt halt, though, when Diane heard the high-pitched whine of a mosquito near her ear. She swatted at the insect.

"I suppose we ought to go." Brushing a final kiss across her lips, Tim slowly withdrew his arm.

Diane straightened. Hoping to drive the mosquito away, she started the ignition and cranked the air conditioner to full blast. Her hair stirred in the breeze that poured out of the vents while one thing weighed heavily on her heart. Reluctant to say anything that might once more threaten their relationship, she considered burying it. Instead, she forced herself to speak calmly. "There's just one thing…"

"Yes?" Tim's window glided up.

"How are we going to make this work—with you in Tampa and me here in Emerald Bay?" She held her breath, knowing this final test had the power to undo their newfound happiness.

Tim turned toward her. He reached for her hands. "I'm willing to do whatever it takes," he said earnestly. "And yes, I've thought about it. I meant it when I said I've thought about nothing else since we talked that night at the restaurant. I've come up with a plan I think will work. It may need a few adjustments here and there. We might have to be flexible…"

"Just say it, Tim." She smiled, softly. It stood to reason that both of them would have to compromise. But their love, their marriage, their family was worth doing whatever it took.

"Warren is a fine partner and a caring dentist." Tim had sold a portion of his practice to the young man a few years back. "He's expressed an interest in buying me out, taking over the entire business when I'm ready to retire. That won't be for another four years."

Diane nodded. Tim had worked hard to build a thriving practice. Now that he had, he dreamed of retiring at fifty-five.

"I'd like to hang on to our house in Tampa until then. Currently, I'm going into the office four days a week. Over the next few years, that'll drop to three and then two and so on. In the meantime, I'll spend as much time as I can here in Emerald Bay. With you. In a house we'll buy here. One big enough to accommodate your accounting business and all of us once I retire and Nick graduates. Assuming he doesn't get a job in Timbuktu or something."

She appreciated his attempt at levity but couldn't laugh when her heart was in her throat. "And Caitlyn?" she asked.

"She'll stay here with you, of course. Go to Emerald Bay High. Play on the soccer team. Do whatever else girls that age do." Tim paused. "As long as she doesn't get involved with some boy and fall in love. You gotta promise me you won't let that happen."

Diane held up her hands. "No promises. She has a mind of her own, after all. But with both of us watching over her, I think we can keep her on the straight and narrow. We're both on the same page. We want her to go to college, make something of her life."

"I like the way you said that. Both of us... together."

Before she could tell him, much less show him, how much she ached for them to be together again in every way, her phone buzzed from its holder on the console. The screen lit up, their daughter's name displayed prominently at the top.

"You better get that," Tim murmured.

Diane punched a button, and Caitlyn's voice filled the car.

"Mom, where are you? You and Dad didn't get into another fight, did you? Are you okay?"

"I'm fine, sweetie, and no, your dad and I weren't fighting."

Anything but.

Wearing a silly grin, Diane rushed to reassure her daughter. "We were talking, and I guess we lost track of time. I'll drop him off at his car, and I'll be there soon."

"Okay. Remember, you promised to take me driving tomorrow morning. We need to get an early start 'cause Coach called a team meeting at ten."

The screen went dark as Caitlyn, having delivered her message, disconnected.

"She's driving now?" Tim sounded shocked.

"She has her learner's permit. She needs to log fifty hours behind the wheel before she can get her license." Diane ran her fingers through her hair. "Which explains why I'm turning gray."

"Huh. I'll take her out tomorrow."

"Sounds good to me." Tim had spent countless hours making sure Nick knew and obeyed the rules of the road.

Tim squeezed her hand. "I guess that means you won't be coming back to my place tonight?"

"Not tonight." She wanted their reunion—when it happened—to be something special. Not some rushed, hurried affair in his room in some nondescript hotel. "But soon," she promised.

And in the meantime, she'd shave her legs and do all the girly things a woman liked to do when she had an important date with the love of her life.

Oh, and start shopping for a house. She'd do that, too. They needed a bigger house, a house she and Tim could make their forever home.

Four

Jen

The line of black ink disappeared as Jen inched the pen across the sheet of kraft paper.

"What? No!"

She scribbled on a scrap left over from the roll she and Nat had purchased. The tip of the pen skipped over the page, leaving nothing behind but spiral indentations. She shook the ink pen and tried again.

Nada.

"Well, phooey." She removed the empty ink cartridge and set the useless pen aside. That had been the last of the refills. No others were available anywhere in Emerald Bay. Not for love or money. Which left her no choice. She'd have to make the long drive to the office supply store in Vero to pick up another cartridge. Or two.

"Make that four," she muttered, her gaze shifting from the stack of completed "treasure" maps to the remaining sheets of plain brown paper.

Straightening, she rotated her shoulders and, with her hands pressed against the base of her spine, arched her back, which had grown stiff. And no wonder. She'd spent the last two hours hunched over the desk in her suite on the back side of the inn. It was worth it, though. After all, what were a few new aches and pains compared with the fun they'd have at the gender reveal party this weekend?

If she finished the maps, that was. It was kind of hard to find a buried treasure without a map, wasn't it?

She rose from the desk, slipped the empty cartridge into the outside pocket of a crossbody purse she'd picked up at a thrift store and headed downstairs, where she intended to grab a bottle of water on her way out the door. Her footsteps faltered when she reached the spacious kitchen, where her sister whirled like a dervish.

Normally the epitome of organization, Kim gave something on the stove a quick stir before she raced to the fridge for a jug of milk, which she abandoned on the counter by the cutting board when she stopped there long enough to scrape a few peels from a carrot. Dropping the peeler, she returned to the stove, stirred rapidly and retraced her steps to the fridge.

"Where's the milk?" she asked holding the door ajar. She glanced, wild-eyed, over her shoulder.

Jen studied the smears of heaven-knew-what on Kim's usually pristine apron, took in the strands of hair that had worked loose from the normally neat bun and let her gaze roam the chaotic kitchen. Something urged her to turn tail and run, to duck back into the hall and pray that by the time she returned from the store in a couple of hours, the devil that had possessed her sister would relinquish its grip.

Okay, possession was a little bit over the top, but something had Kim rushing around like a crazy person. Which was so unlike her usual calm and collected state that Jen didn't quite know how to react.

Kim was the older sister who'd changed her diapers, fixed her bottles and, later, put sliced hot dogs into the macaroni and cheese they ate for dinner on those all-too-frequent nights when their mother left them home alone while she went who-knew-where. It was Kim who'd held

Jen's hand and assured her that everything would be all right the day their mom had dropped them off at the entrance to the Dane Crown Inn with instructions to, "Get on up to the house, girls." She'd disappeared down the road before they'd walked ten feet. And after their mother died, it had been Kim who'd made sure Jen did her homework, brushed her teeth and said her prayers before her big sister read them both a bedtime story each night.

Now, it looked like Kim could use some help. Jen couldn't abandon her in what certainly looked like her hour of need, any more than her sister had abandoned her when they were children. Taking a deep breath, she crossed to the kitchen island and grabbed the milk. Adopting the same slow, calm tone she'd used when customers at the bar had had a wee too much to drink, she held out the jug. "Is this what you're looking for? You left it on the counter."

"I did?" Kim blinked several times. Some of the wildness faded from her gaze. "I guess I did." She eyed Jen as if seeing her for the first time. "Did you need something?"

"No." Jen rushed to reassure her sister. "Nothing at all. I think you might need some help, though." She waved a hand at the dirty bowls and pans piled in the sink.

Kim brushed sweat from her forehead with the back of her hand. "The kale did it."

"Say what now?" Jen flexed her fingers. If her sister thought a bunch of greens had snuck in and wrecked her kitchen, maybe that possession thing wasn't so far-fetched after all.

"The kale," Kim insisted. "I need it for my salads this week. I bought plenty at the grocery store on Monday. This morning, when I opened the bags, it was all slimy. I had to throw every bit away." She pointed to the trash can. "I have to get more. The dinner is ruined without it. I've called everywhere. This time of year, Moss Meadows is the only place that has kale. By the time I drive down there and back, I'll be so far behind on this week's deliveries for Royal Meals that I'll never catch up."

"You couldn't use something else for the salads? Head lettuce? Or romaine?" Jen would have suggested something else, but her knowledge of leafy green vegetables didn't go much deeper.

Kim shook her head. "Kale, goat cheese, cranberries and almond salad with a Dijon vinaigrette," she said as if reciting from the recipe. "It sets the tone for the entire menu. To go with it, I'm making a goat cheese tart, roast pork with a cranberry compote, and salted-caramel almond pralines. If I ditch the kale, I'll have to start over, plan a whole new menu. Then I really won't make my deliveries."

"Okay," Jen said, recognizing the futility of trying to change her sister's mind. "Here's what we're going to do. First, you're going to take a break." She took Kim by the shoulders and steered her to a chair. "Have a cup of coffee or tea. When did you last eat?"

"I had breakfast," came a soft admission.

"That was hours ago. You need sustenance," Jen said in the same tone Kim had once used with her. "I'll grab a granola bar for you to have with your coffee. While you just sit for a bit, I'll do up these dishes. Then you can give me direction to Ma's Meadows—"

"Moss Meadows," Kim corrected. "It's an organic truck farm southwest of Vero."

"Oh, good. I was headed in that direction anyway. I have to pick something up at the office supply store." Jen deliberately avoided any mention of what, exactly, she intended to buy. To maintain the suspense, she and Nat were keeping the details of the gender reveal party under wraps. "While I'm out, I'll get whatever you need."

"You'd do that?" Kim's lower lip trembled, a sure sign she'd been stretched to her limit.

"You'd do it for me, wouldn't you?" Jen asked, not that she needed to. Kim had already done much more for her and many times over. Running an errand for her sister was the least she could do to chip away at a mountain of debt she'd never be able to repay.

"Oh, I could just hug you." Kim jumped from the chair.

"Please don't." Her arms stiff, Jen prevented her sister from getting too close. "I don't know what you've got all over your apron, but if you get any of it on me, I'll have to change my clothes. Sit. Drink. Eat," she directed.

After grabbing a granola bar from the pantry and pouring a cup of coffee, she made sure Kim followed her orders before, moving to the sink, she made quick work of tidying up.

From the outlet center on the outskirts of Vero Beach, Jen headed west on Route 60. On either side of the lightly traveled highway, flat, green farmland stretched for miles, unbroken except for the occasional barn or corrugated metal shed. She was nearly halfway to Yeehaw Junction and certain she'd gone too far when she spotted a weathered sign for Moss Meadows. Slowing, she took the next right-hand turn onto a single-lane road. Beside her on the passenger seat, the plastic bag that held a fresh supply of ink cartridges jostled as her tires bumped over ruts in the dirt-and-gravel track.

Childlike drawings of cucumbers, melons and ears of corn mounted on a series of white-washed boards put a smile on Jen's lips as she headed for the open-sided pole barn that loomed in the distance. There, a sign tacked to one of the structure's wooden posts welcomed visitors to the farm's vegetable stand. She stopped her car and, tucking the wad of Kim's cash into the pocket of her windbreaker, stepped out onto the matted grass that served as a parking lot. Beneath the pavilion's pitched roof, empty wooden crates stood on end, each supporting a bushel basket. The closest one held green heads of broccoli. Others contained clumps of bright red radishes with their tops still attached and several varieties of squash in different sizes, shapes and colors. Determined to get what Kim needed, Jen made a beeline for a basket filled with leafy greens.

"Welcome to Moss Meadows." A woman in a baseball cap and a flannel shirt hailed her from a lawn chair behind a white folding table. "I'm

Lacy. Let me know if I can help ya," she said without bothering to get up.

Pieces of dried gourd clacked together when a gust of wind stirred the strings of several wind chimes that hung from the pole barn's rafters. Lacy shifted her chair closer to the space heater at her feet.

Despite the chill in the air, Jen replied with a smile. "I'm Jen. Let me grab that kale over there, Lacy, and you can tell me what I owe you."

The wrinkles in the clerk's sun-browned face deepened into a frown. "Honey, we ain't got no kale. Sold ever' last bit of it to them boys from Ocean Grill when we opened this morning."

Disappointment flashed through Jen when a closer look inside the basket revealed thin stalks of something that looked more like romaine than the wider, curly leaves she'd driven nearly forty miles to buy. Sure enough, a hand-printed tag identified the contents as mustard greens.

"Are you sure you don't have kale? My sister needs it for her catering business. You might have heard of it—Royal Meals? In Emerald Bay?" Slowly, she walked past baskets filled with pale green cabbages and bunches of spinach without finding what she wanted. Hoping against hope, she eyed wooden crates that held oranges and tangerines.

No luck.

"Emerald Bay, you say?" Lacy pulled a thermos from under the table. "You've come quite a way to walk away empty-handed. Next time, call first and save yourself the drive." Steam rose from the opened container.

"But my sister did call," Jen protested. "Someone promised they'd set some kale aside for her.

"You say she talked to somebody? Musta been Caleb. He's the owner." The woman drew up the collar of her flannel shirt before she poured herself a cup of dark, coffee-colored liquid. "He's pullin' some early carrots. You can check with him if you want." She aimed a thumb at the dirt road. "Just keep going that-a-way till you see his pickup truck. You can't miss 'im."

Jen cupped her hand over her eyes and studied the fields that stretched farther than she could see. She was pretty sure Lacy was mistaken. It was entirely possible, likely even, that she'd never find this Caleb person considering the size of the farm, but what choice did she have? She'd promised Kim she'd bring the kale home, and by all that was holy, she wouldn't quit without giving it her best shot.

"Thanks, I'll do that." Her gaze landed on a basket that held thick green sticks covered in knobby bumps. She peered closer. "Are those…

Brussels sprouts?" she asked, not trying to mask her surprise. "I never knew they grew on stalks." Not that she'd given much thought to the tiny heads that tasted like a mix of her least favorite vegetables—asparagus and cabbage. Nevertheless, she grabbed a couple of pieces to show to Caitlyn.

"How much for these?" At the table, she dug in her pocket for money while the woodsy scent of chicory tickled her nose and reminded her of the time she'd spent in New Orleans.

"Nah, honey." The woman took a sip of the dark brew. "Them's on the house. In case, you know, Caleb ain't got what you want."

He'd better.

Leaving the thought unspoken, Jen forced a smile, thanked Lacy for her kindness and climbed back into her car. Seconds later, she clenched her teeth to keep from chipping a tooth while she sped over the road's washboard surface in search of the farmer.

"Huh. Imagine that. Lacy was right." Jen eyed the battered pickup truck someone had left in the middle of the narrow path that ran between a field of bushy green plants and one filled with something more akin to ground cover. With no room to pull to either side, she parked behind the truck, adjusted her sunglasses and emerged from the warmth of her car. Wishing she'd worn a heavier jacket, she scoured the plots on either side of the road, her gaze eventually landing on a man in overalls. About twenty yards away, he tossed a handful of carrots, leafy tops and all, into a burlap sack before, straightening, he turned toward her.

Not wanting to interrupt his work more than absolutely necessary, Jen headed out to meet him. A plan she reconsidered once she reached the first line of plants. Sprouting from mounds of rich dark soil, they bent and swayed in the breeze. Walking through the rows of carrots without brushing against them would be impossible. She shivered. Who knew what sort of bugs lurked beneath those feathery leaves? There might even be snakes. Another shiver passed through her, leaving her to guess whether it was from the cold or her fears. Refusing to pick just one, she cupped her hands around her mouth.

"Yo! Are you Caleb?" she yelled.

"Yeah." The gunnysack he wore across one shoulder fell to the ground, and he strode toward her.

Jen shaded her eyes against the bright sun of clear winter's day. Though she couldn't put her finger on it, something about the way Caleb moved looked oddly familiar. Did they know each other? Was he a client of Sweet Cakes? Mentally, she shook her head. Though he was too far away for her to see his face, none of the people she'd met while making the bakery's morning deliveries had defined "tall and dark" quite the way Caleb did. He didn't attend their church, either. She'd certainly remember a man with those broad shoulders, that narrow waist. So, no. He wasn't someone she'd met since her return to Emerald Bay.

Which only left the people she'd known when she lived in town nearly thirty years ago, and the idea that he was one of them nearly made her laugh. She didn't have a lot of friends back then. A few acquaintances. A couple of bullies who did their best to make her miserable life worse. Anything more was hard to come by when you were the odd girl out, the kid who spent two weeks in Emerald Bay one year, three months the next. Add the boulder-size chip she carried on her shoulder those days, and it was no wonder that she never fit in. Tired of trying, she struck out on her own the day after graduation and, until recently, she'd never been back.

So, no. She didn't know the man who strode toward her, his golden tan reflecting the midmorning sun, muscular forearms bulging, his face hidden beneath a baseball cap. She didn't, but judging from the way her insides shimmied at the sight of him, she'd like to.

Summoning her brightest smile, she greeted him. "Hi, Caleb. I'm Jen. Sorry to interrupt your work."

Jen's tummy gave another shimmy when Caleb removed his baseball cap and waves of dark hair fell to his shoulders. Her mouth dry, she forced herself to stare around his solid frame at the burlap sack he'd left in the field while he used a red bandana he'd pulled from the pocket of his overalls to mop his forehead. Only when he'd thrust the dampened cloth into a pocket and resettled his hat did she dare look at him again.

Though his ball cap still bathed his face in shadow, she took in a pair of wide-set eyes, unshaven cheeks and a softly rounded jaw. Mesmerized by his lips, which were wide and full, she took a beat or two to react when he asked, "What can I do for you?"

Several answers sprang to mind in response to the deep timbre of his voice. Though it took every bit of willpower she possessed, Jen forced herself to stick to the reason that had brought her to Moss Meadows. "Um, my sister called this morning about some kale. I'm here to pick it up."

"Kale, huh? And here I thought maybe you'd come to see me."

"You?" Her libido, which had admittedly been on the rise, plummeted. If there was one thing she couldn't abide, it was a man who was too full of himself. This one fit the bill if he thought she'd driven all the way here from Emerald Bay for a booty call.

"Well, yeah." He eyed her up and down, his gaze landing on her face and staying there so long she thought it might put down roots. "You're Jennifer, aren't you? Jennifer Dane?"

Behind her sunglasses, Jen felt her eyes widen. The last time someone had called her Jennifer Dane had been two husbands ago. "These days, most people call me Jen. And it's Passel now." Though why she hadn't reverted to her maiden name, she didn't know. She peered up at the man who reminded her of someone she couldn't quite remember. "Do I know you?"

"It's me, Caleb. Caleb Grimes. We went to senior prom together."

Nah. Couldn't be.

If it had been up to her, she'd have skipped the dance, but her Aunt Liz wouldn't hear of such a thing. So instead of curling up in the library with a good book—or, more likely, spending the night sulking in her room—she'd borrowed the gown Belle had worn to her prom several years earlier and joined a misfit group of other losers who didn't have dates.

Had Caleb been one of them?

A vague memory of a lanky teen with a bad haircut and an ill-fitting suit surfaced. She stared up at the man who had very little in common with that boy. In the ensuing years—if indeed this was the same person—he'd shot up at least another six inches and put on sixty pounds of the kind of muscle that came from lifting bales of hay, not weights at a gym. Tilting her chin up, she studied the face that looked down on her from beneath the brim of his baseball hat. The acne that had once marred his skin had either cleared or now hid beneath three-day-old stubble. No help there. It wasn't until her eyes met his that recognition dawned. More green than brown, his hazel orbs focused on her as if the rest of the world no longer mattered.

A delicious zing passed through her.

"Caleb!" Twin helpings of relief and laughter rang in her voice. "My, how you've changed. I would never have recognized you."

"Bigger, older and, hopefully, wiser. But you…" He whistled softly. "You haven't changed a lick."

"Now I know you're lying, but since you're being sweet, I'll forgive you," Jen teased. These days L'Oreal Number Twenty-One kept her hair the same glossy, black color she'd been born with, and daily workouts were absolutely necessary in order to maintain her waspish waist and keep her legs from getting flabby. Her breasts, though, were another story. She'd often boasted they were the "best money could buy," and she meant it. In her line of work, small breasts meant small tips, a situation she'd rectified as soon as she'd saved up enough for a good plastic surgeon.

"Are you back in town for good? Or just come for a visit?" Caleb's gaze intensified.

Jen leaned against his truck. "It started out as a visit. Now I'm not so sure." When Caleb's dark brows knitted, she explained. "My Aunt Margaret needed some help with the inn. She's eighty and, up until recently, was still running the place all by herself. It sounds like we've got everything worked out, though."

"Not in a rush to hurry home to hubby?" Caleb asked.

Jen coughed. "That would be the ex-husband. And no, I'm fine right where I am. At least, for the time being." She gestured toward the field of carrots. "How'd you end up here? I thought you were headed to someplace like Stanford or MIT." Unlike her, Caleb had graduated with honors and seemed destined for a top engineering school.

"Life happens." Caleb peeled heavy work gloves from his hands. "I went to Duke, even worked for one of those big contractors up at the Space Center for a few years. I hated every minute of it." He chuckled, a low, humorless sound. "It was Wilma who introduced me to farming. Her dad owned this place. Soon we were spending weekends and holidays—all our free time, really—helpin' him out. When he died, we inherited the farm, so here I am."

"You're married." She tempered her voice to weed out the surprise.

"Widowed. Lost Wilma to leukemia back in 2000." He stashed his gloves in a back pocket.

"I'm so sorry." She hoped the brief condolence didn't sound as trite to him as it did in her own ears, but she didn't know what else to say.

"It took her quick," he said, as if the thought gave him some comfort.

"And you like farming?" she asked, shifting direction.

"I love it." An easy grin spread across Caleb's face. "Even more since I switched over to organics. Better for the environment. Better for everyone's health—yours and mine."

Oh, why'd he have to go and say that?

Jen felt like she could have stood there for another hour, catching up with Caleb like two old friends who hadn't seen each other in decades might, but the mention of organic farming reminded her why she'd come looking for him in the first place. She cleared her throat. "I hate to cut this short, but Kim—you remember my sister, don't you?"

"She was a couple of years ahead of us, wasn't she?" Caleb resettled his baseball cap.

"Right. Well, she's started a catering business, and she sent me here to pick up the kale she needs for this week's menu. She said you'd set some aside for her?" Jen held her breath, hoping she hadn't wasted the trip all the way out here. Not that any woman in her right mind would ever consider spending time with Caleb a waste.

"Kale. Right." Caleb kicked at a clod of rich, black dirt. "Got it right here in the truck for you. Picked it myself just before you got here." Two strides took him to the pickup, where he hauled a bulging burlap sack from the bed. "Pop your trunk," he directed, nodding at her car. With an effortless grace, he transferred the bag to her car.

"How much do I…"

Caleb held up a hand, his fingers splayed. "No charge."

Jen pursed her lips. "I can't take all that for free. This is your livelihood." She eyed the acres of farmland.

"I insist. It's not every day I get the chance to see the girl who got away." Tossing another killer smile in her direction, he paused. "Of course, if you want to repay me, I wouldn't turn down a drink at the County Line one night." The honkytonk at the Vero Beach city limits had been *the* hottest spot in town when they were in high school and needed fake IDs to make it past the door.

"You know where to find me," she said, slipping behind the wheel and starting the engine. "Give me a call. We'll set something up."

With that, she threw the car into reverse. Slowly, she backed to a spot where the road widened enough to let her make a three-point turn. As she bumped over the track toward the main road, she caught a final glimpse of Caleb standing in the middle of the road watching her go.

Should she invite him to the party this weekend? She laughed dismissively. Taking a man to a gender reveal party on their first date was sure to send him running for the hills. Though, in Caleb's case, maybe that wouldn't be such a bad idea.

She needed to be very careful where he was concerned, she warned herself. The tall farmer was exactly the kind of man she often fell for—

good-looking, with a smoldering sexiness that made her feel all fluttery inside. She had no doubt that they could have a lot of fun together. The problem was, she suspected things with Caleb could go from fun and games to serious in about sixty seconds flat, and a relationship was the last thing she needed in the mess that was her life right now.

Sunday dawned clear and bright, the perfect day to spend time outdoors. Which relieved Jen to no end, considering the whole *reveal* part of their gender reveal party involved tromping through the inn's twenty acres in search of hidden treasure. Which wouldn't be nearly as much fun in the pouring rain or if the temperatures dropped below freezing.

"Is anyone else here?" Nat asked, walking into the kitchen looking her usual adorable self in sweats and a T-shirt.

At the sink, Jen swigged the last of her coffee. "Nope. It's just us chickens." Tim had swung by early this morning to take Diane and Caitlyn out to breakfast before church. The rest had helped themselves to sweet rolls, coffee and orange juice before Kim, Belle and Aunt Margaret left for Sunday school. The church crowd would all go out to lunch at the Pirate's Gold Diner after the eleven o'clock service. While she rinsed her cup and added it to the load of dirty dishes in the dishwasher, Jen silently accounted for the inn's guests, who had scattered in a half dozen different directions, eager to take advantage of a beautiful midwinter day.

Nat yawned and stretched her arms over her head. "I don't think I slept a wink. I kept having nightmares about pirates coming ashore and stealing our treasure chests." Late yesterday afternoon, she'd hidden small boxes filled with pink and blue beads wherever X marked the spot on the maps they'd designed.

Jen laughed. "I doubt if we have to worry about a landing party. I was more concerned about the racoons and squirrels. That's why we left that one box behind the shed all week." Though she'd found paw prints around the spot, the animals had not disturbed the chest.

Nat tucked a wisp of blond hair behind her ear. "I can't wait to see everyone's reaction. What do you think Scott and Fern are hoping for—a boy or a girl?"

"Oh, you know." Jen shrugged. "They'll be happy with either, as long as it's healthy. It's

Sophie I'm concerned about. She's in for a big adjustment." She'd spent two weeks with Kim right after Nat was born. Josh had barely been two at the time. Much as he loved being a big brother, it had been a hard time for the toddler.

"I talked to Fern about that," Nat said. "She wants me to spend a couple of afternoons each week at their house after the baby's born. I'll do crafts with Sophie and Isabella, take them to their dance and music lessons, basically help ease the transition."

Jen reeled back, stunned. "That's awesome, Nat. What a great idea!" Studying her niece, she marveled at the changes that had occurred in the young woman in a few short months. Just as the blue streak that had given Nat a parrotlike look had disappeared, so, too, had the entitled attitude that insisted the world owed her a living. Lately, the girl had been pitching in left and right, updating the inn's website, helping Belle take her music in a different direction and, now, offering to help out with a newborn.

On impulse, she slipped one arm around Nat's waist and gave her a quick squeeze.

"What was that for?" Nat asked when Jen had released her.

"I need an excuse to hug my niece?"

"No, but…"

"No buts. I just wanted you to know how happy I am that we're spending this time together." Truth be told, she hadn't seen much of Nat or Josh in the years since Kim and Frank split up. Not that she'd seen much of Kim, either, but whenever she had managed a visit, the kids had been with their father. Now that she had the chance to make up for lost time with the young woman, she wanted to take advantage of it.

Straightening, she said, "We have a lot to do if we're going to have everything ready by the time Scott and Fern get here. Are you ready to get started?" When Nat's head bobbed, Jen started for the stairs. "I guess we'd better grab the decorations from my room, then." In order to keep the party's theme a secret, she'd tucked all their purchases out of sight in her closet.

Four hours later, tiny Jolly Rogers waved from sticks along the coquina driveway that led from the main road to the inn. A pirate's frigate adorned the welcome banner draped over the railing on the front porch. On a table near the door, old-fashioned script on a parchment scroll directed guests to help themselves from a "treasure trove" of pirate-themed accessories— eye patches, plastic swords and the like. The aged, leather tricorne hat worn by at least two generations of Dane children on countless treasure hunts rested on the newel post at the bottom of the stairs. Outside, Jen and Nat had huffed and puffed until they'd filled several inflatable ships' wheels and anchors, which they placed around the deck. In the shade of an oversize umbrella, a set of old-fashioned brass scales and a ship's log created a weighing station where Margaret would await the return of the treasure hunters.

"I still think we should have borrowed that statue from the diner," Nat said as she ripped open packs of markers at the craft table. "He'd be the perfect addition to our décor."

"Couldn't do it. That thing scares your Aunt Amy to death. One glimpse of it here and she'd probably hightail it right back home, taking our cake with her." Jen didn't understand her cousin's fear, but she could relate to it. She'd no sooner drag the wooden carving of Captain Hook to the inn than she'd stick her hand into a terrarium full of snakes or force Kim to wrestle an alligator.

"Hmmm. I guess there's that—it wouldn't be a party without dessert." Nat glanced toward the kitchen, where tall sticks supported balloons decorated with pirate sharks wearing toothy grins around the empty cake table. "Speaking of which, when's Amy getting here?"

Jen checked her cell phone for messages. "She's leaving the diner now. She says it'll take her fifteen minutes to swing by the bakery. Then she's coming straight over." She propped her hands on her hips and nodded her approval at the decorations. "I'm going to dash upstairs and get ready."

"I'll race you," Nat said with a daring grin.

Jen waved her on. "You go ahead. I'm still out of breath from blowing up all those balloons." Not for the first time, she wished they'd opted to have them filled at the store.

By the time Jen had captured her hair into a ponytail and donned the requisite jeans and white T-shirt, the sounds of footsteps and excited, little-girl shrieks came from downstairs. She rushed down the steps, eager to greet Scott and Fern and their daughters. In no time at all, Nat was helping Sophie into the black vest the child had chosen from the accessory table along with a loot bag filled with plastic coins. Isabella slipped an eye patch over one eye. Jen tried not to laugh when the preteen ripped off the patch after only a few seconds. She quietly exchanged it for a spyglass and a fake cutlass.

No sooner had Amy slipped in through the back door and settled the cake on its special table than the house filled with boisterous greetings as, accompanied by Craig and Max, the rest of the family trooped in from lunch.

"Gather 'round, everyone," Jen called once the women had ooh'd and aah'd over Fern's tiny baby bump and the men had exchanged back slaps and handshakes with Scott. As soon as she had their attention, she cleared her throat. "As you can see, today we're all pirates."

"Arr!" Scott called, swishing the rubber hook he'd attached to his arm through the air.

"Avast, ye maties," Amy said in a guttural voice that sent laughter rippling through the group.

"Arr," Jen echoed. Wiggling her eyebrows, she asked, "And what do all pirates do? They search for treasure," she said, answering her own question before anyone piped up with other, less child-friendly things pirates were known to do. "Now, pirates have to wear something on their heads to keep from getting sunburnt, so we've set up a table in the family room where we can all make and decorate our own three-corner hats." Grinning, she made eye contact with Isabella and Sophie. "Just like a real pirate would wear!"

"Yes!" shouted Isabella.

Standing beside her, Sophie didn't look nearly as excited but, following her big sister's example, she added her own, quieter, "Yes!"

Soon everyone was gathered around the craft table where, following directions Nat had found online, the adults quickly fashioned three-corner hats out of stiff paper. Isabella struggled for a moment, but with Nat's help, she finally managed to make a passable hat. Her younger sister, though, ran into trouble.

"I can't do it!" A double helping of frustration and determination showed on Sophie's face as she crumpled her sheet into a ball when she couldn't get the edges to align.

Fern stepped to her daughter's side. "That's okay, honey. We'll get another piece of paper and try again," she soothed.

"It's no good," Sophie moaned. Her mood shifting, she shoved at the stack of cream-colored paper. "Pirates wear black hats, not white ones."

"Sophie…" her mother said, using the same warning tone used by mothers throughout the world.

"No!" Sophie picked up a black marker and began furiously coloring on a sheet. "I need a black hat."

Jen, who'd been standing close enough to overhear the exchange, suppressed an urge to giggle. Sophie reminded her of herself at that age, and the little girl wasn't wrong. Like all the other bad guys in books, movies and on TV, pirates usually wore black. Jen snapped her fingers. Before she gave herself a chance to think better of the idea, she knelt in front of Sophie.

"What if we let you wear a *real* pirate's hat?"

"Honest?" Her eyes widening, the girl's mouth rounded into an *O* shape.

"You can't keep it. It has to stay here at the inn. But you can wear it for the treasure hunt if you want to."

Sophie blew out a big breath. "Yes, please."

"Okay, then. Let me get it for you." Only then did she glance at Scott, who mouthed a silent, *You're spoiling her*.

Laughing, Jen shrugged. That's what aunts were for, weren't they? She grabbed the old leather tricorne from its perch and plopped it onto a grinning Sophie's head. Then, with the crisis averted, it was time for the treasure hunt.

Cries of "Ho-ho-ho!" and "Arr!" rang through the house as, brandishing plastic swords and wearing eye patches beneath their paper hats, the jovial group of *pirates* moved to the back deck. Nat broke the crowd into teams of two and three. Aunt Margaret took her place at the scales, where she'd agreed to record each team's treasures in the logbook. Jen issued a final admonishment that the success of the reveal depended on each team not only finding their treasure, but bringing it back to be weighed. Then, with maps in hand, six of the teams set off in different directions.

Jen handed Scott the final map as he and Fern started down the steps. Trailing behind her parents, Sophie shot a final look over her shoulder at Jen and froze. One hand holding her hat in place, she tipped her head to her parents. "Can I go with Aunt Jen? Pleeeeze?" she begged.

Jen blinked. She hadn't planned on participating in the treasure hunt. After all, how fair would that be? She'd drawn the maps. She knew where every treasure chest was buried. She was on the verge of telling Sophie *no* when Fern intervened.

"You know what, Soph? I think that's a great idea. Jen, you go with Scott and Sophie. I'll stay here and keep Aunt Margaret company." Fern's hand drifted down over her slightly rounded belly.

Jen swallowed the protest that had formed on her lips while heat rushed up her neck and spread across her cheeks. What had made her think sending a pregnant woman on a trek through twenty acres of gardens, fields and orange groves was a good idea?

"I'm so sorry," she rushed. "I should have thought this through."

"Please." Fern brushed aside Jen's concerns like she was brushing aside a fly. "My doctor encourages me to get plenty of exercise. I work out at the gym every day. A short hike wouldn't hurt me. But I would like to spend more time with Aunt Margaret." She smiled warmly at the older woman, who sat in the shade. "If you don't mind, Aunt Margaret."

"I'd love a chance to chat." Margaret patted the chair beside her.

"There. It's settled," Fern declared. "The three of you go. I'll be fine right here."

"If you're sure." Jen glanced at Scott, who nodded his approval.

Her hand once more pressed over her belly, Fern took her seat beside Margaret. "I am."

The old tricorne listing to one side, Sophie practically tripped down the steps. "We need to hurry so no one else finds our treasure." She tugged urgently on Jen's hand. "Let's go."

Jen's heart expanded two sizes when Sophie's fingers slipped into hers. She smiled, thinking that her mother would have called the little girl who was always cocked and ready to go "a pistol." Though the name fit, Sophie's sweet and adorable moments far outweighed her occasional temper tantrum.

"Are we really going to find the treasure?"

Sophie asked, pushing back the hat far enough that Jen could see tiny furrows in her forehead.

"We will if you'll help your Daddy follow the map," Jen assured her. Since she already knew where every chest was hidden, she decided to lag back.

"Want to hold the map?" Scott asked, taking his cue from Jen.

"Can I?" Sophie bounced on her tippy-toes.

Jen's fingers felt empty when Sophie dropped her hand and rushed to her father's side. Trailing behind, she followed the pair along the pavered walkway that led past the cottages until they reached Regalia. There, the line on the map veered toward the gardens, and Jen sighed with relief when Scott steered them in the right direction. With Sophie stopping to adjust her hat every couple of minutes, it was slow going, but eventually they stepped onto a dirt path that meandered around neatly trimmed patches of bougainvillea and bird of paradise, as well as palm trees whose spiny leaf bases formed a protective barrier around their trunks. Finally, they passed the now-dormant rose garden and arrived at a small clearing.

Scott pointed to the map. "X marks the spot," he announced, tapping the paper with one finger.

Wide-eyed, Sophie spun in a circle. Her hat slid sideways. When she stopped to straighten it, her lower lip trembled. "I don't see an X, Daddy."

"Good point, baby girl," her father said. "But there must be a treasure around here somewhere. Let's see if we can find it."

While Sophie flitted about, scuffing her feet through the short grass, her dad slowly walked around the perimeter of the clearing. A knowing smile formed on his lips when he stopped to stare at a squat palm tree. He waited, patient, until his daughter spied a small treasure chest tucked into one of the lower fronds that jutted out from the trunk.

"Daddy! I found it!" Sophie squealed. Rushing forward, she grabbed the box and pried open the lid. Inside, a collection of blue and pink glass beads glistened. She ran a finger over them. "Oooooh!"

"Be careful not to spill them," Jen cautioned. "Aunt Margaret needs to separate the blue pieces from the pink ones and weigh them."

"I'll be very careful." Sophie snapped the lid closed and pressed the box to her chest with both hands. "Aunt Jen, can you fix my hat?" she asked.

Though she didn't think anything could look more adorable than the girl who wore a lopsided hat and clutched a treasure chest, Jen plucked the old leather tricorne from Sophie's head. But as she started to reposition it, she noticed several thick, dark flakes in the girl's hair. After brushing them off the child, she tipped the hat upside down and peered at the torn and frayed lining.

"Uh-oh," she said, making a face. "The inside of the hat is falling apart. It's making a mess." She brushed the inside of the hat with her fingers. When she held them out to Sophie, they were covered with tiny black flecks. "Maybe you shouldn't wear it until we get it fixed." She waited a beat, hoping her niece wouldn't be too upset.

"That's okay." Sophie's fingers tightened on the little chest. "I have to carry the treasure. I need to be very, very careful with it."

"I'm sure you will, sweetheart," Jen agreed. She tucked the old hat under one arm. Smiling conspiratorially at Sophie, she asked, "What do you think? Should we head back to the house and find out whether you're getting a baby brother or a sister?"

"Can't it be something else? Pleeeze?" Sophie shot a hopeful glance at her dad.

"What do you mean, honey?" Scott peered down at his daughter.

"I been asking Mommy for a kitten, but she always says no," Sophie explained. "She says we hav'ta have a baby." The girl sighed wistfully. "I *really* want a kitten."

This was one battle the headstrong child couldn't win. Jen struggled to swallow the laughter that welled up inside her. Catching sight of the humor that glinted in Scott's eyes didn't help one iota, and she turned away, leaving her cousin to deal with the question of the kitten.

"We always listen to Mommy," Scott said, managing to sound both sympathetic and serious. "And now, I think we should go see her 'cause I heard there's going to be cake later. You don't want to miss out on that, do you?"

"Can I have a really big piece?" Sophie asked, her interest in a kitten quickly fading.

"Tell you what—I'll cut us both a piece of cake and you can choose which one you want."

"I'm going to take the biggest one," Sophie boasted. And, with the treasure chest pressed to her chest, she set out on the path back to the house.

Twenty minutes later, the family crowded close around Margaret's table, where piles of blue and pink glass beads stood in front of six of the seven treasure chests. She opened the lid on the final box. "Is everyone ready?" she asked.

Whispering a prayer that this final part would go according to plan, Jen nodded. She looked to her cousin for confirmation, but for once, Scott was speechless. When her husband didn't answer, Fern gave an enthusiastic *yes* for both of them. While Scott clutched Fern's hand in his, Margaret sorted the remaining stones into two piles and weighed them. She recorded the figures in the log, then tallied the results. Frowning uncertainly, she beckoned Jen, who ran one finger over the numbers.

Relief tightened Jen's throat when the final tally matched the slip of paper in the envelope Fern had delivered after her last doctor appointment. "Perfect," she told her great aunt.

Aunt Margaret's eyes brimmed with happy tears. She dabbed at them with a tissue before, her face wreathed in smiles, she handed the logbook to her nephew. Scott took one look at the bottom of the page, snapped the book closed and, rather than announce the results, swept his wife into a crushing hug.

"Get a room," Amy shouted at her brother when the couple continued to hold one another close.

"Boy or girl?" demanded Kim.

"Let me see that logbook," Diane said, pushing her way to the front of the group.

"Okay, okay," Scott said at last. Planting a final kiss on his wife's cheek, he turned a tearstained face toward the members of his family and their few invited guests. "Well, folks," he said, clearly fighting for control. He slipped one hand protectively over Fern's baby bump. "It looks like the newest addition to our family is a girl."

The words no sooner left his lips than clouds of pink confetti burst from the two poppers Isabella and Sophie wielded under the watchful eyes of their aunts. A chorus of, "Congratulations!" rang through the air. As the noise quieted, Jen leaned down to Sophie, who'd lingered at her side. "You're going to have a baby sister. Isn't that great?"

"Uh-huh." Sophie scuffled her feet. "Can we have cake now?"

This time, Jen didn't try to hide her laughter.

The monk parakeets that lived in the palm trees at the edge of the property had flown to their nests and settled down for the night by the time Scott and Fern herded Isabella and a sugar-hyped Sophie into the big SUV in the parking lot of the Dane Crown Inn. Craig and Max had departed shortly after Scott and his family. Tim had been the last to leave, but eventually, Diane had walked him to his car and seen him on his way back to Tampa.

Tired after the long day, Jen sat at the kitchen table, her feet propped up on the rungs of the empty chair beside her, enjoying the peace and quiet while, behind her, Kim arranged glasses on a tray. As she watched the last bit of sunlight fade from the western sky, Belle slipped out of the family quarters carrying a bottle of nail polish. She closed the door behind her and joined Jen at the table. Soon, Amy and Diane wandered into the kitchen from other parts of the house for the chat that had become a nightly ritual. Nat, her hair still damp from the shower, was the last to join them.

As she slid the tray of glasses onto the table, Kim nudged Jen's shoulder. "Good job today." She nodded at her daughter. "You, too, Nat."

"Thanks," Jen murmured while her sister poured wine from one of the bottles she'd uncorked earlier. "I think everyone had a good time."

"I don't know how you managed to keep the secret, but the reveal was a huge success." Belle whipped a short stack of napkins from the holder and plunked her polish on top of it.

"That's the truth." Nat brushed her fingers through the short ends of her hair. "I didn't know whether it was a boy or a girl, and I even helped fill the treasure chests."

"It wasn't easy," Jen admitted. She'd had to sneak a few blue baubles out of each box after Nat had filled them. "I was so excited, I wanted to tell everyone the minute I found out."

"You know, from Scott's reaction, I thought for sure it was going to be a boy." The acrid scent of polish floated in the air as Belle began painting her nails a soft pink.

"I thought so, too, for a moment." Kim emptied the first wine bottle and reached for a second. "But I'm thrilled we're going to have another girl in the family."

"Do you think Scott and Fern are really happy about having that?" Nat passed one glass of wine to Amy, another to Jen. "I mean, three girls. Don't you think they were hoping for a boy this time?"

"Not really." Amy sipped her drink. "My brother knows how to work a room—it's part of the reason he's such a successful attorney. But I don't think even he could fake the kind of joy I saw today. What do you think, Diane?"

"No doubt about it—he was genuinely

happy. So was Fern." Diane tapped her fingers on the tabletop. "I'm glad I've finally mastered the double crochet." Their Aunt Margaret had been giving her and Caitlyn lessons. "I already picked out some beautiful pink yarn for my baby blanket. I can't wait to see how it turns out."

"Three girls." Kim shook her head. "They'd better start saving for all those weddings."

"Unless they get married here." Nat gestured toward the living room. "You and Aunt Amy could handle the catering and the cake. That's what I'm going to do."

"Oh?" Kim's eyebrows hiked. "Is there someone special in your life I don't know about?"

"How about the youth pastor? Is he *the one*?" Amy made air quotes.

While a protesting Nat blushed all the way to the roots of her hair, Belle chimed in. "I think you've missed the point. We won't own the inn by the time those girls are old enough to start dating, much less get married. Not if we stick to the plan and put the place on the market right after the reunion." Without lifting her head, she painstakingly painted one nail.

Jen's heart sank at the thought of someone else running the inn or, worse, watching the new buyers raze the property for another set of cookie-cutter condos. Unable to trust her voice, she toyed with the stem of her wine glass while she found slim comfort in the fact that she wasn't alone. For several long seconds, no one spoke.

Finally, Nat cleared her throat. "Um, remind me again why Aunt Margaret is selling the inn?"

Knowing it wasn't her place to answer, Jen kept her lips sealed while her sister and cousins stared at one another, each trying to decide who should speak first.

At last, Belle sighed heavily. "Running the inn is too much for Mama to do on her own anymore. And none of us can shoulder that responsibility. It's too much to ask of one person."

"But it wouldn't have to be one person, would it?" Hope edged Nat's voice. "I mean, you all live here now. Couldn't you—oh, I don't know—share the load or something?"

After a pause in which, once again, no one seemed eager to answer, Diane softly explained, "It's not just the work of running the inn, though. The biggest problem is a financial one. There just isn't enough money to keep the place going."

"I thought things were getting better." Nat's smooth brow furrowed.

"They are. The new website really helps," Kim said.

"Plus, all the improvements we've made," Belle added.

"The inn lost money hand over fist for so long that Aunt Margaret nearly depleted her savings to keep it going. She put the last money she had into fixing up the place, but it wasn't enough." Diane's gaze traveled around the table until she singled Belle out. "Belle sold an expensive piece of art to pay for the new carpets. When Deborah bought into Sweet Cakes, Amy put some of that money toward getting the floors redone. I paid this year's insurance premiums from my severance package. That takes care of things for the time being, but repairs are constant. What happens when the inn needs a new roof or a new driveway?"

The question was a sobering one, and they took a minute to let it sink in.

Nat finally sighed. "I guess I'd better not plan on getting married here after all."

"Not unless you're thinking of a June wedding. This June." Kim stared pointedly at her daughter.

"No, ma'am. Not a chance," Nat assured her.

"Whew." Kim exhaled quickly.

With the matter of the inn settled—at least for the time being—Jen reached for the tricorne hat she'd hung behind her on the ear of her chair. "Speaking of expenses…" She twirled the cap on her finger. "Does anyone have any idea where we can get this repaired? Or what it'll cost?" Though she managed to earn a few dollars by making deliveries for Sweet Cakes a couple of times a week, she didn't have much left over after she bought gas for her car.

Diane cast a worried look at the hat she and the others had worn on countless treasure hunts when they were kids. "What's wrong with it?"

Jen held the tricorne up so the others could see the threadbare fabric. "The lining's fallen apart. No wonder. The thing's fifty years old, at least."

"No one knows how old it really is," Belle corrected. "I always thought Grampa Dane made it, but Mama says he swore he found it when he was building the inn. That was in the early Sixties." Her fingers curled inward, she blew softly on the wet polish.

Jen examined the seams. "I think it's hand-stitched, and there's no label." She ran her hand over what was left of the lining until she felt the rough edges of something stiff. "Wait a sec. What's this?" She tugged gently on one end of something that had been wedged into the brim. A tightly folded piece of leather slipped out onto the table.

"Goodness," Amy said. "Something was hidden in there?"

Jen gently unfolded the creased leather. Her breath caught in her throat as she stared down at drawings of trees and rocks some long-ago artist had burned into the smooth surface. A dark stain spread across one corner. A small hole dotted one end. The ragged edges had torn in a couple of places.

"Oh, my gosh," cried Diane. "Is that what I think it is?"

Jen slid the piece to the center of the table where they could all get a better look at it. "I think it's a map," she said, pointing to a faint line that ran between some of the images.

"It's the same one we used for treasure hunts when we were kids," Amy said. "See?" She pointed to wavy lines on either side of a spit of land. "That's the ocean. And that's the river."

"No, no, no," Diane protested. "You've got it backwards." She spun the map in a half circle. "*That's* the ocean," she said, tracing her finger over the lines Amy had called the river. Her hand moved to the other side. "And *that's* the river."

"And *that* explains why we never found a bit of buried treasure when we were kids." Belle screwed the cap on her polish bottle down tight. "We could never agree which end was north or which one was south."

"I doubt there was any treasure to begin with," Kim said. "But we sure had fun looking for it." She grinned.

"I wonder if we'd have better success now that we're older," Diane mused.

Pointing to the aged leather sheet, Amy shook her head. "Those landmarks—none of them exist anymore." She traced her index finger over a spot on the map. "Assuming this end is north and that clump of arrow tips are trees, they're smack dab in the middle of where the cottages were built." Moving to another part of the map, she said, "Daddy and Uncle Eric cleared all these rocks when they planted the orange grove."

"So, you're saying it's useless." Diane's shoulders slumped.

"It's still a piece of our history. Of the inn's history." Belle glanced at the closed door that led to the family quarters. "I know Mama wanted to save the hat for posterity's sake. If everybody agrees, I'd like to put it and the map in a shadow box. We can mount it in the library, near the collection of local history books."

"Good idea!" Diane exclaimed. "But do you mind if I make a copy?"

"You're not still thinking of going on a treasure hunt, are you?" Amy teased her sister.

"Been there, done that, got the T-shirt," Diane said with a mournful glance at the map. "But I'd like a copy just the same."

"I still want to get this lining replaced." A few more scraps of cloth rained down on the table when Jen flipped the hat over. "Anyone know a good leathersmith?"

"Actually, I do." Amy took a sip of wine.

"Well, are you going to tell me or just leave me in suspense?" Jen grumbled.

"Micah Gray. He made the leather turtle that hangs on the wall behind the cash registers at Sweet Cakes." The life-size green sea turtle was a work of art. "He'll be in town next week for the Spring Fling. You should take the hat to his booth. He might be able to fix it while he's here."

"Maybe he can give us an idea of how old it really is." Not that it mattered, Jen thought. Whether their grandfather had made it or it had belonged to an earlier settler, the hat would always be a part of the Dane Crown Inn's heritage.

Five

Kim

"Tell me again why you're feeding every single one of Emerald Bay's employees," her daughter demanded, though Kim didn't catch a trace of malice in Nat's tone.

Plastic covers emitted squeals not unlike the sound fingernails made on a chalkboard when Nat stacked the two large platters of sandwiches on top of one another. The muscles in her arms contracted as she hefted them from the kitchen island and moved toward the door.

Carrying boxes of brownies, Kim trailed behind her daughter. "I'm not the only one. All the restaurants in town are showing their support for the Spring Fling." Normal activities at Town Hall had all but ground to a halt while the entire city council—plus the secretaries, police officers and scores of volunteers—prepared for the annual craft show. "Sweet Cakes provided lunch yesterday. Vivi and Denise are covering tomorrow," she said, referring to the owners of the Pirate's Gold Diner.

"Is it too late to get a job as a crossing guard?" Nat asked.

"A crossing guard?" That seemed like an odd role for her talented daughter.

"I'd be a city employee, wouldn't I? I could get into some of the diner's fried chicken." The dish was a favorite at the Pirate's Gold Diner.

"Sorry to crush your dreams, but crossing guards work for the school board." On the wide pavered walkway that led to the parking area, Kim sped up until she and her daughter walked side by side. "You could always just show up, though. Craig says they need more volunteers."

"Work all day for free just for one piece of chicken? I don't think so." Nat's dangly earrings swung back and forth. "Yours is better, anyway."

"Awww. That's nice to hear," Kim said. "I'll put it on the menu." She'd been considering several options for her next set of Royal Meals deliveries. She couldn't think of a single reason why crispy, oven-fried chicken shouldn't move to the top of her list.

"You're sure you won't need help unloading all this when you get there?" Adding the sandwich trays to the other items already in the trunk of her mom's well-aged Honda, Nat frowned. "It's a lot to carry."

Kim shrugged. Much as she could use an extra pair of hands, Nat had her own responsibilities. "You need to make that airport run." As it usually did in the days leading up to the Spring Fling, the inn had been steadily filling all week. Today's new arrivals had requested an early-afternoon pickup. Kim shrugged. "Besides, Craig will help me."

Nat glanced at the thick cloud cover overhead. "If you're sure you don't need me, I might shoot some exterior shots of the inn before I leave for the airport. I've been wanting to take more pictures for the website now that the painters have finished." The crew had disassembled the last of the scaffolding and removed the paint tarps from the bushes last week. "The lighting is better on gray days like this."

Kim closed the trunk. "Don't you want the pictures to look, um, tropical?" Admittedly, she didn't have her daughter's eye for graphic design, but people usually thought of blue skies and sunshine when they planned a trip to Florida, didn't they?

Nat laughed. "Trust me, it'll look like I took the pictures on a perfect summer's day at the beach by the time I put them up on our website."

"Well, you did a great job with the photos you took for Royal Meals." The pictures on the Royal Meals website were absolutely mouth-watering...and she wasn't the only one who thought so. Thanks to her daughter's talented camera work and, Kim had to admit, word of mouth, her client list had grown from twelve to twenty in a few short weeks. At this rate, she'd be able to buy the pizza oven she'd had her eye on in no time.

"I'll be back soon," she said, slipping behind the wheel. "If anyone asks, I'll be working late tonight." She normally spent Thursdays putting the finishing touches on the heat-and-serve meals for Friday's deliveries, but she'd devoted this morning to fixing lunch for the Spring Fling crew.

Kim sent Craig a quick text to say she was leaving the inn. Then, with a final wave to Nat, she slowly drove down the crushed coquina driveway. A short drive down a road lined with palm trees and palmetto bushes took her to town, where she pulled into an angled parking space in front of the squat, one-story building that served as Emerald Bay's Town Hall. Just as she'd known he would, Craig stepped outside to greet her before she'd even shut off the engine.

Kim wanted nothing more than to leap from the car and kiss the man whose long legs ate up the sidewalk in quick strides. How had she possibly mistaken him for a stuffed shirt the night they'd met on the shuttle bus to Emerald Bay, she wondered. The man was anything but that. Would a man with an inflated ego devote his weekends to taking his fatherless nephew on camping and fishing trips? Or teach the boy the importance of helping those in need by working side by side with him at the soup kitchen or Habitat for Humanity? She thought not. Someone who took their position as mayor too seriously would never stoop to building booths for the Spring Fling. Yet here Craig was, dressed more for swinging a hammer than leading a council meeting. She eyed the jeans and long-sleeved polo that did far too good a job of hiding the lean frame and taut muscles she pretended not to notice whenever they ran along the beach together.

"Mmm, mmm, mmm," she whispered, smiling to herself. The man was the total package.

She still could have resisted him, still could have kept him at arm's length. After all, that's what she'd vowed to do with all men in the aftermath of her disastrous divorce from Frank. But Craig, with his ready smile, innate kindness and, yes, even his tragic past, had broken down every defense she'd erected until, here she was, practically in love with the man.

And which man would that be? Why, it'd be the one who stood beside her car with a most quizzical expression on his face, that's who. Embarrassed that he'd caught her daydreaming, she started.

"Everything all right?" Concern etched on his handsome features, Craig offered her his hand once she'd finally popped the lock. "You looked a little lost there for a moment."

"Lost in thought. I was thinking how much things have changed in such a short time." Only six months ago, she'd been flat broke, estranged from her children and wondering if she'd end up living in her car when she got evicted from her apartment at the end of the month. Her life looked entirely different now. It had taken hard work, but she'd forged new and better relationships with both Nat and Josh. She'd launched a thriving business of her own. She was putting down roots in Emerald Bay, and she loved everything about it. Including the man standing right in front of her.

Wishing she could show him just how much he meant to her, but recognizing that on the steps of the Town Hall was neither the time nor the place, she hugged Craig just a moment or two longer than she normally would when she joined him on the curb. But a glimpse of the folding chairs and tables that leaned against the trunks of tall oak trees in the small, downtown park across the street reminded her that seeing him was not the main reason for her trip into town. Clearing her throat, she broke the embrace. "I guess I'd better get set up," she murmured.

Craig's reluctance to let her go showed in his grudging smile. "Tell me what to do. I'm here to help." He aimed a thumb at his chest.

As they circled the car, she clicked the fob. The trunk opened with a noisy squeak. Inside, platters, bowls and boxes of paper products crowded every inch of the cargo area.

"Oh, man. You really went all out, didn't you?" Craig rubbed his hands in anticipation.

"It's just sandwiches and brownies," Kim protested, though she couldn't help the jolt of warmth that pulsed through her.

"Sandwiches on homemade bread."

"Well, yes. There is that."

She watched as Craig pried up the lid over a platter and helped himself to one of the halves.

Taking a bite, he chewed slowly.

"Is this ham salad?" he asked. "I haven't had any since…" Savoring another bite, he shook his head. "Yours is better than my mom's, and that's saying something." He dusted a crumb or two from his fingers.

Kim pushed the compliments aside. Although the dish did take a fair amount of time—all that ham wasn't going to chop itself— the salad only required three ingredients—ham, mayo and a little pickle relish. Definitely not rocket science.

"Let's get everything else set up before we bring out the food." Grabbing an armload of supplies, she whispered a silent thanks for the chilly spring day that made it possible to leave the sandwiches and salads in the car for a few minutes longer.

In less than a half hour they'd erected tables, covered them with the disposable tablecloths and ferried food from her car to the park. By the time the noon siren sounded twenty minutes later, an ice chest and paper cups sat beside the tea dispensers at the foot of two long tables that had been placed end to end beneath the shade trees. Paper plates, plasticware and napkins stood at the ready. In between, two enormous bowls brimmed with fruit salad while two more held crispy greens dressed in a yummy vinaigrette. Bags of chips lay beside round platters that offered several sandwich choices, including the ham, as well as tuna or egg salad and her own blend of pimento cheese. At the far end, enough brownies to satisfy every sweet tooth in Emerald Bay were available for the taking.

The high-pitched blare of the alarm hadn't completely died before casually dressed secretaries and members of the town council, maintenance workers and volunteers thronged the park.

Sporting a white collar around the neck of his black sweater, Samuel Colter hurried over from the church. The youth minister blessed the food and prayed for a successful Spring Fling with a few short words. His firm, "Amen," served as a starting gun for the hungry workers, who began moving down both sides of the tables, grabbing sandwiches and helping themselves from the bowls and bags. Then, carrying heaping plates, most sat on the folding chairs Kim and Craig had set up in small groupings while a lucky few scored spots at one of several picnic tables scattered throughout the park.

"I need to check in with the team leaders, make sure everything is on track for Saturday," Craig whispered in Kim's ear when only a few people remained in line. "Will you be okay on your own?"

Kim scoffed a laugh. Though she appreciated his concern, she'd been on her own for more years than she could count. This—catering lunch for people who'd spent their morning building booths or hanging signs or doing any of the other myriad tasks involved in hosting the craft fair and the dance that followed—was a piece of cake. She hefted a pitcher she'd filled with sweet tea from one of the dispensers. "You go on. I'm just going to see if anyone needs a refill."

Kim made the rounds, refilling empty glasses, replacing dropped forks from a stash she kept in the pocket of her apron, and, in general, making sure everyone had plenty to eat. She'd just snagged the last of the pimento cheese sandwiches for a young police officer when Betty Lauder beckoned her.

"Kim, dear." The plump, matronly woman broke off a tiny piece of brownie. "Craig tells me your catering business is off to a fine start." She popped the chocolate in her mouth and chewed.

"Yes, ma'am." Kim inhaled the scent of Jean Naté that lingered in the air around the Town Hall receptionist.

"He just raves so much about your food that I

thought I might give it a try. Do you have any openings?"

"A few, as a matter of fact. Would you like a brochure?" Kim patted her back pocket, where she'd stuck a handful of the colorful trifolds Nat had designed for Royal Meals.

"I'd love one. Why don't you give one to Melinda and Honey, too." Her plump upper arm jiggling beneath a lightweight crew-neck sweater, she pointed to the other women who sat in her small circle.

"Of course." Kim doled the papers into waiting hands.

The scene repeated itself twice more before someone blew a whistle, summoning the volunteers and employees back to work. Not quite as quickly it had filled, the park emptied. In their wake, the workers left full trash cans, neatly folded chairs and only a few crumbs in the containers on the serving table.

"Thanks for lunch. It was great!" called a man in jeans as he walked past the tables where Kim stacked the empty salad containers.

"I'm glad you liked it," she said.

Betty Lauder led her little group closer. She peered into the boxes that had held the brownies. "Those were awesome. Do you have any more?" she asked hopefully.

"Not this time," Kim said sympathetically. "They're on the dessert menu for Royal Meals, though."

"My favorite was the pimento cheese—it was to die for," Melinda said.

Kim beamed. The spread was her own blend of peppers, spice and two kinds of cheese.

"You'll be hearing from me." Honey waved the brochure Kim had given her.

"I'll look forward to talking to you," Kim said, her heart expanding with every word of praise until she thought it might burst from sheer overload.

When the last straggler had disappeared, she spied Craig jogging down the steps of Town Hall. "You should hear them inside," he said, grinning practically from ear to ear when he neared the spot where she stood. "You're a hit. Are you sure I can't convince you to take a booth at the Fling this weekend? We had a cancellation. Say the word and it's yours."

"Oh, heavens, no," Kim answered rapidly. Feeling Craig's curiosity, she explained, "I appreciate the offer—seriously, I do—but I couldn't possibly get ready in time." It would take weeks to design a display and print more brochures. And why bother? She nearly had all the business she could handle. If even a few people like Betty and her cohorts signed up, she'd need to hire part-time help.

She grabbed one of the empty boxes and began breaking it down for recycling. "I can't anyway. Caitlyn has a soccer game Saturday morning, and we're going to cheer her on before we come to the craft fair."

"I get it." Craig nodded. "Maybe next year."

"Yeah. Maybe next year," Kim echoed.

She watched as Craig cast a glance at the depleted table. "You didn't get any lunch, did you?"

He gave his head a mournful shake. "No. I got caught up in chasing down a few problems."

"Anything serious?" Kim picked up dishes to take to the car.

"Nah." What was left of the tea sloshed against the sides of the drink dispensers when Craig grabbed them. "A couple of vendors complained about their assigned spots. It took a bit to find new places for them," he said as they started for her car. "And Tom Medford still hasn't given up on having Belle perform at the dance Saturday night. He asked me again if I'd convince her. Like I have any sway with your cousin." Craig shook his head.

Kim nearly missed a step. Belle had turned down the idea when Tom raised it after The

Emeralds' first performance. "Did you want me to ask her?" she asked reluctantly.

"Of course not." Craig's firm response put an end to such nonsense. "Belle made it perfectly clear that she wasn't interested. I respect her decision."

Relieved to know they were on the same page where her cousin was concerned, Kim let out a slow, even breath as she slid the stack of platters and bowls into the car.

"Other than that, everything's going better than I'd hoped," Craig said, wedging the tall tea dispensers into the trunk. "Except I kinda missed lunch. I was sure hoping for more of that ham salad."

"Oh, you." Kim tapped him lightly on the upper arm. "You help me finish up here, and I'll see what I can do."

"Done." He took off for the park at an easy lope.

Working together, they stashed all the dishes and utensils in the trunk, stuffed the tattered tablecloths into trash bags, and left the tables as they'd found them. When they'd finished, Kim handed Craig the small cooler she'd tucked behind her driver's seat.

"Tell me this isn't what I think it is," Craig said, prying open the lid for a quick look inside.

"Okay. It's not what you think it is," Kim

parroted, though she knew for a fact that the cooler contained exactly what he'd hoped for—a ham salad sandwich, chips and not one, but two brownies.

"You want to split this with me?" Craig dug out a plastic baggie and held the sandwich out to her.

"You go ahead. I'll grab something back at the house." She'd stashed a leftover bowl of pimento cheese in the inn's refrigerator before she left this morning.

"You don't have to tell me twice." Craig dug in. When he'd devoured the sandwich and the chips, he waggled his eyebrows. "If you won't take a booth, how about entering something in the Silent Auction? The money all goes to local charities, so you'd be supporting a good cause. And you can count on my bid."

Kim gave the matter a moment's thought. Though her business was off to a good start, she still needed to keep a close watch on her bottom line. "I can't afford to give away a subscription to Royal Meals, but maybe I could do something smaller?"

"A homecooked meal would be good. Say, dinner for two?"

Kim nodded. "That, I could definitely swing. I'll send you all the details this afternoon."

Craig pushed off of the car. "I'd better get back to it." He chuckled. "I'm kinda surprised my phone isn't blowing up already." Leaning forward, he bussed her cheek. "You'll save a dance for me Saturday night, won't you?"

Kim smiled up at him. "You betcha."

As he trotted up the steps and disappeared inside the Town Hall, she traced her fingers along the spot where his lips had pressed against her skin. The man was the total package, all right. He checked all her boxes, and his name was the only one on her dance card.

Aboard one of the shuttle buses that ferried visitors from the high school parking lot to the craft fair, Kim marveled at the change that had struck Emerald Bay over the last two days. When she'd last seen it, the main street had looked no different from that of any sleepy little beach town. But almost overnight, wooden booths, tents and open-sided pavilions had sprung up on either side of the street. Another row of crafters filled the median. The fair stretched for six city blocks before stopping at a stage that had been erected at the end of town.

The bus she was on crawled past a trio of police officers in orange vests who rerouted traffic onto side roads with firm, no-nonsense motions. Kim lurched forward on her seat as, with a whish of air brakes, they stopped in front of sawhorses that had been set up across the road at the town limit. The doors of the bus slid open. Centering a cross-body bag in front of her, Kim followed Jen down the steps and onto the pavement.

"This is crazy, right?" she said when she caught a glimpse of the crowds of shoppers. Nearly shouting to be heard above the scuffle of shoes on pavement, pitchmen who used portable mics to hawk their wares and the hubbub of a thousand different conversations all going on at once, she asked, "How are we supposed to find the others?" Diane and Tim had lingered at the field after Caitlyn's soccer game while Belle, Jason and Nat had boarded an earlier bus.

"No idea." Jen shook her head. "I say we just do our own thing and catch up with everyone at lunch." They'd all agreed to meet at the hot dog stand manned by Emerald Bay High students.

"I don't think we have any other choice. Even if we did find Belle and Nat, it'd be hard to stay together." A cloud of exhaust fumes filled the air as their now-empty bus jolted forward to a spot where some of the craft fair's earlier shoppers waited for rides back to the parking lot. With Jen sticking close, Kim wove through a break in the sawhorses.

Sidestepping couples with baby strollers and doing their best not to get bowled over by those who were on some kind of quest to "do" the craft fair in record time, they browsed a candlemaker's booth and a tent filled with tea towels stamped with cute sayings. Kim considered one that read *She believed she could so she did* but ultimately left it behind when she saw Jen edging toward the exit. Once they had rejoined the crowds, she asked, "Are you looking for anything in particular?"

"That leather worker Amy mentioned. Micah Gray." Jen patted the cloth shopping bag she wore over one shoulder. "I want his opinion on this hat."

"I'll help you look for him." Kim smiled at a toddler who rode on his father's shoulders. When her gaze dropped from the little tyke, it landed on stacks of fresh fruits and vegetables that glistened in farm-stand baskets. She pointed. "That's Moss Meadows' booth, isn't it? Let's stop there." She stepped toward the open-sided pavilion. "Didn't you say the owner harvested our kale himself the other day?"

"Caleb," Jen said.

Was it her imagination, or had Jen replied a hair too quickly? "Who?"

"Caleb Grimes. He owns Moss Meadows."

The name sounded just as oddly familiar as the lilt in her sister's voice. "Well, come on. I want to thank him."

"Uh, you go on. I'll keep looking for the leather smith's booth."

"Oh, no." Kim linked her arm with Jen's. "If we get separated, I'll never find you again in this crowd." As if to prove her point, people scattered left and right when a cluster of power-walking women wearing red hats and purple shirts surged past. Surprised when her sister didn't put up much of a fight, Kim ducked into the shady tent.

"That's right. Everything we grow is all natural, all organic," the tall man behind a roughly constructed counter assured a customer whose hair fell to her waist in tight braids. He folded the top of a crisp paper bag closed over her purchases. When she padded toward the aisle, he turned toward them. "How can I help…" His face brightened. "Jen," he said with a deepening grin.

"Hey, Caleb." Jen threw her shoulders back, her chest out. "This is my sister, Kim. She owns Royal Meals. Kim, this is Caleb."

The big man's eyes left Jen long enough to briefly meet Kim's. She placed her own hand in his calloused one and was rewarded by a firm shake. "I can't thank you enough for picking that kale for us," she said while she had his attention. "Those were some of the best greens I've had in ages. I was wondering if we could make an arrangement with Moss Meadows to supply all the vegetables for Royal Meals." She waited a beat, but Caleb's focus had returned to Jen like a bee returned to a flower blossom.

Beside her, Jen's gaze strayed from Caleb. "You were?"

"Yes," Kim answered. She nodded to the farmer, who didn't have eyes for anyone but her sister. "If we can reach an agreement on prices and delivery schedules."

"I'm sure we can work something out, but, uh…" Caleb's words trailed off when two couples broke away from the passing crowds and joined them under the canopy. "I'll be right with you, folks," he said with barely a glance in their direction.

"You're busy." Kim smiled. "I won't take up any more of your time today. Why don't you give me a call next week, and we can talk about it?" She slipped a Royal Meals business card from the pocket of her jeans.

"I'll do that." Caleb dropped the slip of paper into his shirt pocket. "Hey, uh, will I see you at the dance later?"

Kim bit her tongue. The question had definitely not been directed at her.

"Maybe." Jen scuffed her foot against the plywood floor. "Probably," she amended.

Caleb's grin slanted to one side. "I'll see you there, then."

"Yeah. See ya," Jen said, hooking her arm around Kim's and practically rushing them from the tent. Forcing a young couple to swing wide in order to avoid crashing into them, she plunged into the sea of people.

Kim waited until they'd moved several booths down before she clutched her sister's hand. "What was that all about?" she demanded. "You two have some kind of history?"

"Not really. We were in the same class at Emerald Bay High. I knew him, but Caleb took all honors courses and stuff. We didn't exactly sit together in College Algebra, if you know what I mean."

Kim nodded. Jen was smart—no doubt about that—but she'd hated school with a passion. On her best days, her sister had pulled down average grades. On her worst, well...She had to admit that the entire family had been relieved when Jen had actually earned her diploma.

"Apparently, though, he thinks I'm the one who got away." A faint blush crept up Jen's neck.

A high school crush? That was interesting. Hesitantly, Kim probed. "Is he a good guy? Is he married?"

"Widowed. He inherited Moss Meadows from her side of the family. As for a good guy, I don't know him well enough to answer that question."

"Yet," Kim said insistently. "You don't know him well enough *yet*. Because, if there's one thing I'm sure of, he wants to get to know you a whole lot better."

"Yeah. I kinda figured that out." Jen let out a long, slow breath. "I don't know, though. He might be a too serious for me."

"I could see where you'd think that," Kim said, trying to sound agreeable. "He's a farmer. He's all about roots and you're...not." Jen had been in Emerald Bay since Christmas. She'd lasted two months in Vegas, five in Biloxi before that. Any day now, she expected her sister to announce that it was time for her to pull up stakes and hit the road.

"Maybe it's time for a change. Maybe I'm tired of moving from one place to another." Jen squinted at something up ahead and nudged

Kim. "Hey. There's that leather shop Amy told us about. C'mon." Her pace quickening, she darted to a tent where purses and belts hung from pegs mounted on wooden frames.

Her footsteps as slow as her muddled thoughts, Kim followed. Only a fool would deny there was something going on between Caleb and Jen. The sparks that had flown between them had been so thick, Kim had half expected to see the farmer's tent catch fire. Still, it was hard to wrap her head around the possibility of her sister settling down. And with someone who had strong ties to the community, no less. Was the attraction between them a deep enough basis for a lasting relationship? Or was one of them— Caleb or Jen—about to get burned? A big sister's protective urge surged through her. Determined to snatch her little sister out of danger the minute she smelled smoke, Kim joined Jen in the booth where the only smell drifting in the air was the rich scent of leather.

Her sister and Micah were deep in conversation by the time she reached them. Handling the old tricorne with something akin to reverence, the leather worker agreed to replace the lining and have the hat ready for them in the morning.

With Jen's mission accomplished, they spent

a pleasant hour meandering in and out of the stalls. Not that either of them could afford to buy much. Kim picked up a small, citrus-scented candle as a gift for Aunt Margaret. They split the cost of a pair of earrings they both thought Caitlyn might like for her birthday. Before long, though, it was time to meet the others for lunch.

Belle, her statuesque figure hidden beneath an oversize sweatshirt and her signature red curls tucked into a baseball cap, hailed them in the crowded food court. "We have a table. Diane and Tim are holding it for us. Jason and Max are getting everybody hot dogs and sodas so we don't have to stand in line. Let's grab a seat."

"Tell me again why we're eating hot dogs when there are so many other wonderful choices," Jen grumbled on her way to the table.

"I'll admit it—the smell of those onions and peppers makes my mouth water," Kim said, aiming her chin at a massive open-air tent where a nonprofit group offered freshly prepared sausage-and-pepper subs. "But we're supporting Emerald Bay High."

"Okay. But just between you and me, I'd rather have one of those drumsticks." Jen shot an envious glance at a teenager who wandered past holding a turkey leg before she made a beeline for one end of the table, where she plopped down beside Amy. Belle joined them.

"How's Caitlyn?" Kim asked, gratefully slipping onto the bench across from Diane and Tim. Their favorite player had limped off the field after a rousing victory against St. Leo that morning.

"She's okay," Tim said. "Her team won, so she's happy. And her coach was happy with how the team reacted to St. Leo's poor sportsmanship. Another plus." Parents in the visitors' section had booed loudly when their striker drew a red card after colliding with Caitlyn.

"She has a nasty bruise on her leg where she got kicked," Diane added. "I made sure she put ice on it."

Kim winced. She reached into her bag. "Jen and I picked these out for her birthday. Do you think she'll like them? If you don't, the lady said we can take them back." She was a teensy bit nervous about their choice—it had been a minute since she'd bought a gift for a teenage girl.

"She'll love them," Diane declared after she examined the tiny silver and turquoise butterfly earrings.

"She'd like a car better," Tim chided.

"We agreed. No car. Not till she's had her license for at least six months."

Kim patted her cousin's hand. "I feel for you. I really do," she said, sympathetically. She'd spent a lot of sleepless nights when Josh and Nat had started driving.

Over the hot dogs and soft drinks Jason and Max brought to the table a few minutes later, they discussed their plans for the afternoon.

"Jason's taking me back to the inn. I have to get ready for our performance at four." Belle made a show of fluffing invisible hair. "We'll bring Mama with us when we come back for the concert." Aunt Margaret, who insisted she'd been to enough craft fairs over the years, had opted to stay at the inn this morning.

"I'm going to visit the town council's booth," Kim said. "I want to see how the secret auction is going." In truth, she was half scared to death that no one had bid on her entry.

"I'll hang out with Amy for a while, but I'll meet you backstage at three thirty," Jen told Belle. Though the town was running its own sound system for the dozen or so bands and solo artists who'd perform this afternoon, Jen had offered to stick close.

"We'll wait here," Diane announced. "Caitlyn's shift at the hot dog stand ends at two thirty. We'll see everyone at the concert."

They split up then, each group heading in a

different direction. Though Kim lost sight of the others soon after she left the food court, promptly at three thirty, she stood at the edge of a surprisingly large crowd of onlookers. Waiting for an Elvis impersonator to finish his set, she plotted a course through the families who'd camped out on blankets, the older couples who sat in comfy lawn chairs they'd brought from home and several clusters of preteens who danced with wild abandon without seeming to care whether the performer crooned a love song or rocked out. At last, the man who'd apparently spent more time perfecting his costume than his music gave a final bow and left the stage. While the announcer introduced the next performer, Kim hurried to join her own family in a row up front.

"Craig's not with you?" Nat asked when Kim slid onto one of the seats she'd been saving.

Kim shook her head. Even though Tom Medford was technically in charge, Craig had warned her that, as mayor, he'd be up to his armpits in alligators for both days of the craft fair. When she'd stopped by the town council's booth, she'd only caught a quick glimpse of him as he'd hurried past. "He's coming to the dance tonight, though."

Nat grinned. "I bet you're looking forward to that."

Kim squirmed away when her daughter's sharp elbow poked her ribs. Hoping for a distraction, she glanced over her shoulder. In the short time she'd been chatting with Nat, people had practically filled the seating area. "This is a bigger turnout than I expected for a bunch of no-name bands," she whispered.

"You didn't know?" Nat looked surprised. "Word's gotten around about Belle. I heard people talking about her everywhere I went today."

Kim's stomach sank. "I hope they're not expecting 'Jimmy, Jimmy, Oh.'" Worried about the reception her cousin's new music would receive, she fidgeted with a thumbnail. If the crowd were made up of friends and neighbors from in and around Emerald Bay, she had no doubt that Belle could recite her grocery list into the mic and still get thunderous applause. But thousands from all across Florida and beyond had flocked to this weekend's Spring Fling. If they'd come to the concert expecting to hear the pop star perform numbers from her old repertoire, how would they react?

She shifted uneasily in her seat while the local folk singer who'd followed Elvis on stage wrapped up a final song about snapping turtles and the environment. In a somewhat fitting tribute, applause as light and brief as a summer shower rippled through the audience.

"Tough crowd," Kim murmured.

The announcer stepped to the middle of the stage. With far less fanfare than Kim expected, he said, "And now, folks, it gives me great pleasure to introduce our final group of the day, The Emeralds."

Kim's stomach muscles tightened when Belle, her trademark red curls cascading down her back, stepped out from behind a partition. Daclan followed at her elbow with his hand wrapped around the neck of his grandfather's guitar.

A chorus of, "It's her!" and, "Belle—it's really Belle!" whispered through the crowd. From somewhere near the back, a male voice shouted, "I love you, Belle!"

Smiling and waving, Belle lifted the mic from its stand. "I love you, too. In fact, I love all of you." She swept her hand through the air in an inclusive gesture that drew a deafening response. Belle stood, silent, her head slightly bowed, until the noise faded. At last, she faced the audience again.

"I know many of you are here because you heard I was performing this afternoon. And I appreciate every one of you who came." She paused for a beat, her eyes sweeping over the crowd, her gaze dipping down to linger on one individual here, another there.

Kim felt some of the tension in her shoulders ease. Belle already held the audience in the palm of her hand, and she hadn't sung a single note yet.

"In case you're one of the few people in the country who hasn't read *Variety* or seen the news on your favorite country station," Belle continued, "I'm taking a different approach to music these days. You might say I'm listening to a higher power." She pointed skyward. "I ask that you keep that in mind as we perform for you today. Oh, and before I forget, this fine young man beside me is Daclan Medford, a local boy and one of the most talented guitarists I've ever had the honor of working with." She grinned. "Make sure you applaud for him, if not for me." Ignoring the titters of laughter, she turned to Daclan and asked, "Ready?"

In response, the teen strummed a *G* chord.

Kim's breath stuttered, but the moment her cousin launched into "Better Than A Hallelujah," people all around her surged to their feet. Swaying, clapping and, in some cases, mouthing the words to the popular song along with Belle, the audience instantly proved that they hadn't shown up to watch a pop diva strut across the stage. No sirree. They wanted the new and—if the crowd's reaction was any indication—improved version of a star who'd come full circle.

By the time Belle and Daclan finished their set—and answered the crowd's calls for an encore—Kim wasn't the only one who was wiping tears from her eyes. Wishing Craig were there to share the moment with her, she settled for squeezing her daughter's hand.

"She gets better and better with every performance," Nat gushed as they hurried to catch the shuttle bus shortly after Belle and Daclan left the stage. "I can't wait for Noble Records to come crawling back with their hats in their hands. With their backing, Belle will be right back on top where she belongs."

As Nat tripped up the steps onto the bus, Kim exchanged a look with Jen. The hint of humor in her sister's expression told her they both thought her daughter had stars in her eyes. No doubt, Nat still pictured Belle with all the trappings of success—the entourage of hair-dressers, makeup artists and stylists that would follow her wherever she went, the bevvy of personal assistants. But were fame and fortune what their cousin wanted? Or had she chosen a different path? It was a question that deserved exploring, and Kim tucked it away for the next time they held one of their nighttime chats.

Returning to the stage area a short while later, Kim felt her eyes widen. In the time it had taken Jen, Nat and her to go back to the inn, shower and change, the seating area had been transformed into a dance floor. A locally popular country and western band had taken over the stage and was doing a credible job of belting out a good mix of current favorites and oldie-goldies. Beneath a tent, Betty Lauder and several other town employees sold tickets good for use at any of the food and beverage trucks that had formed a wide semicircle around the stage. Best of all, Craig waited for her by the ticket booth, exactly where he'd said he'd meet her.

"I'll catch you later," she said to Jen and Nat, though she needn't have bothered. Nat had hurriedly joined a group of line dancers who clapped and stomped their feet in time with the music. And Jen didn't even try to take her eyes off a certain farmer who was on his way to her side. Slipping her hand in Craig's, Kim let him whisk her onto the dance floor.

"Did you catch any part of Belle's performance earlier?" she asked as they held each other close when the band changed things up with a slow number.

"I got waylaid by the fire chief." Craig lifted his hand from her waist long enough to gently tuck a stray curl behind her ear. "Tom Medford captured the whole thing on his cell phone, though. He is one proud papa. As he should be. I nearly choked up watching the video."

"It was incredible. She and Daclan were amazing." Kim had been so swept up in the music that she still wasn't sure her feet had touched the ground.

"I should congratulate her and Daclan." Craig's head swiveled. "But I don't see her."

"She's not here. Jason took her and Aunt Margaret back to the inn right after the concert."

"Another time, then." Craig shrugged. "It's good to see Caleb Grimes here tonight." He exchanged nods with the big farmer when he swept past with Jen.

"You know him?" Kim asked, though she shouldn't be surprised. There was no such thing as a stranger in a town the size of Emerald Bay.

"Everybody knows Caleb. He volunteers at the community garden on Wednesdays. He'd give you the shirt off his back if you needed it." Craig cleared his throat.

"He's one of the good guys," Kim said, relieved.

"I'd say so. He could have turned bitter after what he went through with his wife, but he didn't." Craig spoke in low, hoarse tones. "He deserves some happiness."

A hurt note in Craig's voice stirred Kim's concern. She tipped her head to his in time to catch a fleeting whisper of pain in the depths of his gray-blue eyes. And no wonder. Having both lost their wives, Craig and Caleb shared an unenviable history. Words of sympathy gathered on the tip of her tongue. Before she had a chance to say them, though, Craig steered both her and the conversation in a different direction.

"What about those two? Are they back together?" The sadness disappeared from Craig's eyes as he singled out Diane and Tim with a tilt of his head.

"I need to ask her about that." Though the pair had been spending a lot of time together lately, her cousin hadn't made any announcements. Kim laughed softly. "You should have heard them talking about Caitlyn's sixteenth birthday at lunch today. They were bickering like an old, married couple."

Craig spun her around in a circle. His head dipped until she felt his breath sigh softly across the top of her ear. "What about you—do you ever think of making that commitment again?"

The question came from so far out in left field that Kim stumbled. The move proved without a doubt that her feet were on the ground after all.

"Me? Married?" She frowned, her concentration split between following Craig's lead and giving him the right answer. Deciding that honesty was not just the best policy, but the only one, she said, "Right now, I have enough on my plate—Royal Meals, the family reunion, Aunt Margaret and the inn. Marriage is something I haven't really had time to think about." But if and when she did, she added silently as the musicians on stage played the final bars of the song, she already knew there was no one she'd rather spend the rest of her life with than the man who held her in his arms.

Taking a break from the dance floor, they bought beers at one of the beverage trucks and a plate of nachos from a colorfully painted food truck. While they ate, she broached the subject that had been nagging at her since her visit to the town council's booth earlier.

"I was shocked when I saw the bids for my entry in the silent auction," she said before she popped a chip loaded with gooey cheese in her mouth.

"Really?" Concern deepened the creases around Craig's eyes. "Was it too low?"

"Too high," Kim corrected. "Number eighty-seven kept upping the price. Anytime someone else placed a bid, number eighty-seven would top it. The winning bid was over two hundred dollars when I checked. Doesn't that seem a bit...excessive?"

"Not really." Craig took a long pull from his beer mug. "You're a good cook. You're making a name for yourself around town."

"Yeah, but two hundred dollars. For that price, the winner's going to expect surf and turf." An expensive cut of beef and lobster for two was more than she'd bargained for. "I had planned on serving chicken."

Craig chuckled. "It's all for fun and charity. I'm sure the winner will be just as happy with hamburgers. Although, if you threw in some peel-and-eat shrimp, I'm sure they wouldn't mind."

"Oh?" Kim felt her eyebrows rise. "Do you know who my mystery fan is?"

"Yes, but I'm sworn to secrecy." His eyes sparkling, Craig snagged a chip off their plate and broke it into tiny pieces. "Until tomorrow when they announce the winning entries, that is."

He held out his hand when the band played the opening bars of "Bless The Broken Road." "Dance?"

Kim wove her fingers into his, but as they returned to the dance floor, she gave herself a stern warning to go easy on Craig if they ever played poker. The man had a tell, and she could read the sparkle in his eyes from a country mile away.

Six

Amy

"Where are they?" One after the other, Amy pulled socks from her dresser drawer without finding the red pair adorned with images of her cat. The pair Kim had given to her for Christmas. The pair she wanted to wear when Kim and the others came over tonight. But to do that, she had to find the socks. So far, she wasn't having any luck.

Determined to give it the old college try—even though the closest she'd ever come to a university was culinary school—she shoved her hand into the back of the drawer. Her fingers brushed against something hard and square and definitely not a pair of socks. Her eyebrows slammed together.

The ring.

Her engagement ring. It wasn't all that impressive—not much more than a trinket, really—but how had she forgotten its very existence?

Sinking onto the edge of her bed, she tried to recall the last time she'd thought about the ring. She supposed it had been the night she and Max had spoken of their first marriages...and divorces. In the months that had followed, Max had filled up all the empty places in her heart, her mind. No wonder she hadn't given the ring—or Connor—a second's thought since then.

She grasped the small leather box between her thumb and forefinger and drew it to her. Leaning forward, she pried the lid open. The small diamond sparkled just as much as it had the day two burly men had unloaded all her possessions into the house she'd purchased behind the bakery. In the midst of a thousand and one tasks she'd faced as a new homeowner, she'd tucked the jeweler's box in the back of her sock drawer for safekeeping.

She tipped the ring this way and that, examining it from every angle. Perhaps a half carat, the round-cut diamond sat high in a rose gold setting with tiny, sparkling chips embedded on either side. It was a pretty little thing, she admitted. But it hadn't suited her any better than the man who'd slipped it on her finger. The few times she'd worn the ring to work, she'd been forced to spend an hour cleaning the dough out of each crevice and from beneath the stone. As a result, she'd never gotten used to feeling the weight of it on her finger. Oh, she might have, if the marriage had lasted longer, but she'd cut Connor out of her life as neatly as a slice of pie the day she'd caught him cheating.

She snapped the lid closed and set the box on her dresser. Tonight, while they had their wine and snacks, she'd ask what the others thought she should do with it.

Standing, she spied the toe of a red sock in the middle of all the others she'd piled on her dresser. She tugged on it and smiled. She'd finally found what she was looking for.

"Come in. Come in and get warm." Crisp, salt-scented air rushed into the house when Amy held the door wide and motioned to her cousins.

Two by two, the women hurried up the steps and onto the small front porch, their breath forming clouds as they walked. Once inside, Jen shucked her jacket and made a beeline for the fireplace, where two small logs burned cheerily.

When she didn't spot her sister behind the others, Amy lobbed a question at Kim. "Diane didn't ride with you?"

"She'll be along soon." Kim slipped off a bulky sweater and hung it on the coat rack. "She took Caitlyn out for a driving lesson."

"Poor Diane," Amy said, recalling her first time behind the wheel of her dad's 1985 Chevy 4x4. The truck had a standard transmission and, much to her father's chagrin, she'd burned out the clutch before she got her license.

Turning, she greeted the next arrival. "You didn't wear a sweater, Nat? Aren't you cold?"

"Nah. I'm used to living in New York. It's freezing up there. Right, Belle?" Despite her protests, the youngest member of the group followed Jen's example and perched on a small ottoman by the fire.

"Yes, but I'm a Florida girl, born and bred. I break out my winter clothes when the thermometer dips below seventy." Belle slipped off a stylish cloak to reveal a creamy cashmere sweater paired with a pair of winter-white wool slacks. "Mmm. Your house always smells so good, Amy."

"It's probably the candles." Two vanilla-scented candles burned cheerily on the mantle.

Amy felt her gaze drift from Belle's outfit to Socks's favorite spot on the couch cushions. Glad the black-and-white cat had made himself scarce, and even happier that she'd run the roller over all the furniture just moments earlier, she added Belle's cloak to the coat rack.

When a timer dinged, she pointed to the bottles and glasses on the coffee table. "Help yourself to the wine while I get the snacks. I hope you brought your appetites," she said over her shoulder.

Belle groaned in response. "You and Kim are such good cooks, I'm never going to lose any weight."

"Don't worry. This is a calorie-free zone," she called from the kitchen, where she shut off the timer and slipped a pan of crisp potato crostini from the oven. The dab of brie she'd placed on top of each round had melted nicely. She added tiny sprigs of rosemary and transferred them to a serving dish. Taking a tray of ham biscuits from the warming drawer, she carried both platters to the living room, where the others waited.

Nat hurriedly pushed the glasses and bottles aside to make room for the dishes. "What's this?" she asked when her hand brushed against the tiny box Amy had left on the coffee table. She flipped the lid without waiting for an answer.

"Whew!" she whistled. "Sweet ring." Her eyes rounding, she stared at Amy. "Did Max propose?"

Belle squealed. "What? Let me see!" She held out her hand. When Nat immediately complied, disappointment flickered in the redhead's green eyes. "This isn't from Max. It's your old engagement ring, isn't it?"

"You were engaged?" Shock lifted Nat's voice.

Kim frowned at her daughter. "Don't look so surprised. Your Aunt Amy was engaged and married."

"And divorced before the ink on the marriage certificate dried," Amy added. She snagged one of the crostini and popped it in her mouth.

"Belle's the only holdout," Jen said, smiling at her cousin. "Never been married. Never been kissed."

"I wouldn't go that far." In mock offense, Belle swept her hair over her shoulder with one hand as she reached for one of the potato rounds.

"Oh, my goodness!" Kim chewed thoughtfully on a ham biscuit. "These are wonderful. What's in the sauce?"

"Apricot jam and two kinds of mustard— whole grain and Dijon," Amy answered, smiling. She'd been certain her cousin would like it.

"I *need* this recipe," Kim insisted. "It would be incredible on a pork roast."

"Sure. No problem," Amy said, but her focus had drifted. "Now about that." She pointed to the box Belle held. "What should I do with it?"

Belle slipped the ring from its holder and held it up to the light. "It's real, right? Not zirconia? A half carat, give or take?"

Amy blinked. Her cousin sure knew her way around jewelry. Not that she should be surprised. Not when, for the past thirty years, Belle showed up to every gala and awards show dripping in diamonds and precious stones.

Belle took a small bite of the crostini while she considered the ring. "You could probably get a couple of grand for it."

"Whoa. That much? That's way more than Connor paid for it." Amy swigged her wine. In order to buy the ring, her future husband had taken two hundred dollars from the money they'd been saving to open their own bakery. She had not been pleased.

"How long have you had it? Twenty years? Prices have gone up considerably in that amount of time," Belle said with the confidence of someone who regularly visited the jewelry stores on Fifth Avenue.

"Do you have a sentimental attachment to it?"

Jen asked. "Of course, you do," she said, answering her own question. "You wouldn't have hung on to it if you didn't."

"Actually, no." Amy cupped her chin. "I kind of forgot I had it. I probably should have gotten rid of it a long time ago."

"Then sell it," Kim and Nat said in unison.

"I'm with Kim and Nat. Sell it." Her fingers clenched in a fist, Jen jerked her thumb through the air. "It's outta here."

"Hold that thought," Amy said when she heard a car door slam shut. She rose from her perch on the arm of a chair to let her sister in while Kim whispered to Jen.

"Pour Diane a glass of wine, won't you?" Kim's gaze shifted to her sister. "Remember when I was trying to teach you how to drive?"

"Hey! It wasn't that bad," Jen protested.

"Yes, it was," came Kim's quick retort. "You drove Uncle Eric's car into a tree."

Laughter rippled about the room. Though their uncle had straightened the front bumper with ease, the trunk of the palm tree at the entrance to the Dane Crown Inn still bore a jagged scar.

Glad she'd never been forced to sit in the passenger seat beside an inexperienced young driver, Amy greeted her sister with the usual hugs and kisses. Seconds later, air whooshed out of the sofa cushion when a harried looking Diane collapsed onto the couch. Flexing her fingers like someone who'd held a steering wheel in a tight grip for far too long, she reached for the nearly full glass Jen handed her.

"Thank you. You're a godsend." Diane drained half the wine in one long sip. "You don't know how much I needed that." She sighed gratefully.

"C'mon," Amy chided. "Caitlyn's a good kid. It couldn't have been that bad."

"Ha! Surely, you jest." Diane rolled her eyes. "For a girl who never takes her eyes off the ball during an entire soccer match, your niece has the attention span of a gnat when she's behind the wheel. Tonight, she drove straight past a stop sign. Didn't even slow down. Next time, some-one else can take her driving."

"Not me!" Amy threw up her hands. If Caitlyn wanted to learn how to make the perfect loaf of bread, she'd gladly spend all day in the kitchen with the teen. But she knew her limits. Giving driving lessons was way beyond them.

"How much more practice does she need?" Belle asked.

"She has thirty of her fifty hours, but we're just starting with nighttime driving. She needs ten of that." Diane sighed and sipped her wine.

Florida had rather stringent requirements when it came to issuing licenses to young drivers, and for good reason. "I really should make Tim give her the next lesson when he comes over this weekend."

Amy froze when her sister's comment raised several pairs of eyebrows. Whispering a silent prayer that the rest of the family would support her sister's decision, she watched as Kim and Jen exchanged silent glances. Kim must have drawn the short straw because she cleared her throat.

"Speaking of Tim, we're all wondering what's going on with him and you."

"Yeah, you two were thick as thieves at the Spring Fling," Jen added.

Several long seconds stretched out while Diane stared at Amy, who nodded a silent *I've got your back* in response to her sister's searching gaze. Her heart clenched when Diane's eyes filled.

Diane set her wineglass on the table and folded her hands atop one knee. "I haven't wanted to say anything because I didn't want you to think less of me," she whispered.

"No one here would ever do that," Amy said. She scanned the room, making eye contact with each of her cousins, daring them to contradict her.

No one did.

Belle uncrossed and recrossed her ankles. "It's your marriage. Your family. Your decision. We're only here to support you," she said.

"Thanks," Diane said softly. "I needed to hear that."

Amy felt her own shoulders relax as she watched her sister's posture soften.

Retrieving her wineglass, Diane rolled the stem gently between her fingertips while she explained, "Tim asked—no, he begged—he begged me to forgive him. And, after a lot of thought and prayer, I have."

"You're giving him a second chance?"

Ready to weigh in on her sister's behalf at the slightest hint of condemnation, Amy shied away from saying anything when she detected only a mix of concern and surprise in Kim's voice.

"Not really." Diane's expression turned pensive. "Saying I'm giving him a second chance implies that I'd always be watching, waiting for him to screw up again. I don't want to do that. I can't live like that. This has to be more. We both have to make a real commitment. To our marriage. Our children. Ourselves. It's a forever kind of deal."

"It's like going all in," Jen said. "Win or lose, there's no going back."

Diane's head bobbed. "Right."

Kim held out her glass. "Then here's to Diane and Tim. I'm so very happy for you."

"Hear, hear," chimed Belle and Nat.

"Me, too," Amy added, glad her sister had finally shared the news she'd been keeping under wraps for days. After they drank to the toast, though, she sobered. The reunion did have one drawback.

"As happy as I am about you and Tim getting back together," she said, looking at Diane, "there *is* one thing I need to tell you."

"Yeah?"

"I hate that you'll be moving back to Tampa. I've loved having you and Caitlyn around."

"We'll *all* miss you," Belle said.

"What about your new accounting business, Aunt Diane?" Nat asked. "I thought you were excited about that."

"I am," Diane said, choosing to address the last question. "And no one is going to miss me—or Caitlyn—because we're staying right here."

"What?" Amy noted the same confusion she felt on the faces of the others. "How's that going to work?"

"Tim and I have talked about it and hashed out all the details. Caitlyn and I will stay here. She'll go to Emerald Bay High. I'll open my accounting business. Tim…" She took a deep breath. "He needs to hang on to his dental practice for another four years until he can take early retirement. In the meantime, we'll buy a house here in town. He'll work in Tampa during the week and come over on weekends and holidays."

"Whoa," Amy cried. "I didn't see that coming." Although, when she thought about it, she told herself she should have. Her sister loved Emerald Bay, and Caitlyn's whole outlook on life had improved since mother and daughter had moved here. A warm rush of happiness filled her as the realization that her sister wasn't leaving sank in. She supposed the others felt the same way because a giddy happiness circulated around the room.

"Well, I have news, of sorts," Belle said when the hugs and congratulations had died down and more than a few tears had dried.

"Do tell," Amy said, hoping for more good news.

"Jason called earlier this afternoon." Though he'd flown down for the concert, he'd caught the red-eye back to Manhattan that night.

"He had to be pleased with how well the audience reacted to The Emeralds at the Spring Fling," Jen said.

"I don't mind telling you, I was a little nervous when I saw the size of the crowd," Kim admitted. "Especially after Nat said word had gotten out that you were going to perform.

"About that…" Belle's face scrunched. "No one was supposed to know. But I think we have Tom Medford to thank for the leak. He'd been pestering me to sing at the dance that night. He probably thought if enough people knew I was going to be there, he could pressure me into singing some of my old songs."

"Well, that sure backfired," Jen said. "I didn't hear one negative comment about your new music."

"Yeah, Aunt Belle. If anything, people wanted more of Belle Dane, Full Circle," Nat said.

Belle's face flushed. She pressed her hands together in a prayerful gesture. "It was humbling and exhilarating all at the same time."

"So what did Jason have to say?" Amy prompted.

"He said the feedback he's been getting about The Emeralds has been quite favorable. He says it won't be long before the record companies are knocking at our door, and we need to be ready. He even suggested that Daclan and I get an agent—sooner rather than later."

Propping her elbows on her knees, Nat

leaned forward. "Does that mean you're going back to New York? Or moving to Tennessee?"

Amy studied the young woman's reaction. Was that concern, or hope, furrowing Nat's forehead?

"Uh-uh." Belle's curls shook. In a firm voice, she said, "This is where I belong." Her demeanor softening, she grinned. "For one thing, my guitarist is only sixteen. He can't go anywhere until he graduates from high school, so I'm stuck."

"And the other reason?" Diane asked.

"Oh, there are several, but Emerald Bay is my home. It always will be," Belle answered.

As much as she wanted to believe Belle, Amy wondered if her cousin had taken the big change that loomed on the horizon into consideration. "Even after Aunt Margaret sells the inn?"

Sadness touched Belle's eyes, but her voice didn't waver in the slightest. "Even then," she said.

Despite her cousin's response, Amy couldn't help but notice that the hint of regret she'd seen in Belle's eyes mirrored her own feelings about putting the Dane Crown Inn on the market. Was anyone else thinking along the same lines?

The question had barely formed in her mind before Kim stood. Carrying her empty wineglass into the kitchen, she said, "I'm going to have to call it a night, I'm afraid. I have a busy day tomorrow."

"How so?" Amy asked, hating to see the evening draw to a close. "You usually have weekends off, don't you?" Once Kim made the deliveries for Royal Meals each Friday, she spent most Saturdays relaxing and catching up on her personal chores. Sundays were for church and family activities.

"I'm making dinner for Craig tomorrow night," Kim said, returning to the living room. "He won my dinner-for-two entry in the silent auction."

Amy whistled. The charity auction had been wildly successful. Kim's donation alone had raised almost four hundred dollars. By contrast, Sweet Cakes' custom-designed birthday cake had brought in half that amount. "He must really love your cooking," she said, suppressing a twinge of envy.

"Or he's planning a special date." Jen's brows knitted in concentration. "Ooooh, how long have you two been seeing each other?" Kim and Craig had started dating before she arrived at Christmas.

"I don't know." Kim slid her arms into the sweater she took from the coat rack. "Six months, I guess. Maybe a little longer."

"Girl," Diane said, "you'd better pull out all the stops."

"And shave...everything." Repeating the advice she'd been given during their spa day, Amy circled a finger through the air below her waist.

"You guys." Kim waved a dismissive hand. "He's not having dinner with me. It's business."

"Monkey business?"

The question was so unlike Belle that even Kim had to laugh. She was still giggling when she grabbed her purse and headed for the door.

"Oh, shoot," Jen said. "She's my ride." She jumped to her feet. Seconds later, the sisters were on their way down the sidewalk to Kim's car. The others quickly followed in a hail of hugs and promises to get together again soon.

Once she'd locked and bolted the door behind them, Amy surveyed the glasses and trays that cluttered the coffee table. She smiled at the few scraps that remained in the serving dishes. Knowing her sister and cousins had enjoyed the snacks filled her heart.

When she began to clear the dishes, though, she spied the small box on the end table. Picking it up before Socks could mistake it for a toy and hide it somewhere she'd never find it, she opened the box. Her good mood faltered as she eyed the stone. Was it the only engagement ring she'd ever wear? She snapped the lid closed. Whether it was or not, it was time to let go of the old and move forward. The next time she was in Vero, she'd make a point of taking the ring to a jeweler there who handled consignment sales.

But as she puttered about, loading the wineglasses and the platters into the dishwasher, filling Socks's bowl with an extra-large helping of the salmon flakes he loved, turning out the lights and such, she felt oddly unsettled, adrift. Knowing she'd toss and turn all night if she didn't figure out what was bothering her, she sank onto the couch. As if sensing her distress, Socks hopped down from the counter where he'd been enjoying his favorite treat and leapt onto her lap. He nudged her hand, demanding to be petted. Complying, she let her thoughts drift.

She lived a pretty good life. Sure, she'd had a few lemons roll her way, Connor and her failed marriage among them. But mostly, there'd been more sweet moments than sour ones. She had a wonderful family who loved her as much as she loved them. She had a great job doing what she truly loved to do, a passion she'd turned into a successful business—so successful, in fact, that she was in the middle of opening a second location. She owned her own house. She had very little debt. And she had Socks, she added, giving the cat a belly rub.

So, why wasn't she content? Why had she begun to feel like there was something missing in her life? That she wanted something more than just her family, her bakery and her cat. That she wanted Max.

Was he the missing ingredient that would make her life complete?

Seven

Kim

"Good grief, what is that heavenly smell? And when is dinner?" Jen asked on her way through the kitchen of the Dane Crown Inn in ragged jeans and a well-worn sweatshirt.

"Dinner is whenever you want. Everyone is on their own tonight. As for what smells so good…" Kim's gaze shifted between the pans on the big Aga range. The mushroom duxelles, an herby blend of mushrooms and shallots, sizzled on the back burner, while on the front burner, she was using her best cast iron skillet to sear two of the prettiest pieces of beef tenderloin she'd seen in a long time. She supposed traces of thyme from the vinaigrette she'd prepared earlier might still linger. Meanwhile, because

Craig had declared it his absolute favorite dessert, the apple pie baking in the oven perfumed the air with the delicious smells of spice and sugar. She pointed to the stove. "This is the dinner Craig won in the silent auction."

Jen's sneakers skidded to a halt on the oversize Mexican floor tiles. Looking positively glum, she said, "You mean none of that is for us? That's cruel and unusual punishment."

Kim laughed. "You donate four hundred dollars to charity, and I'll fix beef Wellington for you, too."

"Sorry. No can do. When it comes to charity, I'm more likely to end up on the receiving end, not the giving end. I'll make do with leftovers." She paused. "Unless Caleb takes me out to dinner," she added, her voice carrying the slightest tinge of hope.

"You're meeting Caleb dressed like that?" Kim aimed a wooden spoon at her sister's work clothes.

"Oh, you mean this old thing?" Thrusting out one hip, Jen plucked at her sweatshirt. "He's not really coming over to see me. He's going to help me start an organic garden."

"You? Digging in the dirt?" She'd never known her kid sister to show an interest in gardening of any kind. Of course, that was before

Jen met Caleb. "You kill potted plants."

"No time like the present to learn better. Don't worry. We're going to start small. Caleb says we should see if I have the knack for it before we go hog-wild."

"That sounds like good advice." *Whether they were talking about farming...or the farmer.*

A bubble of air formed under the mushroom mixture. Kim gave it a quick stir to avoid getting ground mushrooms splattered all over the stovetop.

"You cleared this gardening business with Aunt Margaret, didn't you?" Kim flipped the tenderloins over with a pair of tongs. The meat had developed the perfect char on both sides. She turned off the heat and transferred the beef to a warm plate, where it would rest for twenty minutes while she finished the other dishes.

"Of course. She suggested using a small plot down by the orange grove. Where guests of the inn won't see it."

A distant motor rumbled. Jen's head swung. "There's Caleb." Her feet in motion, she called, "Don't forget to wear something sexy for your big night." She sashayed through the French doors just as Caleb strolled into view.

"Big night, indeed," Kim muttered as she watched her sister's shorter legs pistoning to keep up with Caleb's longer strides. No matter how many times she repeated that this was not *the night* for her and Craig, her sister—like her cousins—refused to believe it. But they'd see. Tomorrow, when she regaled them with stories of the big client Craig had wined and dined, they'd have to accept that she'd been right all along. Still, on the off chance, the very rare chance, that Jen and all the others proved her wrong after all, she'd dutifully shaved her legs and taken special care with all her lady bits *just in case*. As for the slinky little black dress she'd pulled from the back of her closet, black was the preferred color of wait staff, wasn't it?

By the time the grandfather clock in the living room struck the six o'clock hour, Kim had finished all the preparations for a dinner guaranteed to impress Craig's client, whoever he might be. In the refrigerator, a fan of spinach leaves held a heap of hand-torn mixed greens topped with a fine dice of carrots, peppers and corn. A bottle of her special vinaigrette stood on the shelf beside the salad. Two individual beef Wellingtons rested in a roaster pan, ready to pop into Craig's oven. Fresh rolls and a couple of vegetable dishes rounded out the meal that would end with apple pie and homemade ice cream.

Enlisting Nat to ferry the food to the car, Kim dashed upstairs for a quick shower. Her reappearance a half hour later elicited a low whistle from her daughter, who lit an imaginary matchstick and blew out the pretend flame.

"Hot!" she exclaimed as if Kim hadn't interpreted Nat's clues.

Okay, so she might have spent longer than usual curling her lashes and applying her lipstick, but she had to look her best in case Craig introduced her to his client, didn't she? And she couldn't help it if the LBD fit her like a glove. She was only dressing to fit the occasion.

The occasion that definitely was not a date, she reminded herself.

"Fourteen thirty-two...fourteen thirty-four... fourteen thirty-six."

Kim drove through the residential neighborhood made up of one-story cement block houses, a style of construction that had been popular along the coast in the Fifties and Sixties. Despite the age of the houses, the area had a definite upscale vibe. Maybe it was all the BMW SUVs and Lexus sedans parked in the driveways. Or maybe it was the glimpses of boat docks and pool screens she caught in between the houses. Regardless, she had to admire the mature trees that dotted the wide, rectangular lots. And the neatly mowed lawns of thick St. Augustine grass that stretched between hedges of copperleaf, buttonwood or ficus, though here and there, an owner had opted for a privacy fence.

At 1438 Bay Drive, she took in the beige exterior walls paired with chocolate trim before she turned onto the poured concrete driveway and slowly drove to the end where, according to his directions, Craig had left the back door unlocked for her. Turning off the engine, she sat for a moment, soaking in a stunning view of the Indian River. The sinking sun had set a low cloud bank ablaze, and she felt an urge to walk out on the wooden dock to watch until the sky darkened. But she resisted. Craig had asked her to have dinner ready to serve at seven thirty. With an hour to go, she had no time to waste. Wanting to get a look at his kitchen before she started unloading, she mounted the two steps that led to a tidy addition at the back of the house.

The fresh scent of soap and softener mingled in the air of the serviceable utility room that housed the usual washer, dryer and what looked like a storage closet for cleaning supplies. Above a built-in folding table, coat hangers hung ready and waiting for the next laundry day.

Stepping into the roomy kitchen, she was pleased to note the top-of-the-line appliances, tall pecan cabinets and gorgeous, cream-colored granite counters flecked with gold. A wall of floor-to-ceiling glass offered an incredible view of the river on one side while, on the other side, an L-shaped island separated the kitchen from a spacious living area done in earth tones. A barn door off the living room probably led to the dining area but, wanting to get dinner under-way, she decided to check it out later.

Beneath the cedar beams of a pitched roof-line, the air-conditioned air carried a faint trace of disinfectant but no lingering scent of last night's dinner. And no wonder. The shelves of a double-door refrigerator held little more than cartons of orange juice and creamer, a bottle of champagne on a wire rack and two plastic takeout containers from the Pirate's Gold Diner. Once she'd slid the latter to the rear of a shelf, she returned to her car.

She laughed as she shoved stacks of TV dinners aside to make room in the freezer for the container of ice cream. Craig had mentioned once that he considered the peanut butter and jelly sandwiches he ate for lunch nearly every day the extent of his culinary prowess. Judging from the contents of his refrigerator and freezer, he hadn't been kidding.

Working from her To Do list, she began the final preparations for his dinner, and soon the twin beef Wellingtons roasting in the oven began to fill the house with their wonderful aroma. The rich wine and mushroom gravy barely simmering on top of the stove supplied another layer. Those alone were wonderful, but the honeyed carrots sizzling in another saucepan contributed to the blend of fragrances, as did the triangles of garlic bread that waited for a last-minute run under the broiler.

Kim had just added freshly chopped red pepper and onions to a bowl of avocado and mango cubes when she heard someone rattle the doorknob in the laundry room. She looked up from the salsa she intended to serve as an appetizer with the toast points. "Hello?"

"Hey. It's just me." Craig's voice drifted from the other room.

Kim gave the counter a quick swipe to erase any stray drops of juice and barely had time to retie the apron she wore over the LBD before Craig breezed into the kitchen.

"Sorry I'm late." He set his briefcase down on

a barstool on the opposite side of the wide granite island. "I meant to be here earlier, but a meeting with the town treasurer went longer than expected. Did you find everything you needed?"

"Sure did. You have a very nice home." Kim tossed a glance toward the window and the darkening sky beyond it. "If I could watch the sunset from these windows, I might cook dinner every night."

"What's the point of living on the river if you can't enjoy it, right?" Craig asked. "The house was a wedding present from my folks. After my wife died, I needed a change, so I had the entire place remodeled. It was either that or sell it, and I couldn't bear to move away from the river. I put floor-to-ceiling windows in every room to take advantage of the views. The kitchens and bathrooms were showing their age, so I gutted them and replaced everything else while I was at it."

"I haven't made it past the kitchen, but you made some excellent choices in here." She especially liked that he'd chosen a neutral palate instead of going with a more nautical theme.

Craig loosened his tie. "Gosh, everything looks and smells amazing." His gray-blue eyes took in the pots bubbling on the stove, the serving dishes she'd lined up on the counter. "I can't thank you enough."

"It's the least I can do after the contribution you made to the silent auction," Kim said.

"I didn't have much choice. People kept outbidding me."

Craig's grin threatened to turn her insides to mush. She was pretty sure a kiss would finish the job, but he lingered on his side of the island.

"Are we all set for seven thirty?" he asked.

"Yep," she assured him. She'd planned everything down to the tiniest detail. Setting the table and steaming the broccoli were the only big items left on her to-do list. Oh, and sharing a kiss or two. She'd factored in enough time for that, too. Opening a nearby drawer, she began gathering silverware. "Is the dining room through there?" She aimed her chin toward the barn door.

"Yes, but I set the table before I left this morning. You won't need to do anything in there."

Mentally checking that item off of her list, she asked, "Would you like me to serve dinner? Or do you want me to dish everything up and make myself scarce?" Her donation had included full dinner service, but if Craig and his guest needed to discuss business matters in private, she could certainly make that happen.

"I'm all thumbs in the kitchen," Craig confessed. "I'd feel better if you handled everything."

"No problem." Kim added a drizzle of olive oil and a pinch of finely chopped cilantro to the salsa.

"Good." Craig let out a long, slow breath, but he still didn't come around the island for their usual kiss. "I don't mind telling you, tonight is very important to me."

"Nothing like a little pressure," Kim grumbled. She added a smile to show she was up to the challenge.

"That didn't come out right. A good meal will go a long way toward a successful evening—but I know you have that covered. I'm the one who needs to make a really good impression."

"Do you mind if I ask about your guest?" She had her money riding on some business deal he had in the works.

"An old friend. Someone I fell out of touch with long ago." A soft smile tugged at the corners of Craig's mouth while he stared into the deepening night beyond the windowpanes.

Not business, then, she surmised. But not the relationship-changing moment Belle and Amy and been hoping for, either. She considered asking him the name of his mystery guest, but before she could, the crow's feet at the corners of Craig's eyes tightened.

"I think I'd better run in and take a quick shower." He pushed away from the counter. "Are you good here?"

When Craig still made no move to kiss her, Kim chalked the oversight up to his concerns about reconnecting with his old friend. "Don't worry," she said, hoping to reassure him. "I have everything under control and on schedule."

"Okay, then. I won't be long." The sound of Craig's footsteps soon faded as his long strides carried him into another part of the house.

With fifteen minutes to go before showtime, Kim reviewed her list. The only item she hadn't checked off herself was the dining room, and she glanced toward the barn door. What if Craig hadn't included steak knives in the place settings? Were cups and saucers available for coffee? Or would she need to bring them when she served dessert? Knowing how important it was to him that the evening go smoothly, she decided to see for herself.

At the entrance to the dining room, she gave the door a slight push. It glided open to reveal eight upholstered dining chairs evenly spaced around a polished wooden table. At one end, a red runner carved out an intimate dining space for two. Kim's heart thudded as she took in the red roses and baby's breath that filled a short, square vase. Her breathing hitched when she saw the silver wine bucket and two slender champagne glasses. She forgot to breathe altogether when she spotted the mounds of rose petals at the base of several candles that stood, waiting for someone to light them. She tore her gaze away from the romantic setting as tears stung her eyes. But looking away did no good. With the night sky as a backdrop, the windows reflected the tableau.

"Idiot," she whispered to her own reflection, which, thanks to her tears, wavered. "You are such an idiot."

She eased the door closed. Not wanting to get caught anywhere near the dining room, she hurried back to the kitchen. There, her hands splayed on the countertop, she leaned forward, letting her outstretched arms support her. When he'd said he'd asked an old friend to stop by for dinner, she'd assumed he meant one of the members of his high school baseball team. Or a roommate from his days at college. Well, she'd been wrong about that. As wrong as a gal could be. Whoever Craig was having dinner with, *she* was no mere friend. Champagne? Roses? Candles? It didn't get much more romantic than that. She scoffed.

You're a fool, Kim. She'd thought they were in an exclusive relationship.

Apparently, it was only one-sided. True, neither of them had ever said the words aloud, but she'd thought their deepening feelings for one another were obvious.

How had she misjudged her relationship with Craig so completely?

With a sinking heart, she flipped through her memories of the last six months. The weekend they'd spent painting the inn's cottages. The time they'd spent cleaning up after the workmen had refinished the floors. The holiday dinners, the celebrations, the Sundays they'd attended church together, the soccer games where they'd cheered Caitlyn's team to victory—she'd seen them as dates, but perhaps that old saw was right.

Hindsight was twenty-twenty.

Now, looking back, she had to admit that she and Craig hadn't spent a lot of time together as a couple, just the two of them. On the rare occasions when they were alone—in her current, frazzled state, New Year's Eve was the only example she could recall—Craig had never pushed to take their relationship to the next level. Oh, he'd been kind and encouraging and helpful. A real Boy Scout. And yes, they'd kissed—they'd kissed a lot, actually—but he'd never tried to take things beyond that. Never attempted to sweep her off her feet and into the bedroom.

From the looks of things in the dining room, though, romance was definitely on Craig's mind. Only she was not the one he wanted.

A door closed somewhere in the house. Footsteps on the floor tiles signaled Craig's approach.

Kim whirled away from the counter. Facing the stove, she hastily wiped her eyes.

"How are we doing on time?" Craig asked. He opened a wine cooler built into one end of the crook of the L-shaped island and pulled out a bottle.

Glimpsing the label out of the corner of her eye, Kim stifled a groan. The pinot gris he'd chosen was one he'd introduced her to. It had quickly become their date-night favorite. At least, she'd thought they were date nights. Apparently, that was another thing she'd been wrong about. She cleared her throat.

"Everything's all set," she said, struggling to remain calm when her breaking heart urged her to start throwing dishes and upending furniture. "I'll need five minutes' warning to run the toast points under the broiler. The salads are in the fridge. It's just a matter of plating the rest whenever you're ready for the next course."

"Why don't you go ahead and fix the appetizer and bring it into the living room." Craig opened the bottle of wine.

Kim blinked. "You don't want to wait for your guest to arrive?"

"I think we'll be all right.

A smile Kim could only describe as bemused played across Craig's face as he took two glasses from a cabinet by the fridge and threaded the stems through his fingers. Taking the bottle from the counter in his free hand, he sauntered into the other room.

She stared after him, wondering if the man was totally clueless. Didn't he have any idea how hard this evening was going to be for her? Anyone who'd ever watched a single episode of reality-based TV knew that introducing their current girlfriend to the next woman on their list wouldn't end well. Apparently, though, Craig had never considered her his girlfriend in the first place, so maybe he simply didn't see the problem. Or how badly he'd hurt her.

Well, she wouldn't give him the satisfaction of finding out.

Wishing she'd stuck to black slacks and a crisp white blouse—her usual working uniform—she tugged at the hem of her LBD and thanked the good Lord above that she'd at least donned a bibbed apron over the ridiculous dress. Then, glad for the opportunity to do something else, to think of something else, Kim turned on the broiler and listened to the slight whoosh of the flames. She slid the tray of garlic bread onto the top shelf and told herself she needed to get through this night. No matter what happened, no matter how badly her heart was breaking, she'd maintain a professional, respectful decorum. Because, from this night on, her career was the only thing she had going for her.

Her expression a mask of chiseled granite, she slid the bowl of colorful salsa and the basket of toast points onto a coffee table that was all smoked glass and sculpted metal. Carefully, she stacked napkins between the two wineglasses and turned to retrace her steps.

"Wait. Where are you going?" Craig's deep voice held a hint of surprise.

"To the kitchen," she answered, as if it wasn't obvious. To Craig, she was nothing more than the hired help, someone to spend time with until a better option came along. Fine. If that was the way he felt about her, she'd act like it.

Craig patted the cushion beside him. "Sit with me. Have a glass of wine. You deserve to relax a bit after all the effort you put into this meal."

Was he crazy? Or simply delusional?

"Your guest will be here any minute," she said, in case he needed the reminder. "I don't think she'd appreciate finding me sitting here with you." She wagged her finger between them.

"You keep talking about my guest. What guest?" Craig pointed to the salsa. "This is all for you."

Kim stopped in midstride. She retraced her steps. "Say what now?"

"This is all for you. For us." Craig ran a hand through thick, wavy hair. "I wanted us to enjoy an evening together. Just the two of us." His voice turned sheepish. "I thought you'd like that."

Kim's mind filled with so many questions, she didn't know where to start. "But—but your guest," she stammered. "You said she was someone you hadn't seen in a long time."

"I believe I said we'd fallen out of touch." A hank of hair fell onto Craig's forehead. He shook it back. "Like you and I had fallen out of touch."

Doubt crept into his voice. "You didn't know you were the one I meant?"

Kim's knees wobbled. Unable to remain standing, she sank onto the couch beside Craig. Had she misread the entire situation? "Let me get this straight," she said, pausing to catch her breath. "You outbid everyone else in the silent auction, all those other people, so we could have a *date*?"

"When you put it that way, it does sound kind of silly. But yeah, that was part of it." He rubbed his chin. "Much as I like your family— and I do. Seriously, I do. But much as I like being around them, I wanted us to have some time alone."

"You could have just said so," she murmured. "We could have gone out to eat. Taken a long walk along the beach. I could have made popcorn, and we could have watched a movie right here in your living room." She pointed to the wide-screen TV mounted on the wall. "You didn't need to spend so much money just to see me."

Color stained Craig's cheeks. "It was for charity, too."

Kim clamped a hand over her mouth, not sure whether she should laugh or cry. Until tonight, she'd thought she and Craig told each other everything. They'd bared their past—the tragedies, the disappointments, as well as the good times. They'd talked about their business prospects, their hopes for the future. He'd been her staunchest supporter when she launched Royal Meals. She'd encouraged him to run for mayor the next time elections rolled around. And yet this one thing, this inability to say, *I want you all to myself*, had nearly destroyed them.

Thinking of how close she'd come to walking out his front door and never looking back, she felt her breath shudder. "You should know I thought there was someone else. Some other woman in your life. It hurt me terribly to think that you'd have me fix a fancy meal for you and…her."

Craig paled. He couldn't have looked any more stricken if she'd hauled off and slapped him. "I swear. There is no one else. I thought for sure you were just playing along, asking me questions about my dinner guest to prolong the suspense. I never dreamed…Oh, Kim, I'm so sorry." He mopped his face with his hand. "There is no one else. No one," he repeated. "You mean the world to me. I hope, I pray, you feel the same way about me."

She exhaled, her breath ragged with the last vestiges of her anger and disappointment. "I do.

I, um, I think that's why it hurt so much when I thought you had developed feelings for someone else. Because it broke my heart to think I'd lost you." She clasped her hands in front of her.

Craig cupped her hands in his. "Do you think...I mean, I know it's a lot to ask, but...Do you think we could start tonight over?"

"You mean, like a do-over?" Kim laughed despite herself.

"Yeah. Do you think we could?"

One glance at the tender, hopeful expression on Craig's face melted any resistance she might have held on to. "Let me, um...Give me a minute to check on things in the kitchen and freshen up a bit. Okay?"

"Sure. Anything. I'll do anything to make things right between us."

Slipping into the kitchen a minute later, Kim made quick work of shutting off burners and ovens so the special dinner she'd worked so hard on wouldn't get ruined completely. That done, she untied her apron strings and ducked into the half bath off the laundry room, where she blew her nose, splashed water on her face and finger-combed her hair. Leaving the apron hanging from a handy hook, she smoothed her hands over the LBD before she eased the back door open and slipped outside. Race-walking down the concrete sidewalk, she circled around to the front of the house, where she rang the doorbell.

"Can I he—" Craig's voice stalled the instant he caught sight of her standing in front of him. His eyes filled with a cautious optimism. "Hey, Kim. Come on in." He stepped aside to let her in.

"Hey, yourself," she answered. Pretending she was seeing his house for the first time, she took a moment. "You have a lovely home," she said at last. "I'm so glad you invited me to dinner."

Craig's smile widened. Without another word, he drew her into his arms for a kiss that went on forever and yet left them both breathless and wanting more.

An hour later, as they lingered over dishes that were, by her estimation, more than a wee bit overdone and Craig had declared absolute perfection, Kim studied the man seated across the table from her. As painful as it had been to stand on the brink of breaking up with Craig, she knew she wouldn't change a thing about tonight. If nothing else, the prospect of seeing their relationship crash and burn had deepened her awareness of how much she loved him, how much it would hurt if they ever did call it quits. From his gray-blue eyes to the gray at his temples that gave him a distinguished air, she loved everything about him. She loved the laugh lines around his mouth, the tiny cleft in his chin, his broad shoulders, slim hips and beyond. She loved his humor and the humility that clung to him like a warm blanket on a winter's night. Most of all, she loved…

"A penny for your thoughts."

Craig's voice broke into her reverie, and she couldn't have stopped smiling if she wanted to. Any more than she could have stopped the words that dropped like pebbles into the silence of the room.

"I was just thinking about how much I love you."

Even as the words slipped out, she braced herself. Though she knew Craig cared for her deeply—if nothing else, this evening had shown her that much—had she spoken too soon?

Craig's quiet, "I love you, too, Kim," banished all her concerns and put her doubts to rest. She watched as he seemed to be mulling something over. At last, he said, "I was saving this for later, after we'd had dessert, but I don't think I can wait another minute."

While Kim watched, Craig slowly set his napkin aside. The legs of his chair squeaked softly against the tiled floor when he pushed away from the table and stood. The soles of his shoes made shushing noises as he rounded the table and came toward her. Pretty sure she was about to be on the receiving end of one of Craig's amazing kisses, Kim tipped her head up. She swore her heart stopped when the man she loved more than any other man she'd ever known went down on one knee.

"Kimberly Ann Dane," he said, his eyes fixed on hers, "I know some people would say that six months isn't long enough to fall in love. But they'd be wrong about that. I fell in love with you the instant I saw you the night we both took the shuttle bus to Emerald Bay. I think Fate put us together that night. I pray we never part. I love you with all my heart, my soul, and I'm asking you, Kim Dane, will you do me the honor of marrying me, of making me the happiest man on earth?"

Kim's heart thudded. "Yes," she whispered, barely able to breathe. She forced herself to inhale. "Yes," she said, louder this time. "Yes. You are the love of my life, Craig Mitchell. Yes, I'll marry you."

When Craig continued to kneel before her, she noticed the black velvet box that lay in the palm of his hand. Tucked into a shiny white pillow, a diamond in a platinum setting sparkled like the morning sun.

"Oh, my," she whispered, her mouth going dry.

"If you don't like it…"

Kim shushed him. "I love it."

A fleeting kiss, little more than the brush of his lips across hers, followed. He slipped the ring on her finger.

"How did you know my size?" she asked, holding out her hand and admiring how the stone caught the light.

"That was the easiest part. You take your rings off and set them on the windowsill whenever you wash dishes. I just had to bide my time until there was no one else around and make a quick impression of one."

"Clever fellow."

With that, ice clinked and shifted as he pulled the bottle of champagne from the wine bucket. Swiftly, he wrapped the bottle in a towel and popped the cork. He poured the pale gold liquid into two waiting glasses. Handing one to her, he clinked their glasses softly.

"Here's to us, our future, our happiness."

The bubbles tickled her nose and throat.

The kisses that followed rekindled sensations she hadn't expected to ever feel again.

Later, padding barefoot into the kitchen for a glass of water, she remembered that they'd never gotten around to dessert. She cut two slices of the apple pie, added generous scoops of homemade ice cream and carried them back to the bedroom, where the man she loved with all her heart waited.

Eight

Diane

"I can't believe he wants to marry...me."

Seated across the table on the inn's back deck, Diane watched her cousin extend her hand to examine the gorgeous diamond she wore on her ring finger.

"Why would you doubt it? It's as plain as the nose on your face—the man is crazy in love with you," Margaret quipped. "I knew that the day he stopped by our table at Sweet Cakes."

Diane laughed. She remembered Kim's account of that lunch quite differently. Hadn't her cousin practically given Craig the cold shoulder after he'd made disparaging comments about the Dane Crown Inn? She'd gone so far as to compare him to her first husband. Fortunately, it hadn't taken Kim long to recognize that Craig and Frank had been cut from two entirely different pieces of cloth.

"He's lucky to have you," Diane insisted.

"Have you two lovebirds set a date?" Nat asked. Fruit bobbed and ice cubes clinked as she swirled her glass of sangria. The women had opted to take advantage of the early spring evening by gathering around the table on the back deck of the inn.

"Neither of us wants a long engagement." Kim picked up her own glass. "We thought maybe we'd have a simple ceremony during the reunion. What do you think? Is it too soon? Would it be too much extra work?"

"I think it's an excellent idea," Diane said firmly. "The whole family will be here to celebrate with you. What's wrong with that?"

Kim's expression still bore doubts. She turned to her daughter. "What about you, Nat? Do you need more time?"

Nat reared back in her chair. "To get used to the idea of you getting married again? Are you nuts? I'm excited for you! Craig is such a good guy, and it's clear he worships the ground you walk on."

Diane thought her heart just might melt when Nat stood and walked to her mother's side. Slinging her arms around Kim, the younger woman embraced her mom tightly. Tears shone in the eyes of everyone at the table when Nat added, "And, before you ask, Josh is just as happy about Craig and you as I am."

"Hear, hear," Diane said, lifting her glass to Kim as Nat returned to her place at the table.

"To Craig and Kim," Amy added.

As the last bit of tension drained from her sister's face, Jen asked, "What did you have in mind? A formal wedding with all the bells and whistles? Or something a bit more casual?"

"*Very* casual," Kim said, putting added stress on the first word. "I'd be happy if we went to the courthouse tomorrow and said our vows in front of the Justice of the Peace. Craig thinks we should have something more than that, but neither of us wants some big over-the-top affair."

"Still, you'll need a venue, a cake, flowers, a minister, the usual stuff," Diane said, ticking the items off on her fingertips.

"I can handle the cake," Amy blurted. "The end of May kicks off our bridal season, and the bakery is booked solid. My staff has been turning away brides for a couple of months already." She grinned. "But for *you*, I'll make an exception."

Kim leaned across the table to squeeze her cousin's hand. "Thanks, but nothing fancy. Just a sheet cake will be fine."

"Sheet cake. Got it." Amy nodded.

Belle sipped the ice water she'd opted for instead of sangria. "If you're getting married over the Memorial Day weekend, Daclan and I will provide the music." With the reunion in mind, she'd deliberately kept their calendar clear at the end of May.

Kim clasped her fingers together. "That'd be wonderful, Belle."

"Caleb says everything is in bloom in May. I'll be able to make some awesome floral arrangements using flowers from the inn's gardens. Unless home-grown isn't good enough," Jen hedged.

"I've always thought a bouquet of canna lilies and bird of paradise would be beautiful," Kim said. Both plants grew in masses behind the inn.

The back of Diane's throat ached with unshed tears. Everyone else had something special to contribute to the wedding, but she had nothing. "I'll pitch in and help wherever I'm needed," she offered.

Kim swung to face her. "You're a notary, right?"

Diane blinked. "Yeah?"

"Would you be willing to perform the wedding ceremony?"

Diane gripped the sides of her chair. "Me?

Don't you want Pastor Collier or Samuel to marry you?"

"Any other weekend, possibly. Because it's a holiday, the church has back-to-back weddings and services from Friday through Monday night. Neither minister is available."

"And you want me?" Though she and Tim had recommitted to each other, no one would mistake them for the poster couple for a good marriage.

"This last year may have been rough, but you and Tim have made it through twenty-five years of wedded bliss. Except for Aunt Margaret, no one else sitting at this table can make that claim. I can't think of anyone else I'd rather have in charge of my wedding." Kim swung a look around the table. "Can you?"

When a chorus of *no*'s sounded, Diane pressed a hand over her heart. "I'd be honored," she said.

"Okay, that about wraps it up, doesn't it?" Jen asked.

"Nooo," Nat said rather insistently. "She needs a dress." She turned to her mother. "Don't tell me you're going to walk down the aisle wearing a Royal Meals apron."

Diane chuckled at the image. "How about you and I take a ride down to Fort Lauderdale and pick out something at Zola Keller?" The high-end shop featured bridal gowns and special occasion dresses.

But Kim was already shaking her head. "Hmm. If it's all right with Belle, I'd love to borrow the dress I wore for New Year's."

"Of course, you can." Belle's eyebrows rose. "But Craig has already seen you in that one. I have plenty of others. You can take your pick."

"Thanks, but that's the one. Craig loves it almost as much as I do."

"Works for me. It can be your something borrowed." Belle sipped some water.

"A dress. Flowers. A cake. Music and an officiant. I think we broke the record for planning a wedding. Didn't we?" Amy asked.

"Well, there is just one more thing." Kim held up a finger. Turning to their aunt, her expression softened. "Aunt Margaret, in all the excitement, I'm afraid I overlooked the most important question of all—would it be all right with *you* if Craig and I held our wedding here the week of the family reunion?"

"What do you mean, would it be all right with me? Where else would you have it? This is your home, honey. Of course, you can have your wedding here."

"You don't think it will interfere with the reunion?"

"I think a wedding would be the perfect way to cap off the week, don't you? It might be the last Dane wedding we have here." Margaret's voice cracked. "Oh, my. Now I'm getting all weepy." She brushed her eyes.

Six sets of hands rushed to grab napkins from the heart-shaped holder on the Lazy Susan. Belle gave several to her mom. Around the table, more thin sheets fluttered as the rest of the women mopped tears from their eyes. No one needed to say the words aloud. They all knew the rapidly approaching reunion also meant the time to put the inn on the market was just around the corner. For a long minute, silence reigned over the table as each of them wrestled with her own thoughts.

When the stillness threatened to cast a pall over Kim's wedding plans, Diane cleared her throat. "I have something else to discuss with everyone tonight."

As if she'd flipped the light switch in a darkened room, the others turned hopeful faces toward hers.

"Caitlyn's sixteenth birthday is next week. We'd love to throw a party for her here at the inn the following weekend. If that's okay with everyone."

"What a fine idea," Margaret proclaimed. "The more things we have to celebrate, the better."

"A Sweet Sixteen birthday party?" Belle brightened. "With boys in suits and girls in fancy dresses?"

Diane couldn't help it; she laughed out loud. "Can you imagine Caitlyn in ribbons and bows?"

"Well, no," Belle admitted. The teen definitely preferred shorts and T-shirts.

"What'd you have in mind?" Margaret asked.

"Caitlyn wants to invite the girls from her soccer team, plus a few friends like Toby and Harper." Craig's nephew and the minister's daughter had been Caitlyn's first friends in Emerald Bay. "We'd have the party here in the backyard." Diane gestured toward the open space off the deck. "Tim and I will handle all the food."

Her husband had offered to fix hamburgers and hot dogs, but Caitlyn asked for Diane's chicken tacos and her dad's street corn instead. The request stirred bittersweet memories. The meal had once been a favorite at their house in Tampa, but the last time Diane fixed it, things had not gone well. A last-minute crisis at work had demanded her attention, attention that should have been focused on her family. Later that night, Tim packed his bags and moved out. She'd wondered at the time if she'd ever eat another bite of the spicy chicken dish, but a lot had changed since then. They'd all changed. After realizing the strain it had placed on her family, she'd walked away from her demanding job and quietly begun offering accounting services for select clients here in Emerald Bay. It had taken hard work and more than a few tears, but she and Tim had resolved their differences and were carving out a new future for themselves, together again. Equally important, Caitlyn appeared to be thriving in her new school and with her new friends.

"Sounds like fun. Are we invited?" Amy asked.

The question derailed Diane's walk down memory lane. She straightened. "Of course," she answered. Her arm swept through the air. "You all are."

Because a milestone like a sixteenth birthday cried out for a celebration. And there was no better way to hold one than surrounded by family and close friends.

Behind the inn, Diane gripped the deck rail as she watched her daughter and the other girls from Emerald Bay High's varsity soccer team crowd around Krystal Morshe. Wearing the bright blue uniform of her current pro team, the former World Cup goalkeeper walked through one of the footwork drills she ran each day. When she finished, she tapped Caitlyn on the shoulder.

"Okay, birthday girl, show us how it's done." Krystal tossed the soccer ball to the ground at Caitlyn's feet.

Diane's heart swelled with pride as her daughter flawlessly executed the movements the soccer superstar had demonstrated.

"Great!" Krystal indicated her approval with a nod that sent her blond ponytail swaying and brought a flush to Caitlyn's face. "Next player."

While the high schoolers hung on Krystal's every word, the tall, athletically built young woman spent the next half hour teaching more drills to the team. When she finished, she took the time to speak one-on-one with each of Caitlyn's teammates, offering the girls words of advice or encouragement before she posed for individual pictures. After an hour, Krystal's assistant doled out the team's blue jerseys, which Krystal graciously autographed.

As she was leaving, the superstar clapped Caitlyn on the shoulder and began walking the teen toward the long black limo that idled in the parking area. Diane was too far away to hear what transpired as Krystal shook Tim's hand a moment later, but both her husband and her daughter were beaming on their way back from seeing the soccer player off. Satisfied that all had gone well, Diane flashed them both a thumbs-up sign before she hurried back into the kitchen, where dinner preparations were in full swing.

"Who was that?" Kim stood at the stove, expertly adding the last of the pan-fried chicken strips to a veritable mountain of others. Marinated and blackened, the strips would serve as the key ingredient in Diane's tacos.

"*That* was Krystal Morshe. She's the top women's goalkeeper in the country. Word has it, she's a shoo-in for the Olympic soccer team."

"Whoa! Did you know she was going to show up at Caitlyn's birthday party?" Kim waved the spatula.

Diane swung her head. "Nope. Tim made all the arrangements without telling me." She glanced out the window. "However he did it, I'm impressed." But her own shock was nothing compared with Caitlyn's or the other girls'.

Focusing her attention on the job at hand, Diane clapped her hands. "Okay, where are we? Is everything ready? Those girls are bound to be starving after all that excitement."

"All set to put it on the table," Kim assured her. "Jen, let's start carrying things outside."

The guacamole and salsa Diane had made from scratch the night before sat in the fridge. Jen removed the two enormous bowls and started for the French doors that opened onto the deck while, at the stove, Kim began scooping refried beans from a skillet into a waiting bowl. Carrying the containers of tomatoes, onions and lettuce she'd chopped earlier, Diane followed her cousin onto the deck. As if he'd read her mind, Tim lifted ears of corn from the grill, doused them with his special sauce and dusted them with cotija cheese. Carrying a towering platter of the still sizzling corn, he joined them on the deck, where miniature soccer balls anchored blue and white cloths to folding tables.

Diane stared into her husband's eyes while she leaned over the platter and inhaled deeply. The heavenly mix of spice and cheese made her mouth water. She shifted the taco fixings to one side to make way for the corn. Her voice low, she asked, "How in the world did you get Krystal Morshe to show up for Caitlyn's birthday? And why didn't you tell me she was coming?"

"I treated her once for a dental emergency." Careful not to tip the platter lest he send the ears rolling, Tim settled the plate on the table.

Straightening, he added, "And I didn't tell you, or Caitlyn, in case it didn't work out."

Tim shuffled his feet against the wooden planks, a move he made whenever he had something to hide. Determined to ferret out the whole truth, Diane let her eyes narrow. "What kind of emergency?" she asked.

Tim winced. "I met Krystal and her boyfriend on the cruise." The statement hung in the air between them for a moment before the rest of the story spilled from his lips in a torrent. "She'd dislodged a crown on a sticky bun and didn't want to run around snaggle-toothed for the rest of the trip. I was able to make a temporary repair. It was simple, really, just a little bonding agent. But she was so grateful she said if I ever needed anything…" Tim shrugged. "So I asked her to show up at Caitlyn's birthday party."

Diane waited for the sharp pinch of heart-break she'd felt whenever Tim mentioned the two-week cruise he took after he left her. This time, though, only happiness swirled in her chest. She certainly couldn't fault him for arranging for their daughter—and her friends—to meet one of Caitlyn's role models. Nor did she want to. She supposed that meant they had well and truly put their troubles behind them, and she smiled up at him.

"Thanks for doing that. I've never seen Caitlyn so happy."

"Oh, she was." Tim leaned down to whisper in her ear. "There's more, but she wants to tell you the rest herself. I've been sworn to silence." Pressing his thumb and forefinger together, he zipped his lips.

Forcing down her own curiosity for the time being, Diane gave the dinner preparations a final survey. Lanterns hung from the branches of the trees. Festive garland twined around the deck's railing. Balloons decorated like soccer balls formed an arch over the stairs. More balloons danced in the light breeze from the ends of tables scattered about the yard, where they provided plenty of seating options for all the girls, family members and a few close friends.

"Happy?" Tim nudged her elbow.

"It looks nice, doesn't it?" Diane asked. "This is what I wanted to do, what I should have done, that night we had Marty and Sara over for dinner." But instead of hanging lights from the branches of the old oak tree in their backyard, she'd put in another all-nighter at work.

"Water under the bridge," Tim murmured. "We can't undo the past."

"No," Diane admitted. "And I wouldn't want to. We weathered a storm —"

"A bad one," Tim put in.

"Right. There's no denying it. But we came out the other side together. I think our marriage is stronger because of what we've been through."

"I'm glad to hear you say that." Tim slipped his arm around her waist. "I feel the same way, but…" He smiled down at her.

"But?"

"But a horde of hungry young women is gonna stampede up these steps the minute they get a whiff of your chicken tacos."

Diane laughed. "And your corn. I can't believe you bought an entire bushel." She pushed lightly on his chest. Casting a look over her shoulder at the tables that were crowded with food, she said, "I guess we'd better tell everyone it's time to eat before it gets cold. You get the girls started, and I'll let Aunt Margaret and the others know."

For the next hour, Diane rushed back and forth, replenishing bowls and platters as quickly as they were emptied. Which was no small feat, considering the amount of food twenty active teenagers could put away. To say nothing of the assorted friends and family who'd gathered to help Caitlyn celebrate her special day. By the time everyone had had their fill, a lone taco sat all by itself on a tray and every single ear of corn had disappeared.

Diane gave everyone a few minutes to let their meal settle before she signaled Amy and the others. They burst through the French doors wheeling a trolley that held a large one-layer cake in Caitlyn's favorite flavor, carrot. Belle led everyone in singing the birthday song, as Caitlyn, her face glowing with happiness, blew out all sixteen candles in one breath.

As the girls lined up for cake and ice cream, Diane overheard more than one of Caitlyn's teammates declare this the best birthday party ever, which made it worth every bit of the time and effort she and Tim and her family had poured into it.

"Did you have a good birthday, sweetheart?" Diane gave Caitlyn a one-armed hug as they stood at the end of the parking area and waved goodbye to the last of her guests.

"I still can't believe Krystal Morshe came to *my* birthday party. I'll never have another one as good as this one. Thanks, Mom!" Caitlyn's arm wrapped around Diane's waist.

"Much as I'd like to take all the credit, it's

your dad who deserves it. He's the one who arranged for Krystal to be here."

"I already thanked him. Like a hundred times. But you fixed the chicken tacos. They were awesome." Stepping back, Caitlyn rubbed her tummy. "Everything else was, too."

"It takes a village," Diane said, never meaning it more than she did at that moment. "Your Aunt Amy baked the cake. Aunt Kim and Aunt Jen helped with the cooking. Aunt Belle sang 'Happy Birthday.' Nat took pictures." The young woman had documented every moment, from the arrival of the first guest to the departure of the last one.

As they stepped onto the pavered walkway that led back to the inn, Diane posed the same question she usually asked at the end of the school year, after they'd watched a movie, or on special occasions like this one. "What was the best part of your birthday?"

She fully expected Caitlyn to name Krystal's visit as the highlight of her day, but there was always the possibility that her daughter's shiny new driver's license might take top billing.

"I think..." Caitlyn's voice hitched. She kicked a pebble off one of the pavers.

"What, sweetheart?"

"Seeing you and Daddy...happy again...is

the best birthday present ever," Caitlyn said, her voice strained and halting.

"Aww." Tears flooded Diane's eyes. Reaching for Caitlyn's hand, she gave it a tight squeeze. "It's a pretty wonderful thing for us, too."

Up ahead, Tim walked toward them, his footsteps jaunty. "Did you tell her?" he asked, looking straight at Caitlyn once he come close enough to be heard over the distant roar of waves crashing on the beach.

"Tell me what?" Diane asked.

Excitement glowed on Caitlyn's face when she gushed, "Krystal Morshe invited me to a summer camp her alma mater runs for prospective players. It's for two weeks, and I'd stay on campus in a dorm. There's three-a-day practices, and I'd get to work one-on-one with Krystal and Coach Widdingham."

"Widdingham?" Diane's brows knitted. The name sounded vaguely familiar.

"Florida State," Tim said, the words rolling off his tongue with near reverence. "Widdingham coaches the goalkeepers."

Diane sucked in a breath. The school regularly placed in the top ten for women's soccer and had claimed more than one national championship. Not only that, but the university boasted an excellent academic program. As an added bonus,

Caitlyn would qualify for in-state tuition, in case she failed to land a scholarship. "When is this?"

"It's at the end of July. Please say I can go, Mom. Please, please?"

Diane glanced at Tim, who nodded. Putting her trust in her husband, Diane took a deep breath. "As long as your dad says it's all right, of course you can go."

"Awesome!" Caitlyn pronounced while she bounced on her toes. "I have to call Stacey. Krystal invited her, too. It'll be fun having someone else I know at camp."

Over the top of their daughter's head, Diane shared a glance with Tim. Silently, they agreed that it was time for the final surprise of the day.

Tim jangled the keys in his pocket. "Before you make that call, your mom and I want to show you something."

"Is it a car?" Caitlyn stopped dead in her tracks, her eyes widening until her brows disappeared under her bangs.

"No," Diane said, firmly quashing that idea. She and Tim had decided that their daughter needed more time behind the wheel before they'd consider buying her a car of her own. "But you can drive mine to school on the days you have soccer practice."

"Oh. Okay." Caitlyn took the news in stride.

"So what do you want to show me?"

"You'll see. Let's go for a drive," Tim said. He tossed his keys to Caitlyn, who deftly caught them.

"Pull in there." From the passenger's seat, Tim pointed to a circular driveway made of peach-colored bricks. Mature trees shaded a shallow front yard in front of the two-story house that sat in a neighborhood of widely spaced homes.

"Whose house is this? Do they know we're coming?" Caitlyn pulled to a stop before an inviting front door flanked by tall, round columns.

"The house is vacant because it's on the market," Diane answered from her spot behind the driver's seat.

"The front yard isn't very big, but wait till you see the back," Tim said. "The lot is a full acre. Even with the pool, there's plenty of room for a practice field."

"For soccer?" Caitlyn stared at the front door. "You're buying this house?"

"Only if you like it, Caitlyn," Diane said

without unbuckling her seat belt. In the rearview mirror, she caught a glimpse of her daughter quietly tugging her lower lip through her even front teeth.

"I wouldn't have to change schools again, would I?" the teen asked while the engine continued to purr.

"No," her father said with the firm assurance of a man who'd already double-checked the school boundaries. "The kids in this area attend Emerald Bay High."

Caitlyn's voice softened. "What about you, Daddy?

Leaning forward, Diane slipped her hand onto Tim's shoulder. "Your father and I have decided it's time to let go of the past and move on to the future…together…as a family."

"You're moving here, Daddy?" Disbelief and hope warred for control in Caitlyn's voice.

"Yes and no. It's a little bit complicated because I still have the dental practice," Tim said like someone cautiously testing the temperature of the bath water. "I need to be in Tampa Monday through Thursday. You and your mom can come there for a visit anytime you want. Your brother, too. Fridays, I'll hop in the car and drive to Emerald Bay, where I'll spend the weekends and holidays. Eventually—once I retire and Warren takes over the practice—we'll sell the house in Tampa. Your mom and I want to make Emerald Bay our permanent home."

Caitlyn's head bobbed up and down in a thoughtful nod. "I like that plan. I mean, I wish you could be here all the time, but a lot of my friends' parents don't live together. Evy's dad is in the Army. He's stationed overseas. Carol Ann's mom is a travel nurse. She's gone for three months at a time." She shrugged. "I can live with weekends."

"Good," Tim said, sounding somewhat relieved.

Diane exhaled a slow, steady breath. Like her daughter, she didn't relish the thought of living apart from Tim through the work week. But as solutions went, it was the best either of them could come up with.

"I think you might like this place, Caitlyn. Your dad already mentioned the yard; that was a big factor in choosing this house. But it has a lot more going for it. It's about the size of our other house. There are four bedrooms, but in this one, each bedroom has its own separate bath." The bathroom Caitlyn had shared with Nick on the second floor had been a bone of contention between her children from the time her daughter had been in training pants. She pointed to the wing that jutted out from the main house opposite the garage. "That's an in-law suite, a separate living quarters that I'd convert into a home office." She paused before adding, "If we buy it, that is."

Caitlyn shut off the engine. Her seat belt retracted into its holder with a sharp *snick*. "What are we waiting for? We'd better check it out."

Diane trailed Tim and Caitlyn up the short walkway that led to a small porch. At the door, her husband used the key the Realtor had provided to let them inside.

They stepped onto Brazilian koa hardwood flooring that added a depth of color and interest to the empty rooms with their plain, beige walls. To their right, a set of double doors opened into a spacious master suite, complete with its own sitting room. Light from the setting sun streamed through large windows in the living room on the left. An open floor plan meant the living room blended into a recently updated kitchen. Beyond it, sliding glass doors led from a family room onto a spacious screen enclosure that surrounded a kidney-shaped pool.

"A pool?" Caitlyn's mouth dropped open. "With a waterfall? That does it. I'm sold. When do we move in?"

"You haven't even seen your room yet,"

Diane protested. "What if it's the size of a postage stamp?"

"Doesn't matter. This house has a pool!"

Diane smiled. Her daughter had long and loudly lamented the fact that she had to use the pool at the community center in their old Tampa neighborhood. "Still, we ought to at least look upstairs."

Caitlyn dutifully tromped up the stairs with her parents. On the second-floor landing, doors opened onto three upstairs suites, each with its own full bath. Their daughter's forehead furrowed. "So these rooms are for me and Nick?"

"We'll turn the leftover one into a guest room," Tim said.

"I want the biggest one!" Caitlyn darted into a room that was twice the size of the bedroom she'd had in Tampa.

"Great. We'll give Nick the one on the other end and save the middle room for guests," Diane said, certain their son wouldn't mind the slightly smaller room whenever he visited.

The decision made, they piled back into the car a few minutes later. This time, eager to call Stacey, Caitlyn slipped into the back seat. In no time at all, the two girls were engaged in an excited chatter that lasted all the way back to the inn.

"Guess what? Stacey only lives about a mile from our new house," Caitlyn announced as Tim parked the car. "She doesn't have a pool, but she does have a practice pitch in her backyard. We can practice at her place and then cool off in our pool."

"Sounds like you two have things all worked out." Tim's hands lingered on the steering wheel. "I'll call the Realtor on my way back to Tampa, tell her to go ahead with the offer and we want to settle as soon as possible. If there are any changes, I'll let you know."

"Perfect." Diane crossed her fingers. "I hope this goes through." The house checked all the boxes on her rather lengthy list of must-haves. Reaching for her door handle, she peered at her husband. "Are you going to come in?"

"I'd better hit the road." He checked his watch. "If I leave now, I can be back by nine. If I come inside…"

Diane chortled. "It'll be midnight," she finished for him. Leaning toward him, she kissed his cheek. "Take care. I'll see you next weekend."

Caitlyn slung her arms around her father's neck. "See you soon, Daddy," she said, giving him a backwards hug. "Love you, Daddy. This was the best birthday ever."

"You deserved it, honey."

Diane's heart clenched when Tim's eyes took on a misty look as he met his daughter's gaze in the rearview mirror. Moments later, she and Caitlyn stood at the edge of the parking area and waved goodbye while Tim's car rumbled down the coquina driveway toward the main road. When his taillights had disappeared, she turned to Caitlyn.

"I'm in the mood for another piece of birthday cake. How about you?"

"Yeah. That sounds great."

Side by side, they started for the main house, but as they rounded the hedge that lined the parking area, Caitlyn's footsteps faltered.

"Is everything all right?" Diane asked when her daughter gazed at the inn with a puzzled expression on her face.

"I think I just realized that if we're moving, it means we won't be living here anymore. I'm gonna miss being around Aunt Belle and Aunt Kim and Aunt Jen. Especially Aunt Margaret. Don't you think she'll be lonely without us?"

Diane's breath caught in her throat. Their move wasn't the only change on the horizon. Though she'd made no effort to keep Margaret's plans for the future a secret, she wondered how much Caitlyn had really thought about them.

"Honey, you know that Aunt Margaret is

going to sell the inn, don't you?" she asked softly. "She can't run this place on her own anymore. She's already fallen a couple of times. If she falls again while she's alone, she could get hurt. It might be hours before someone finds her." Which was exactly what had happened the night Margaret had broken her arm.

"But she's not alone," Caitlyn protested. "Aunt Belle lives here now. So does Aunt Kim and Aunt Jen. They can help her with reservations and taking care of the guests and stuff."

"Oh, I don't know about that. Singing with The Emeralds keeps your Aunt Belle pretty busy. Aunt Kim has to run Royal Meals. Once she and Craig get married, she'll probably move into his house."

"Yeah, but…"

Diane couldn't fault her daughter for looking at the way things were today and assuming they'd stay that way forever. She, though, knew how quickly change could come about when you least expected it. She tried to explain. "The Emeralds are good. Very good. The more people hear about them, the busier they're going to be. Aunt Belle won't have time to sing with the band and help take care of the inn. The same holds true for Aunt Kim and Royal Meals." As for Jen, the only thing Diane knew for sure about her youngest cousin was that she never stayed in one place for more than a few months.

"Yeah, but if everyone helped Aunt Margaret a little bit…" Caitlyn began.

The concept was an intriguing one, Diane admitted even as she shook her head. "This is a very complex problem. The decision to sell the inn was not easy. Another part of the problem is that it takes a lot of money to run a place like this, and the inn's been losing money for so long that there's not enough left to keep it open."

"You and Daddy can't help?"

"We have. We all have. Aunt Belle sold an expensive piece of art in order to pay for new carpets. Aunt Amy had the floors refinished. Your dad and I paid the insurance bill. Aunt Margaret used the last of her savings to have the house painted and make a bunch of other improvements. We just—there just isn't enough to keep things going for very much longer."

Caitlyn's face paled. "What's Aunt Margaret going to do?"

"She's decided to put the inn on the market right after the reunion. She'll make enough money from selling the property to last her the rest of her life. She's already picked out a room at Emerald Oaks."

Caitlyn chewed on that idea for a long moment. At last, she said, "Now that I have my driver's license, I'll be able to visit her every day, won't I?"

"Absolutely," Diane said.

"Do you think Aunt Margaret has some things she wants to do before she moves? I could help her do them," Caitlyn offered.

"You mean like a bucket list?" Diane asked. She blinked. Her daughter was chock full of good ideas this evening.

"Yeah. Like maybe she'd like to visit the orange grove one more time. I could borrow a golf cart and take her there. Or maybe she'd want to go for a walk in the gardens. We could do that together."

It was a good idea, and Diane told her daughter as much while they slowly resumed their trek to the house.

Come to think of it, a bucket list wasn't just a good idea; it was a great one. Especially since there were a few things she'd like to put on her own list before someone else took possession of the home where she'd been born and raised.

Nine

Diane

"The airboat ride was exhilarating! Oh, my word! We saw alligators. *Live* alligators! And the birds! There were millions of them."

Diane rounded the corner in time to see the chatty guest, a woman wearing a Hawaiian shirt over baggy Bermuda shorts, wave her arms. Her motions were so quick, they threatened to dislodge the sun hat that sat on top of her white curls.

"So many colors," the woman exclaimed. "It was incredible!"

"Sounds like it was a hit." Jen smiled up from her seat behind a desk just off the entryway. "I'm so glad you enjoyed it, Mrs. Leffew."

With a silent nod to her cousin, Diane sank

onto a nearby club chair to wait while the two women finished up. Though she'd argued against spending the money, she had to admit that Jen had been right when she insisted on redesigning the registration area. Gone was the ancient, scarred podium their Aunt Margaret had stood behind while she greeted new arrivals. In its place, a small desk crafted from leather-wrapped raffia and rattan, a tidy rack of brochures featuring some of the more popular attractions in the area, and two armchairs created an inviting welcome spot.

"Then we took your other suggestion and had lunch at Marsh Landing." With only slightly less enthusiasm than she'd had for the airboat ride, Mrs. Leffew declared their visit to the local watering hole *fantastic*. "We ate frogs' legs, catfish and fried green tomatoes. I feel like a real Southern gal now, don't you know. I can't wait to tell my friends back home. They'll all want to book their own trips to Florida."

"Make sure you tell them to stay with us when they come," Jen said. Taking a card from a small stack, she passed one to their guest. "If they mention your name when they make their reservations, you'll get ten percent off on your next stay at the Dane Crown Inn."

"Well, I'll definitely tell them." The woman

slipped the card into the pocket of her rumpled shorts. "You know," she said peering down at Jen, "you've really made our visit here a success. Thank you for all your help."

"My pleasure, Mrs. Leffew. Where are you off to tomorrow?"

For the first time, their guest's enthusiasm flagged. "Deep sea fishing. My husband booked that charter you mentioned out of Sebastian. I just hope I don't get seasick."

"Stop by the drugstore when you go out for dinner tonight," Jen counseled. "Ask the pharmacist what you should take. He'll make sure you get the right medicine."

"Well, I declare. That's another great idea." Mrs. Leffew resettled her hat on her head. "Toodles!" she said, waving her fingers as she turned to leave.

Diane stayed put until she heard the creak of Mrs. Leffew's shoes on the stairs. "You were wonderful with her," she said when the woman was out of earshot.

"Aw, she's a sweetheart. Most of our guests are." Jen straightened the small stack of discount cards before she slipped them into a desk drawer.

"Still, I don't think I'd have the patience."

Jen shrugged. "We all have our talents. I like

working with people. That's probably why I enjoyed waitressing so much." She tapped the desk. "This is even more fun. Plus, I don't spend ten hours in heels every day. No more soaking my feet in ice baths."

"That sounds like torture," Diane said as she stood. "Kim sent me to get you. She says she has a new punch recipe she wants to try out on us tonight. Are you all done here?"

"Let me just grab a pager." Jen retrieved one of the small devices from a different desk drawer, along with a placard advising guests who needed assistance to send a text. After propping the card against a vase of flowers picked from the inn's garden, she clipped the pager to her pocket and dusted her hands. "Okay, let's go see about that punch," she said, linking her arm with Diane's.

As they threaded their way through the house, Diane once again marveled at the transformation the inn had undergone since her arrival nearly six months earlier. She and her cousins had banished the scatter rugs that had covered worn spots or, in some cases, bona fide holes in the hardwood floors. "Those evil trip hazards," as Kim called them, were no longer necessary now that the floors gleamed evenly throughout the house. Fresh paint and new wallpaper brightened every room. Threadbare carpets had been replaced, as had worn bed linens and towels. A robust Internet provided service in every suite, and flat-screen televisions expanded the entertainment options. Nor were the changes limited to the interior. Outside, the inn no longer resembled a badly aging beauty queen. With its trimmed hedges and flowering plants, sturdy railings and bright welcome sign, she thought the place once more lived up to its claim to fame as "The Jewel of Florida's Treasure Coast."

The only problem was, having worked so hard to restore the inn to its former beauty, the family wouldn't be able to enjoy it much longer. Though Caitlyn's suggestion about sharing the workload had stirred her hopes that they could hold on to the place, the dream hadn't lasted long. Once Diane had gone over the inn's books with a fine-tooth comb, she gave up on the idea entirely. Between the unexpected bump in the insurance premiums and the generally higher costs of everything else these days, the inn simply couldn't generate enough income to cover all its expenses.

Oh, they could eke along for a while. Another year, two at the most. But by the time they had their backs against the wall, the inn would have lost some of its glow. In two years, the exterior paint would begin to fade under Florida's relentless sun. Towels and linens would need to be replaced...again. Worse—heaven forbid—a hurricane could take aim at their little corner of the world. That could inflict all kinds of damage...and send their insurance rates through the roof.

No, it was better to sell the property now while it was in tip-top shape. Getting a good price for the inn was the only way to secure Aunt Margaret's future. And that was the whole point, wasn't it?

Walking past the staircase, Diane trailed her fingers across the top of the newel post. The Dane Crown Inn had had a good run. Nearly sixty years as one of the East Coast's premier resorts. But, she supposed, all good things came to an end eventually. Still, she was going to miss this place. And not just for herself. She tamped down a profound longing that swirled in her chest, an ache for the memories her grandchildren would never have the chance to create. Nick's children would never slide down the staircase banister like he had. Caitlyn's children would never pick oranges in the grove at the end of the property or fish along the river's edge. They wouldn't roast marshmallows at the firepit or search for buried treasure following a handmade map, whether it had belonged to a survivor of the 1715 shipwreck or not.

"You've gotten awfully quiet." Jen's elbow dug into Diane's ribs. "You doing okay?"

"Just thinking about the future." She considered the announcement she planned to make tonight and the changes it would bring. "No matter how much I look forward to taking the next step, it's hard to leave the past behind."

"I hear ya. That's why we have to enjoy the here and now." A teasing grin spreading across her face, Jen swung open the door that led onto the back deck. "And right now, I'm looking forward to hanging out with my besties."

Diane laughed out loud. Her cousin always knew the right thing to say. "Have I told you how much I love you?" she asked.

"Yes, but I don't mind hearing you repeat it." Jen slid onto one of the two vacant seats at the table. Rubbing her hands together like a greedy kid, she asked, "What's new, everybody? And what did I hear about something to drink?"

Diane let her gaze flit among the faces of those gathered at the oblong table. Reaching toward Belle, she pulled a pencil from the masses of curls piled atop her cousin's head. "Nice accessory," she said, rolling the wooden stick across the table.

Chuckling, Belle snatched up the pencil and slipped it into the pocket of her sweatpants. "I was working on a new song," she explained.

"Can't wait to hear it," Diane said, with heart-felt sincerity. In her mind, Belle's new music far surpassed "Jimmy, Jimmy, Oh," her biggest hit.

"Did your mom turn in already?" Though Margaret normally skipped their nightly get-togethers, Diane had hoped she'd join them tonight and hear her news firsthand.

"You know Mama. She's a creature of habit."

Diane nodded. Her Aunt Margaret liked nothing more than to read her Bible for a bit before she went to sleep each night.

Seated beside Belle, Kim began handing out short tumblers filled with an icy brew. As she did, the ring on her finger sparkled in the low light, which stirred a giddy feeling in Diane's insides. Her cousin deserved happiness, and she couldn't be more delighted that Kim and Craig had found it in each other. Gratefully, she took one of the glasses and sniffed the fragrant mix of pineapple and orange. "Mmm. Yummy," she said. "Is that rum I smell?"

Kim nodded. "And a touch of grenadine." She passed the rest of the drinks to Nat, Jen and Amy, who'd claimed the spot at the foot of the table.

Not that her sister was sitting still. Far from it. Amy normally kept her cool—even when smoke poured from one of Sweet Cakes' ovens. Tonight, though, she fairly danced in her seat. Her constant motion reminded Diane of a kernel of popcorn on the brink of bursting.

Eyeing her sister, she lifted her glass to the others. "I have news to share," she said. "But I think Amy might explode if we make her wait, so we better hear what she has to say first." She grinned at her older sister. "Age before beauty."

For once, Amy ignored the jibe. Instead, she scooted forward in her chair. A broad smile on her face, she plunged straight in. "After a few hiccups, Deborah and I closed on the property in Sebastian this morning," she announced. "Sweet Cakes Two is finally happening."

The announcement triggered a chorus of congratulations and best wishes.

"When will you open?" Nat asked.

"May 18th," Amy said firmly. "I had hoped to do it a couple of weeks earlier, but the counters we ordered are taking longer than we'd planned."

"I'm so happy for you," Diane said. "Just think, a couple of years ago you were working out of your kitchen, and now, here you are, opening a second location." Not that success had come easily or overnight. Her sister had worked hard to achieve her dreams.

"Excellent news, Amy!" Kim's grin stretched from ear to ear. "I bet Deborah is thrilled."

Though it didn't seem possible that Amy could look any happier, her smile widened. "I think she's even more excited than I am. She's looking forward to running the new place."

"To Amy and Deborah and Sweet Cakes Two!" Belle said, lifting her glass in a toast.

For the next few minutes, Diane sat on her own announcement while questions and answers about the bakery's new location flew around the table. Slowly sipping her punch, she waited until the commotion had died down before she cleared her throat.

"Uh, hmm. Amy's not the only one with news." She paused, letting the tension build. "Tim and I bought a house today."

Amy's eyes widened. "You did? Where?"

"Yeah, where, Aunt Diane? You're not moving back to Tampa, are you?" Nat asked.

Diane shook her head. "No, it's in Emerald Bay. About two miles from here, actually."

Belle's fingers fluttered while she fanned herself. "I'm not sure I can take much more excitement.

"Tell us about it," Jen demanded.

Diane quickly hit the highlights. "It has four bedrooms with a pool and a big backyard. The kitchen and bathrooms have all been updated. Plus, there's a mother-in-law suite I'll be able to use as my office. Once she found out she'd still be able to attend Emerald Bay High, Caitlyn gave the place two thumbs up. Her friend Stacey lives close by, and the two of them are already cooking up plans together."

"That sounds wonderful." Sincerity shone in Amy's eyes.

"When do you move in?" Kim asked.

"Thirty days. We should be all settled before the reunion." By plunking the rest of the money from her severance package down on the new house, she and Tim had avoided the lengthy wait for mortgage approval.

"Oh!" Belle exclaimed. "That's quick."

"I know, right?" Diane had expected negotiations to drag on a bit longer. "Turns out, the current owners are nearly as anxious to sell as we are to buy. I was shocked when they accepted our offer. I thought for sure they'd counter."

Jen pressed a hand over her heart. "I can't believe you're moving."

"Not far. We'll be back and forth all the time. Plus, there's an upside. With Caitlyn and I moving out, the inn will have two more suites available for guests." No one was more aware than Diane how much that added income would come in handy.

"It also means there'll be two extra rooms during the reunion," Jen pointed out.

"Speaking of which, is everything all set?" Belle asked. Less than six weeks remained before the entire Dane clan would descend on the inn for the long Memorial Day weekend.

"The bakery has breads, rolls, pastries and cookies covered," Amy reported. "We've been making extras and freezing them for the last couple of months." She smiled at Kim. "The design for your wedding cake is finished. It's going to be beautiful."

Kim twisted her engagement ring. "I have no doubts," she assured her cousin.

"I've taken care of all the room assignments, though I'll go through them again now that we'll have Beryl and Quartz available," Diane said.

"The menus are all set." Kim had taken charge of coordinating food for the horde. "Sandwiches at lunch. Friday night, we'll grill hamburgers and hot dogs. Saturday will be make-your-own pizzas. Sunday is baked ziti and salad. And—ta da! Craig got a couple of boys from the Kiwanis Club to hold an old-fashioned fish fry and shrimp boil to close out the weekend on Monday."

Amy grinned. "Max and Caleb are thrilled. They volunteered to catch the fish. I told them I'd fill up the tank of Max's boat and pay for the beer."

"They'll clean them, too, won't they?"

A note of concern edged Kim's voice and no wonder, thought Diane. Cleaning enough fish to feed all the people expected for the reunion was a dirty, smelly undertaking.

"It cost me another six pack of beer, but yeah," Amy said, humor dancing in her eyes.

"The lawn games—darts, croquet, badminton and volleyball—are all in good shape," Jen said. "I've printed off copies of the map for anyone who wants to go on a treasure hunt."

"I'll take one," Diane blurted. She immediately felt the color rise in her cheeks and hurried to explain. "Caitlyn asked if Aunt Margaret had anything she wanted to accomplish before she sells the inn. It made me stop and think about my own bucket list. Just in case that old map is real, I'd like to take another crack at it."

"You didn't go on enough treasure hunts when we were kids?" Amy asked. "We went on so many I lost count. Every one ended the same—we were hot, sweaty and had nothing in our pockets but sand and seashells."

"They were fun, though," Diane protested.

"If you call bickering with Scott about who got to wear the hat or who got to hold the map *fun*," Kim said.

"He always wanted to be in charge, didn't he?" Her brother was a born leader, a trait he'd put to good use as a lawyer. Diane turned to Belle. "How about you? Up for a hunt?"

The redhead's curls shook. "Sorry. Daclan and I have back-to-back gigs this weekend. I'll be spending all my free time getting ready for that."

"Don't look at me," Kim said, throwing up her hands. "I'll be busy with Royal Meals all week."

"Caleb promised to help me with the garden. We're going to plant tomatoes," Jen said dreamily.

Diane smothered a sigh. She'd explore the grounds on her own if she had to, but having someone else along made the trek more interesting.

"I'll go with you, Aunt Diane." Nat's soft voice broke the stillness.

"Really?" Diane didn't try to mask her surprise. The prissy, self-styled New Yorker who'd shocked everyone with her appearance at

Christmas was the last person she'd expect to want to embark on what was an admittedly fruitless treasure hunt.

"When Josh and I were little, Mom told us stories about growing up here in Emerald Bay. She made hunting for buried treasure sound so wonderful—like something straight out of the adventures of Peter Pan and the Lost Boys. I don't think the one we went on for the gender reveal party counted."

"We probably won't find anything," Diane cautioned.

"That's what makes it so exciting...knowing we won't but hoping we will."

Diane grinned at her niece. She mentally flipped through her calendar. Tomorrow, she'd promised to contact the power and utility companies to open accounts for the new house. "How about first thing Friday morning?" she asked.

"Could we make it Monday? I told Samuel I'd help him prep for Vacation Bible School on Friday."

"That works," Diane said, not minding at all. As long as she crossed the item off her bucket list before her aunt sold the inn that had been in her family for three generations, one day was as good as the next.

"Aunt Diane, I've been looking at this map and…"

"And?" Her hand on the water bottle she intended to tuck into her backpack, Diane looked up at the sound of Nat's voice.

"What are you doing?" Unease flickered in the younger woman's eyes as she studied the first aid and snake bite kits, the can of bug repellent, the granola bars and water bottles Diane had laid out on the dining room table.

"Packing for our treasure hunt." She gave the supplies a quick glance before deciding she was packing no more or less than usual.

"We're only going to be gone for a couple of hours, right?" Trepidation bordering on outright fear edged Nat's tone.

"Right, but we don't want to get dehydrated or hungry. And you never know about critters. This is Florida, after all." While the odds were against either of them getting bitten by a poisonous viper, the kit also contained a venom extractor in the far more likely case of a bee sting or a spider bite.

Diane shrugged aside her niece's horrified

expression. Growing up, she'd grown used to her siblings' and cousins' unmerciful teasing over her preparations for their treasure hunts. But they'd all sung a very different tune an hour or so into their hikes, when all of them were hot and thirsty. Nat, no doubt, would see the wisdom of her choices soon enough.

Unless, that is, she'd changed her mind about going altogether. She shot her niece a questioning look. "Are you still coming?"

"Oh, yes. I wouldn't miss it. But what else do we need to bring?"

Diane ran down her usual list. "Walking sticks. Garden clippers, in case we have to cut branches and stuff. A hand trowel for, you know, *buried* treasure. Be sure to wear a hat and sunblock."

"I slathered myself earlier." Nat pulled a floppy bucket hat from the back pocket of her shorts. She clamped the broad-brimmed cover over her blond curls. "Will this do?"

"Perfect," Diane declared. Her brow furrowed. "I think we got sidetracked. Did you have something you wanted to show me?"

Nat's blue eyes widened. "Yes! Mom told me you and the rest of the gang never could figure out the landmarks because north and south aren't marked on the original map."

"True," Diane admitted. Using magnifying glasses, she and the others had pored over the drawings and lines etched into the old leather without finding an *N* or an *S* anywhere. "The story goes that our grandfather found the map hidden in a clump of palmetto bushes. He was clearing the land for the front steps at the time, so we mostly used that as our starting point."

"Would it help if the map had a compass rose?"

Duh!

Diane reined in the sarcastic retort. Trying to follow directions without a compass was like figuring out a budget for someone without knowing their income or expenses. Where did you start?

"It would," she acknowledged.

A full-fledged grin lifted the corners of Nat's mouth. "I think I found one."

"What?" The announcement demanded Diane's attention. Her head swung.

"Look here." Nat spread a photocopy of the map on the table. "The original map has a small hole right here." She pointed to a spot in the upper left corner. "But when Aunt Jen made the copies, she had to place the map upside down on the printer. She must have poked at the edges around that hole and smoothed them into place, 'cause I'm pretty sure that's a compass rose." She tapped a dot on the printout.

Excitement fluttered in Diane's chest. Leaving the water bottle, she moved to Nat's side. Together, they peered down at the map. Sure enough, thin lines radiated out from the center of a circle no larger than an eraser head in one corner.

Diane blinked. She and Amy and Scott, along with Kim and Belle and Jen, had gone on hundreds of treasure hunts. They'd examined the old map countless times. How was it that none of them had ever seen the compass?

"How did we miss this?" she whispered.

"You couldn't have seen it. I know a thing or two about leather, and I'm willing to bet the edges had rolled in on themselves. Jen must have pressed them back into place and—voilà!"

Diane clutched her niece's upper arm. "Do you have any idea what this means?"

"That we know how the map is oriented?"

"We do." Diane spun the paper on the table until the heaviest line in the compass rose pointed north. "We've been looking at this upside down all these years." She pointed at the wavy lines on either side of the map. "What we thought was the ocean is really the river, and vice versa."

"That certainly changes things," Nat agreed.

"You've seen those big rocks on the beach just south of the house?" Diane ran her finger across the paper to some lines that looked like misshapen half circles. "We always thought these humps were those rocks. You've probably seen them on your morning walks."

"Yeah." Nat nodded. "The seagulls like to gather on them."

"But with the map turned this way, the rocks are north of the house, on the river side." Diane closed her eyes. The memory of a day her brother had taken her fishing floated back. "I think I know where these rocks are. We fished there once, but our hooks kept getting stuck." Unlike the sandy riverbanks along the rest of the river, some force of nature had created a pile of coquina at a particular bend in the river.

From the rocks, a line snaked across the map to what looked like the drawing of a bush. A closer look revealed a trunk. Not a bush, then. "This tree…"

Her mouth went dry. She grabbed the bottle of water, opened it and drank deeply. Recapping the bottle, she said, "There's an old oak just this side of the property line. When I was in high school, one of our guests was an arborist. He came here specifically to look at it. He said it might be five hundred years old."

"So, it would have been there when the map was drawn?" Awe filled Nat's voice.

"Yeah," Diane said absently. The oak had been a mature, stately landmark for hundreds of years.

She stared at the map. Try as she might, she couldn't remember a single time when their childhood treasure hunts had taken them beyond the orange grove that lay to the north, to the area where X just might mark a spot between the river and an ancient oak tree.

Had they been wrong all this time?

In their efforts to find the spot marked with an X on the map, she and Scott and Amy and their cousins had practically sifted every grain of sand in the dunes that ran along the beach. Years of fruitless searching had convinced them that the spot didn't exist, that the map was a fake, something their grandfather had created to entertain his children—Margaret and Liz and their brother Edward. That he hadn't buried anything for them to find.

But what if the so-called treasure really did exist and they'd just been looking for it in the wrong place? What if…

Her thoughts came to a crashing halt.

What if the map was older than they'd

imagined? What if it dated back to the wreck of the Spanish treasure fleet?

Her heart pounding, she dredged up every fact she could recall about the famous disaster of 1715. That fateful July, eleven ships laden with gold and jewels for King Philip's court left Havana and set sail for Spain. But just off the coast of Florida, the fleet encountered a massive hurricane. The storm destroyed ten of the ships, sending millions of dollars' worth of valuable cargo to the bottom of the ocean.

A few survivors made it ashore lugging bags and chests filled with gold doubloons, precious gems or jewelry intended for the king's bride. But their problems were far from over. Stranded in an inhospitable land without food or water, many died. Others began the nearly two-hundred-mile trek north to the Spanish fort, Castillo de San Marcos, located in present-day St. Augustine. To lighten their load or protect it from marauding pirates, some hid their loot along the way.

Could the map belong to one of those long-ago survivors?

"Jeez," Diane whispered as the ramifications swelled within her. The amount of gold and jewels yet to be recovered from the wreck of the Spanish treasure fleet made her head spin.

She shook her head to clear it. She was letting her imagination get away from her. There probably was no treasure, and if there was, it almost certainly wasn't a hidden stash of gold from a three-hundred-year-old shipwreck. To believe otherwise was pure foolishness. No, if and when they found the spot marked on the map, they'd most likely find a coffee can containing some costume jewelry or, at most, a few quarters.

Beside her, Nat shifted impatiently. "Why don't we check it out? Let's go here." She pointed to the faded X.

"The last thing I want to do is go off on another wild goose chase," Diane said dryly. She'd been on enough of those to last a lifetime. "Let's not get ahead of ourselves. It's been a long time since I've explored the northern end of the property. It could be teeming with alligators." It was mating season for the big reptiles, after all. "We'll start at Point A and follow the map as far as we can."

"Okay by me." Nat shrugged. "Where's Point A?"

Diane pointed to the symbol of a tree near what they now knew was the beach. Unlike the bushy drawing at the opposite end of the map, this one stood straight and narrow. "I'm thinking that might have been a pine tree. Or a tall palm."

Nat's lips pursed. "There aren't any trees that close to the beach."

"Not now. But things change. Trees get chopped down for firewood or lumber. They get knocked over or struck by lightning in storms."

"So, we're looking for a tree that doesn't exist anymore?" Doubt freighted Nat's words.

Diane laughed. "Not necessarily. See this line?" She pointed to a faint mark. "It leads from the tree straight to the river. We could start there and follow the map north." Another half-dozen lines designated a path of sorts.

"I'm game. What are we waiting for? Let's go find us some treasure."

"Do you have your camera?" On the off chance that they did discover something, even if it wasn't gold or silver, even if it was her grandfather's lunch box, Diane wanted to document the moment for future generations.

Nat brushed her fingers over a slouchy shoulder bag. "Do I go anywhere without it?"

Diane quickly finished loading her backpack. Once she'd slipped her arms through the straps and settled the weight, she smiled tightly. "Okay. We're off."

"I think we're in the right spot." Pointing to a wiggly line that resembled a shallow beach, Nat held out her copy of the map. "See? It looks the same, doesn't it?"

Diane eyed the place where they were standing on the river's edge. To their left, a breeze riffled the surface of the water, sending tiny waves lapping against a yard-wide strip of gray sand. A fish—probably a mullet—broke the surface and leaped into the air. Seconds later, it landed with a splash and disappeared. A trio of gulls on their morning hunt skimmed low over the waves, their wings making a soft swooshing sound. Other birds called or chirped from the trees. She spied a blue heron that stood like a statue atop a fallen log, waiting for its breakfast to swim within reach.

"You could be right," she said, though she lacked conviction. Growing up, she'd fished for trout from the shore often enough to know that dozens of small clearings like this one lined the river. As far as starting points for a treasure hunt went, though, this was as good as any.

Keeping the river to their left, they headed north. Their boots scuffed through the grass. Chatting, they made no effort to be quiet. Still, in case the noise they made hadn't already encouraged the occasional snake to slither deeper into the bushes, Diane insisted they prod each downed branch or pile of leaves with their walking sticks before they stepped on or over it. The extra effort slowed their progress, but if it helped to avoid a run-in with a rattler, she deemed it worthwhile.

"How far is it to the oak?" Nat asked when they reached a thick clump of palmettos and were forced to detour around them.

"About a half a mile. Less than an hour's hike."

"When you're walking on the beach or a city sidewalk, maybe. It's going to take all day to get there at this rate." Nat paused long enough to snap a picture of an impressive spiderweb that stretched between two trees.

"I don't think it'll take more than an hour if we keep moving." Of course, if her niece insisted on photographing everything in sight like she'd been doing, they could be out here until nightfall. "Do you want something to drink?" Swinging her backpack around in front of her, Diane withdrew two bottles. She handed one to Nat.

"Thanks," the younger woman said. She guzzled water while she consulted the map. "Shouldn't we reach this lake soon?" she asked. "These are cattails, aren't they?"

Diane swatted at a mosquito that buzzed incessantly around her hat despite the liberal dose of bug spray she'd applied before they left the house. "There is a small pond over there." She waved in the general direction of a pool of murky water that was home to frogs and alligators. "The one on the drawing looks larger, but it would be bigger during the rainy season." Like it would be in July—the time of year when the Spanish treasure fleet sank—and it rained nearly every day.

"Something stinks," Nat complained. She stopped as if afraid she might inadvertently step into something rotten.

Diane sniffed. The air carried a sulfurous scent that would grow worse in the summer. "It's seagrass and algae. Sometimes a storm will stir it up and wash it ashore. When the sun bakes it, it smells like rotten eggs."

"Oh, gross," Nat moaned. She looked over her shoulder, apparently judging the distance back to the house.

Preferring not to hike alone through an uncleared section of Florida's landscape, Diane sought to distract her niece. Nat had worked late at the church yesterday and skipped the nightly get-together with her mom and aunts. A situation which was ripe for all kinds of questions. She chose one or two. "So how'd things go with you and Samuel yesterday? Has he asked you out yet?"

Beneath her sun hat, Nat's eyebrows hiked. "Samuel's a nice guy. I like him...as a friend."

"Nothing more?" Reaching a sandy area shaded by scrub oaks that hugged the waterline, Diane lengthened her stride a bit. "You two seem to be hanging out a lot together."

"There aren't many guys to choose from in Emerald Bay," Nat countered.

"You might have a point there," Diane conceded. Young people tended not to remain in the small beachside community. Of the three hundred students in her graduating class at Emerald Bay High, only a handful had stuck around. Most had gone on to college and, from there, to wherever their jobs had taken them. A few, like Johnny Ito, whose parents owned an appliance store in Vero Beach, had joined the family business. "We don't have the nightlife that Orlando or Tampa can offer. The ones who do stay or who, like me, have moved back, really have to like life in a small town."

"Or, like Samuel, they've been sent here to learn the ropes. In a few years, he'll probably move on to a bigger church, in a bigger city."

"You don't think he likes it here?" As far as she knew, everyone in the church thought the young pastor was a good fit and would be happy if he stayed on permanently.

"That's not really for me to say. But this is his first assignment. He's still figuring out what kind of ministry he wants." Nat's feet slowed to a stop. "Ugh. More palmettos. We can't go through these, can we?"

Diane shook her head. The sawtooth-like spines that edged the plants' fanlike leaves would cut them to ribbons. As she turned to go around them, she asked, "What about you? You think you'll stick around after your mom and Craig get married?"

"For now, at least. In spite of the heat and the bugs." Nat wiped a bead of sweat from her brow. "I love working with Belle. But if I did make Emerald Bay my home, I'd need a steady source of income."

"Do you think you could make a living doing website design, helping people maintain their social media presence?"

"You mean like I've been doing for Belle and the inn?"

"You built your mom's website, too," Diane reminded her.

"Maybe." Nat adjusted her hat. "I'll have to think about it."

Diane looked forward to making easier progress when they rounded the last of the palmettos and emerged into a small clearing. Intending to take advantage of the easier terrain as they worked their way back to the river's edge, she was reaching for her water bottle when Nat yelped.

"Aaaah!" the girl screeched. "Ticks! I'm covered in ticks!" Nat stared down at her socks, which were dotted with little brown specs. In an instant, she was in motion, hopping from one foot to the other, stomping her feet. No matter what she did, not a single one of the brown spots fell off.

"Wait, wait, wait." Diane reached out a restraining hand. Squatting, she studied her own socks. Tiny brown burrs only slightly larger than a pinhead clung to the nubby white cloth. Gingerly, she grasped one between her finger-nails. It took some tugging, but she finally held one in her hand. "These aren't ticks," she announced. "They're beggar's lice."

"Lice!" Nat screeched again.

"Relax. They aren't bugs. They're seeds.

292

Some people call them Spanish needles or stickseeds because they stick like Velcro. They're the very devil to get rid of—we'll be better off throwing our socks in the trash than trying to salvage them. But they're harmless."

"Are you sure?" Nat's voice trembled. "They're not bugs? You're positive?"

"I'm not saying we shouldn't check for ticks when we get back to the house. You should do that anytime you go for a walk in the woods." Bending, Diane grasped one bootlace and ran it through her fingers. Her efforts produced a thimbleful of beggar's lice. She held them out for Nat to see. "But these are harmless seeds."

"Oh, my goodness. I nearly had heart failure." Nat fanned herself. Squatting, she began plucking the seeds from her socks one by one.

"Don't bother." Diane put her hand on the girl's shoulder. "You'll have that many more by the time we're done."

"I guess you're right." Standing, Nat brushed her hands on the back of her pants. As she did, she glanced toward the river. "Hey. Aunt Diane, aren't those the rocks you were talking about?" she asked, her voice rising.

Diane followed her niece's gaze to the uneven piles of boulder-size pinkish stones along the river's edge. "Yep. That's them." She swung in the opposite direction and pointed. "And there's the tree."

Fifty yards away, the majestic oak stood more than seventy feet tall. With a canopy twice as wide as its height, it dwarfed everything in sight.

"Wow!" Nat gasped. "That's impressive. When you said it was big, I had no idea."

Though Diane had visited the tree on several occasions, it never failed to take her breath away. Wanting Nat to have the same experience, she lingered in the clearing. Her niece, meanwhile, aimed her camera toward the oak. The shutter clicked with each step she took through the knee-high grass until she was ten yards closer to the tree.

"Yikes!" Nat called suddenly.

Worry shot through Diane as her niece's arms wheeled in the air. She stumbled forward a step or two before she caught her balance.

"You okay?"

"My boot caught on something. I nearly went splat, but I'm okay. I'm okay."

Relieved that nothing had bitten the girl, Diane breathed easier. She watched as Nat bent to examine something on the ground.

"There are a bunch of rocks here. Be careful. You don't want to trip over them."

"What?" Diane hurried toward her niece. Reaching her, she used her walking stick to part the long stalks of weeds. Sure enough, dozens of fist-size stones were scattered on the ground at Nat's feet.

Diane picked up one of the rocks and examined it. "This didn't come from around here," she announced. Unlike porous coquina, which often contained bits of crushed shells and had a rough surface, these stones were smooth and round and hard as, well, rocks. Excitement shivered through her. Tapping the ground with the end of her walking stick, she moved in an ever-widening circle.

"What are you doing?" Nat asked.

"Looking for the base. My grandfather said he found the map and the tricorne hat beneath a cairn. It stands to reason there'd be another one where X marks the spot."

Not that she had much hope of finding it intact. More than sixty years had passed since her grandparents had moved to Florida. If her grandfather had drawn the map and piled stones over his supposed treasure, a curious squirrel had probably knocked the cairn over in that amount of time. If not that, then surely one of the hurricanes that had blown through the area would have. But the bottom layer, now that was a different story. The base stood a much better chance of remaining put.

"I wouldn't expect to find a pile of rocks still standing in the middle of a field after…" She caught herself before she could say *three hundred years*. "After all this time," she amended.

A few minutes later, she found what she'd been looking for.

"Here!" she said, unable to mask her excitement when she discovered several stones peeking out from beneath the dirt. Yanking handfuls of thick thatch away from the spot, she exposed a rough square shape less than five feet from where Nat had stumbled over the first rock.

"You found it?" Nat hurried to Diane's side.

"Maybe." The word came out in more of a whisper than the firm answer Diane had intended. Her breath stalled, her chest refusing to move, as she stared down at the spot.

Could it be this simple? After all these years, had they really found where X marked the spot? More important, who had brought the stones here? And what lay beneath them?

"Aunt Diane? Are you all right? You look like you've seen a ghost."

The feel of Nat's fingers plucking at her T-shirt snapped Diane out of her daze. She swallowed. "I'm okay. Just excited, I guess.

We've searched for this for so long…"

She straightened. Drawing in a deep breath, she pointed to the rocks. "We should take pictures. Document everything." Aunt Margaret and the others would want to see what they'd found.

But Nat had already whipped out her camera and was snapping photos from every angle. Once she finished, Diane slipped her backpack from her shoulders. She took two trowels from one of the side pockets and handed one to her niece.

"Let's go slowly. We probably won't find anything. Or maybe we'll unearth my grandfather's toolbox." Nervous laughter bubbled up from her insides as she pried one stone from the square. "If we're very lucky, there'll be something inside it."

"Oooh. That'd be cool," Nat said with all the awe of a kid on Christmas morning. "Like a time capsule."

"Yeah," Diane agreed, though she doubted they'd find anything of any significance. Paper dissolved over time. Wood rotted. Iron rusted. Very few substances would remain intact after even a short period underground. Much less sixty years.

Or three hundred, her stubborn heart added.

Slowly, carefully, she removed another one of the stones. On the opposite side of the square, Nat mimicked her actions. When they'd cleared all the rocks out of the way, they took turns scooping up some dirt. Nothing but gray sand slid from their trowels as they sifted the contents into a pile. They kept digging.

The sound of the breeze rustling through the grass, the cheerful chirps of the birds, and the buzz of insects faded. Their small shovels bit into the dirt with a slight hiss. At first, sand rained down when they dumped each load. Later, as they dug deeper, the ground grew more compact and the dirt fell in thicker clumps.

"Have you found anything?" Diane asked when they'd gone about a foot deep. By then, sand and dirt coated her arms and hands. Sweat dampened her T-shirt.

"Nothing," Nat said.

"Same here. Time for a break," she declared.

Scrubbing her hands through the grass, Diane wiped away as much of the grit as she could. Once her fingers were reasonably clean, she rooted through the backpack she'd discarded nearby. Coming up with two bottles of water and a couple of granola bars, she handed one of each to her niece.

"Thanks. How deep do you think we should

go?" Nat stared at their handiwork while she chugged water like a college boy drank beer at a frat party.

Buying some time to think, Diane uncapped her bottle and took a swallow before she answered. Assuming her grandfather had drawn the map, he'd wanted his children—or his grand-children—to find the spot, hadn't he? Whatever he'd left here, whether it still existed after all this time or not, he wouldn't have buried it too deeply. On the other hand, *if*—and she admitted, it was highly unlikely—but if a survivor from one of the ships lost in 1715 had buried something of value here, he'd have been in a hurry. And he'd probably planned on retrieving his stash as soon as possible. All of which meant, he wouldn't have spent all day digging a hole.

"Let's go down another foot. I think after that, it's safe to assume that whatever was here—if anything ever was—it doesn't exist anymore."

Nat chewed thoughtfully on the last bit of her granola bar before she washed it down with a final sip of water. "That works for me," she said. Her expression turned serious. "Before we go on, though, I want you to know I've had fun. Whether we find anything at all or not, I finally got to go on a real-live treasure hunt." She grinned. "How many people get to say that?"

"Outside our family?" Diane laughed softly. "Not many, I guess. Are you ready to get back to it?"

"Yep."

Diane took the empty water bottle and wrapper Nat handed her. Adding her own, she tucked the trash inside her bag. "Okay, then," she said when she'd zipped the backpack closed. "Let's get to it."

The midday sun warmed their backs as they once more bent over the hole. They quickly fell into a now-familiar routine, each taking turns scooping up dirt and sorting through the contents of their trowels before they dumped the soil onto a growing pile. The first foot or so had been easy enough. Dig, sift, dump, repeat. But the deeper they dug, the more they had to stretch, and soon, Diane felt the muscles in her back tighten.

"I'm going to be so sore tomorrow." Setting her trowel down, she rubbed her lower back.

"It's just another couple of inches," Nat said. "I'll do it if you're too old or too tired." With a sly smile, she plunged her small shovel into the hole.

"Challenge accepted," Diane countered. She grabbed her own trowel. While Nat sifted the contents of her most recent scoop, Diane sank her spade another inch deeper into the dirt. She jerked in surprise when the blade struck something hard. The chink of metal against metal rose from the hole. "What the…"

Nat spun toward her. "Did you find something?"

"I, um, I think…Maybe?" Diane sat back on her haunches. Her mind spun with possibilities. Was it just another rock? Had she discovered her grandfather's treasure? Or was there something even more valuable buried here? She turned to Nat. "You want to take a picture or two before we see what this is?"

Seconds later, Nat's camera clicked, and a sudden burst of light brightened the dark hole. Something glinted in the bottom.

Diane's breath caught. She stared down. Was she imagining things? "I guess we keep doing what we're doing," she said slowly.

"Sure," Nat agreed. "I'll take a few more shots while you keep digging."

"Okay." Hoping to steady her nerves, Diane took a deep breath. A sense of anticipation shook her as she retrieved her trowel. She scooped up a shovelful and brought it to the surface.

"Oh, my," she whispered. She stared at the thick chain that dangled from the end of the blade. Her hand trembled. The movement loosened bits of sand and dirt that clung to the thick links of gleaming gold. "Oh, my."

"That can't be real," Nat said in a reasonable tone. "That has to be somebody's idea of a joke, right?"

"Right," Diane echoed, unable to wrench her gaze away from the yellow metal. Half-expecting the necklace to be as light as a feather, she plucked it from the end of the trowel. The weight surprised her so much that she nearly dropped it. The chain had heft. Whatever it was, the jewelry wasn't made of plastic.

"Na-at," she said, slowly drawing out the name while she tried without success to quell her racing heartbeat. "There's a towel in my back-pack. Can you get it?"

An eternity of seconds seemed to pass before Nat brandished the rolled-up terrycloth.

"What do you want me to do with it?"

"Could you put it right here next to the hole?"

Without waiting to be told, Nat tromped back and forth over the grass, mashing the tall green stalks to the ground. When she'd created a fairly level surface, she spread out the towel. Once that was done, Diane gingerly placed the chain in the center of the cloth. Gently, she brushed away the dirt to reveal a gold chain made up of thick links.

"Can I touch it?" Nat asked.

"Of course," Diane said, determined to at least sound calm, though she felt like she was about to jump out of her skin.

"It's heavy," Nat said, letting the necklace dangle from her fingertips before she laid it flat on the towel. "It's not real, though. Probably just gold paint, right?" When Diane didn't answer, she peered up at her aunt. "It is just paint, right?"

"I have no idea," Diane said in all honesty. She took a breath. "When we were kids, we dreamed of finding a stash of gold doubloons or a king's ransom in jewels buried on the property somewhere. We were convinced the map had belonged to a pirate or a survivor from one of the Spanish treasure ships destroyed by a hurricane in 1715. As we grew older, we realized those scenarios were pretty far-fetched." She shook her head. "Aunt Margaret said Grandpa insisted he'd found the map. It was far more likely that he'd drawn it himself. But this..." She glanced at the chain, her eyes narrowing. "I'm not sure what to make of it. If this is nothing more than make-believe, my grandfather spent an awful lot of time and effort on convincing his children they'd found a real treasure trove."

Nat grew silent. "You know what I think?" she asked at last. "I think your grandfather—my great-grandfather—had a wicked sense of adventure. I mean, seriously. He went to all the trouble of making a fake gold necklace, burying it out here in the middle of nowhere, and creating a treasure map so his kids would find it. If they gave out Father of the Year awards back then, I'd vote for him."

"You might be right," Diane conceded. Her niece was probably right about the rest, too. The map was most likely her grandfather's way of entertaining his children. As for the necklace, she'd try to ignore the fact that real gold was one of the few metals that didn't rust or corrode. Instead, she'd do her best to convince herself that the gold paint he'd used had lasted more than sixty years below ground. Picking up her trowel, she tapped it against the palm of her hand. "I guess we ought to see if there's anything else buried here."

"You think there might be more?"

"There's only one way to find out. I'll dig down another inch while you take pictures. Then, we'll swap places."

But Diane had barely scraped away a thin layer of dirt when she felt the tip of her shovel strike something solid. Setting the trowel aside for the moment, she cautiously dug with her fingers until she unearthed a pile of some sort of flat disks. She plucked one up and lifted it into the light, holding it out so she and Nat could both get a good look at it.

Diane felt her stomach plummet when sunlight glinted off an odd-looking cross in the center of the round gold piece.

"It looks like a coin, but the edges aren't smooth," Nat observed. "And I've never seen one with that design."

"Uh-huh." Diane nodded wordlessly. She'd visited the Mel Fisher Museum in Key West a number of years ago. The coin she held in her hand looked eerily similar to some of the ones on display there...coins that had been salvaged from a three-hundred-year-old shipwreck off the coast of Florida.

"Are there any more?" Nat bent over the hole.

"Quite a few, I think." After placing the piece on the towel, Diane felt around in the bottom of the hole. Metal shifted beneath her touch. Rather than grabbing more of the loose disks, she gently brushed dirt and debris from the pile. "There's a flashlight in my backpack. You want to grab it?"

"I'm on it." Nat scrambled for the bag.

Seconds later, gold coins sparkled in the beam of light. Another chain, this one encrusted with green stones, snaked through the pile. A yellow wedge of something long and slender poked out of the ground in one corner.

"What the…" Nat's jaw worked, but no words came out. She turned questioning eyes toward Diane, who simply shrugged.

Putting every bit of effort she could afford into speaking, she whispered, "We might need a bigger towel."

It took two hours of careful excavation to remove everything from the spot. Wanting to be sure they'd gotten it all, she and Nat spent another hour enlarging the hole in every direction. By the time they agreed that there was nothing left to find, gold coins, bejeweled necklaces and earrings, along with one long, gold bar, formed an impressive mound that reminded Diane of something straight out of a dragon's lair. Scattered throughout the pile, another dozen disks were made of some darker metal.

Nat chortled merrily as she ran her fingers through the pile. "I'm rich. Rich, I say. Rich!" She lifted a handful of coins and sifted them through her fingers.

"Whoa, girl." Diane caught a coin before it fell into the hole. She returned it to the pile.

Nat's face pinked beneath the brim of her hat. "I know. I know. None of this is real. But a girl can dream, can't she?"

"It couldn't hurt to pretend a little," Diane said, willing to indulge in the fantasy. Following

Nat's example, she pulled a strand of what were probably cut-glass beads from the mound and draped them around her neck. Striking a haughty pose, she asked, "Whoever said diamonds were a girl's best friend was wrong, dah-ling. I prefer emeralds, myself."

Nat rooted through the stash until she found a pair of dangly earrings that matched Diane's necklace. "Here, take these. Hold them up to your ears."

Diane followed her niece's directions and grinned while Nat snapped a picture. They traded the camera back and forth, each taking photos until Nat pretended to eat the gold bar like an ear of corn.

"Oh, now we're just being silly." Whether they were or not, Diane still captured the moment.

"That was fun," Nat said as she tossed her latest prop onto the pile. She stretched. "What time is it? I'm getting hungry."

Diane scanned the sky. "No wonder," she said. The late afternoon sun hung a lot lower than she'd expected. "We ought to start back soon."

Nat eyed the hole they'd dug. "We can't just leave it like that, can we?" she asked doubtfully.

"We probably should fill it in. I'd feel awful if

one of our guests stumbled across it and twisted an ankle."

"Or if a deer stepped in it and broke a leg," Nat added.

Together, they began scooping all the sand and dirt back into place. When they were finished, they piled as many of the rocks as they could find on top. The sun hovered just above the horizon by the time they'd dumped the contents of the bag on the ground to make room for their discoveries. Securing the towel around their find, they crammed the whole thing into Diane's backpack. She slipped her shoulders through the straps and hoisted the bag. Metal clinked as the pack settled heavily against her hips. She turned to Nat. "Ready?"

Her niece finished scouring the area for their empty water bottles and wrappers from the granola bars. Smashing the bottles, she stuffed the trash into her pockets. At last, she retrieved their walking sticks and handed one to Diane. "Let's book it."

Questions, like the clouds of mosquitoes that would rise from every puddle or pond as soon as the sun went down, crowded Diane's thoughts the minute they began to retrace their steps to the inn. Was Nat right? Were the *treasures* they'd found nothing more than make-believe? Or, as improbable as it seemed, were they artifacts salvaged from a centuries-old shipwreck? Doubts and probabilities buzzed through her mind, but in their midst, one stood out.

How could she convince Nat to keep their adventure a secret long enough for them to figure out the truth?

Ten

Diane

"Aunt Diane. Hold up a sec."

Just beyond the palm trees that had become home to a flock of monk parakeets, Nat's tug on the strap of her backpack stopped Diane in midstride. Gratefully, she eased the heavy bag from her shoulders. The pieces inside shifted, the clank of metal against metal muted by the towel.

Was it gold? Silver? Iron?

Diane studied the hundred yards or so they still needed to cover before full dark enveloped them. More than once, she'd heard the high-pitched whine of mosquitoes buzzing about her face on their trek back from the large oak tree at the north end of the property. So far, she didn't think she'd been bitten. But she and Nat needed to get inside soon or they'd both be covered in itchy welts by morning.

"Make it quick," she cautioned. As if it had been waiting for them to slow down long enough to pounce, a mosquito landed on her bare arm. She swatted it away.

"I was just wondering…" Despite her aunt's warning, Nat heaved a sigh. "It's probably nothing, but…"

"Hold on." Diane unzipped one of the backpack's side pockets and whipped out her emergency supply of bug spray. Quickly, she spritzed her hat, clothes and socks before doing the same to Nat's. "That should buy us a few minutes," she said when she'd finished. "Now, what did you want to know?"

"I was just thinking, if there's any possibility that the coins and jewelry we found today are worth anything…If they have more than sentimental value, that is…"

"You mean, if they're from one of the ships that sank in 1715?" Diane prodded.

"Yeah. I guess. I mean, that's not possible, is it?"

This time it was Diane's turn to sigh. "It's highly unlikely, but…" She let the word hang between them. She took a breath. "It's been well documented that about half of the ships' crewmen survived. The ones who made it ashore camped along the coast, gradually moving north toward the Spanish fort in St. Augustine. Along the way, they had to fight off attacks by pirates and other hostiles. It's not outside the realm of possibility that one of those survivors buried a stash of coins and jewelry near the tree. It's unlikely, but it is possible."

"Well, then, I..." Nat's voice trailed off again.

"You what?"

"All I know is that when we were fooling around earlier, there was a moment when I actually convinced myself the gold and the gems were real. I know it's silly, but I was really, *really* crushed when I came to my senses. I wouldn't want anyone else to feel that way." She kicked her foot through the grass. "If we go inside and dump all we found on the kitchen table, I'm pretty sure people will get their hopes up. We'd be setting them up for a huge letdown when it all turns out to be worthless."

Diane peered at the girl through the deepening gloom. She hoped they'd both reached the same conclusion about sharing their discovery with the others, but she refused to put the words in Nat's mouth. "What exactly are you saying?"

"I don't think we should tell anybody what

we found today. Not until we know more about it. Not until we know, for sure, whether those coins are real or just worthless trinkets."

Diane felt her chest swell. "You have a really good heart, Natalie. More than that, you're very smart. I was thinking exactly the same thing, but I didn't know how to say it. I'm so glad you did." Mindful of how dirty and sweaty she was, she gave her niece a quick hug. "We're in agreement, then?" she asked when they stepped apart. "We won't breathe a word to anyone until we verify whether Grampa Dane buried the treasure or not?"

"That sounds like the safest approach."

Despite the smell of bug spray that still lingered in the air, Diane heard the whine of a mosquito nearby. She shouldered the backpack. "Let's go inside. I'll stick this in the bottom of my closet for tonight We can figure out what else to do about it tomorrow."

"Um, what are we going to tell the others? Won't they be suspicious?"

Diane chuckled. "You forget that I've come back empty-handed from dozens of treasure hunts over the years. No one will give it so much as a second thought if we march straight up to our rooms and jump in the shower. I doubt if anyone will even ask if we had any luck."

Nat chewed her bottom lip. "If you say so," she said doubtfully.

Diane grinned. "Follow my lead, kiddo. I'll show you how it's done."

Diane stood at the front porch railing and sipped coffee from a heavy mug. In the distance, two figures emerged from the beach onto the boardwalk that cut through the dunes. Squinting, she shaded her eyes against the shafts of golden light that radiated from the rising sun. Recognizing Kim and Belle on their way back from their morning run, she groaned inwardly. Her cousins were bound to give her grief about skipping her daily walk, but every bone and muscle in her body ached after yesterday's adventures. She squeezed her eyes closed, trying to block the rush of memories, but she might as well have tried to stop an incoming tide for all the good it did.

Darn.

She'd come out here precisely because she didn't want to think about the discovery she and Nat had made. Hadn't she worried that topic to death last night while she'd tossed and turned as lightning flashed and thunder boomed overhead? The storm hadn't helped her banish the images of shipwrecks and pirates that crowded her head. Not one iota. Yet here she was—going over it all again, stirring up another rush of conflicting emotions.

She should be happy, she told herself. After all these years, she'd finally found the spot marked on their grandfather's map. Had finally unearthed the pile of costume jewelry he'd buried soon after he'd purchased the land for the Dane Crown Inn.

Or had she?

After studying the photos on various websites devoted to the 1715 treasure fleet, she had to admit that a few of the pieces in her backpack bore an uncanny similarity to other necklaces and earrings salvaged from the wrecks. And those coins with their strange crosses? They looked exactly like pictures of other gold coins from that era.

What if, instead of some worthless trinkets, she and Nat had stumbled on an honest-to-gosh fortune?

The possibility made her dizzy. She shook her head to clear away the crazy thoughts as well as the cobwebs that came from a lack of sleep. She refused to fool herself. The odds were astronomically against the likelihood that any of the coins, jewelry or gems they'd dug up were anything more than painted metal, paste and cut glass.

Still, she couldn't help but ask, *What if?*

"Hey, lazybones."

Diane reeled in her wandering thoughts. She looked up to find that Kim and Belle had closed the distance between them while she was woolgathering. "Nice run?" she asked.

"Yeah. You missed a good one. The beach was spectacular. That storm last night washed up a bunch of shells. I found a calico scallop to add to my collection." Belle pulled a round shell with striated pink markings from her pocket.

"Pretty," Diane said.

"The Treasure Seekers are out in full force," Kim said, referring to members of a local club who regularly scoured the beach for items a storm might have washed ashore. "One of our guests was out there with a metal detector. He'd found several coins and a ring already this morning."

A sudden interest lifted Diane's eyebrows. The awkward-looking devices helped their owners locate metal—from bottle caps to iron beams—buried beneath the sand. "Anything valuable?"

"He didn't think so, but he's still looking."

Diane shielded her eyes and gazed past the dunes. "Who's the guest?"

"Gary William. Aunt Margaret says he and his wife stay here for a week every year. They spend another week on the west coast."

Diane made a mental note of the man's name. It stood to reason that anyone serious about metal detecting would know a thing or two about how to evaluate coins. Though she wouldn't discuss specifics with a relative stranger, perhaps this Mr. William could give her a few pointers.

She took another fortifying sip of coffee. "What are the plans for the day?" she asked as Kim and Belle mounted the steps and joined her on the porch. She was itching to catalog the contents of her backpack and find out, one way or another, just how much their *treasure* was worth.

"I'm knee-deep in butter beans and corn," Kim said. The two vegetables were on the Royal Meals menu this week. "Since it's Thursday, I'll be busy prepping for tomorrow's deliveries all day."

"I have chauffeur duty this morning. Mama has a hair appointment, and she's meeting a few of her friends for lunch at Sugar Cakes afterwards." Belle examined her manicure.

"When he gets out of school, Daclan, Jen and I have a practice session."

Diane nodded. She'd overheard Belle humming her latest tune and couldn't wait to catch The Emeralds' next performance.

Kim's focus shifted to Diane. "How about you?"

"More coffee." Diane lifted her nearly empty mug. "I'll spend a couple of hours on the books for Papaya this morning." The owner of the Emerald Bay dress shop was her newest client. "At some point, I need to talk with Max about converting the mother-in-law suite at the new house into an office."

Plans she didn't want to share with her cousins—at least, not yet—made up the rest of her day. After a few hours' work, she'd devote the afternoon to learning as much as she could about the contents of her backpack. A call to a trusted jeweler seemed like the logical first step, but that would have to wait until she came up with a plausible explanation. One that did not start with *I stumbled across a cache of gold doubloons*.

"Nothing else?" Kim prodded.

"I might work on the baby blanket for my new niece." Which wasn't a lie, Diane told herself. She might crochet some. She probably wouldn't, but she might.

When Belle studied her with a doubtful look, Diane decided it was time to direct the conversation elsewhere. "How about Jen? What's she up to?" she asked.

Kim's eyebrows knitted. "I saw her climb into Caleb's truck this morning before we went to the beach. I think they were getting a load of plants for the garden. But she'll be back soon. Several guests are checking in this afternoon. She promised Aunt Margaret she'd be here to help them." Kim smiled. "We'll have a full house this weekend."

"That's a nice change." Not that it mattered in the long term. The truth was, even at full occupancy, the inn couldn't generate enough income to stay afloat. Not without doubling or even tripling their rates. Which they couldn't justify without providing amenities like a full breakfast, private butler service and a day spa.

Stifling a sigh, Diane swigged the last of her coffee. "I'm going to get another cup," she announced. "How about you?"

"Shower first," Belle announced. Using the hand towel she'd draped around her shoulders, she blotted her neck and chin.

"Same," Kim said.

"Well, let me grab that cup of coffee, and then I'll be upstairs if anyone needs me." Hoping the hot spray would ease her sore muscles, Diane had showered and dressed for the day before she'd seen Caitlyn off to school earlier.

Inside, they peeled off, Kim heading for her suite and Belle to the family quarters while Diane meandered into the dining area to refill her cup. The odor of freshly brewed coffee mingled with scent of cinnamon-y goodness that rose from the tray of sweet rolls Amy had delivered before dawn. She nodded at the lone guest who lingered over coffee and a pastry at the table.

"Good morning." Diane summoned a smile for the woman whose hair and makeup were far too perfect for this early in the day. She tugged on a strand of her own chin-length hair and thanked the Lord she'd run a comb through the straight bob before coming downstairs. In answer to the woman's curious glance, she introduced herself. "I'm Diane. My aunt owns the inn."

"Oh, hello. I'm Sandy. My husband and I are from Savannah." Her gaze dropped to her plate. With an unhappy sniff, Sandy pressed the tines of her fork into a bit of loose icing.

Diane's concern flared. Their guest did not look thrilled with her breakfast. "Can I get you anything? More coffee?" She eyed the pastry the woman had barely touched. "A different sweet roll?"

"Oh, no. I don't want to be a bother." Sandy pushed her plate aside. "I'm not sure what this is, but I don't care for the taste."

"Guava isn't for everyone," Diane commiserated. Some people claimed the fruit tasted like a mix of pineapple and strawberries. Others, like herself, thought it smelled like overly sweetened bubblegum. "Here, let me get you a different one. How about cinnamon?"

"Oh, that's so nice. Yes, I'd love another roll."

Diane grabbed a handy pair of tongs and dished one of the rich buns onto a clean plate. As she worked, she tried to make their guest feel welcome. "Is this your first time staying at the Dane Crown Inn?"

"Oh, my goodness, no," Sandy answered, her Georgia accent thickening with every word. "We've been coming here for years. Gary, that's my husband, he insists on spending a week metal-detecting here every spring. He's absolutely convinced he'll find a Spanish doubloon one of these days."

"He must be the man my cousins spoke with on the beach earlier. You'll have to let us know if he finds anything good."

Looking as if she had something else on her mind, Sandy stirred her coffee. "I must say, I was pleasantly surprised by the improvements y'all have made since our last visit. We just *love* Ms. Margaret, but our room was so shabby last year, I was afraid we were going to have to find somewhere else to stay."

"I'm so glad you gave us another chance," Diane said with heartfelt sincerity. After all the time, elbow grease and money she and her family had poured into the inn, it was more than nice to hear that their guests appreciated the effort.

"Oh, we'll definitely be back again next year," Sandy gushed.

While Diane certainly hoped that was so, it pained her to think that the inn would probably have new owners by the time Sandy and her husband returned. As long as they were here, though, she'd help to make the Williams' stay as comfortable as possible. Holding the dish in one hand and a carafe of hot coffee in the other, she turned away from the sideboard. A moment later, she slid the fresh breakfast treat in front of their guest. "More coffee?" She wiggled the carafe.

"How'd you know?" Sandy shoved her cup forward an inch or two.

"We caffeine addicts can always tell." Smiling, Diane poured, but her hand froze when she glimpsed the sparkling chain around the other woman's neck.

"Careful, darlin'," Sandy called.

"Oops!" Still staring at the woman's jewelry, Diane whipped the carafe upright in the nick of time. "Sorry," she apologized. "I was mesmerized by your necklace. It's beautiful."

"This?" Sandy ran her fingers along the thick, gold strand that was quite similar to one in Diane's backpack. "It is pretty, isn't it? They call it a money chain because in the olden days, people would remove a section or two to pay for things like food or clothing or rent."

"You don't say." Diane supposed that explained the tiny opening in each of the links. "Do you mind my asking, did your husband find the necklace while he was metal-detecting?"

"Don't I wish. Then it'd really be worth something. Sadly, no." Sandy lifted her cup without spilling a single drop. "It's a replica. Gary bought it for me at this specialty shop in Sebastian."

"At Mel Fisher's?" The family of the renowned salvage operator ran one store in Sebastian and a larger one in Key West.

"I've been there, but no. This is a coin shop. Let me think. What's the name of it? East Bay? East Cove," she corrected. "East Cove Trading Post. Wyatt Porcher—he's the owner—he knows everything there is to know about all the ships that have sunk off the coast of Florida over the years. And he makes these darling copies."

Sandy straightened a slight kink in the necklace with perfectly manicured fingers. "I told Gary not to buy it. I told him, 'We could make two mortgage payments with what this necklace cost,' but he said I was worth it for putting up with him and his hobby." Soft, musical laughter spilled from her lips.

Sandy seemed to have a wealth of infor-mation stored under her perfectly teased hair. Eager to learn as much as she could from the woman, Diane pulled out a chair at the table and took a seat. "Your husband does a lot of metal-detecting, does he?"

"Only if you consider every day it isn't pouring rain *a lot*." Sandy's smile deepened. "A friend of ours owns a hundred acres outside Savannah. It was the site of a Union camp during the Civil War. I can't count the number of uniform buttons Gary's found out there. We have jars of them at home. Plus, we go out to Tybee Island quite often. You wouldn't believe how much stuff people lose at the beach. He finds bracelets and watches all the time. Coins by the handful. Old bottle tops. Last fall, he found an engagement ring. That was exciting for a minute, but it turned out the stone was cubic zirconia and only worth a hundred bucks."

Diane clucked sympathetically.

"Gary saves whatever he finds throughout the year. We bring it with us when we come to Florida, and we take it to Trading Post before we leave. Wyatt gives us a fair price for our little treasures. That man is as honest as the day is long. None of the people in Gary's metal-detecting club would dream of using anyone else."

"You say this store is in Sebastian?" This Porcher fellow was sounding more and more like someone Diane wanted to get to know.

"Mm-hmm." Sandy chewed thoughtfully on a bite of her cinnamon bun. After she'd washed it down with a sip of coffee, she said, "You ought to visit his shop sometime. It's like a cross between a jewelry store and a museum."

"My sister is opening a small bakery in Sebastian next month. We'll all be going up there for the ribbon-cutting. I'll make a point of stopping in at the Trading Post," Diane said.

A scuffle of feet in the hallway put their conversation on hold.

"Hey, darlin'. I'm done for this morning." A burly-chested man with curly, salt-and-pepper hair stood in the doorway. His accent as thick as Sandy's, he explained, "The tide's comin' in. I'll grab a shower and we can go get us some lunch."

"Mind your manners, honey. You need to say hello to one of our hostesses. This is Diane." Sandy lifted a languid hand in Diane's direction. "And this messy man tracking sand all through the house is the love of my life, Gary."

"Hey. You raised me better than that." Despite the gruff protest, kindness shone in Gary's dark eyes. "I took off my shoes and rinsed myself off with the hose while I was cleaning my equipment." His attention shifted to Diane. "I left everything drying on the deck out back. That's all right, isn't it?"

"Of course," Diane assured their guest. "I'm very pleased to meet you, Gary. Did you find anything interesting while you were out at the beach today?"

"This might be my lucky day." Gary stuck his hand in his shorts pocket and pulled out a circle of blackened material a little bigger than a quarter. "If I'm right, underneath all that crud is a silver *real*—a coin. Maybe from one of the Spanish wrecks."

"How exciting!" Sandy clapped her hands. A speculative gleam lit her eyes. "You're sure it isn't gold?"

"Nah, honey. If it was gold, it'd be as shiny as the day it went into the water. Salt water corrodes silver, though. It gets this black stuff all over it. We'll have to see what it looks like after I clean it up. But speaking of cleaning up, I gotta get upstairs so we can go out to lunch before you plumb waste away." Beckoning his wife with a sly grin, Gary touched the brim of his hat and disappeared.

In answer, Sandy scarfed down the last of her roll. Turning to Diane, she said, "If you'll excuse me, I'd better, um, freshen up before lunch."

Diane wisely kept her chuckle to herself when the woman whose flawless makeup and hair needed no attention whatsoever hurried after her husband. Gathering the dishes Sandy left behind, she carted them into the kitchen, where she loaded them into the dishwasher.

While she worked, she considered the next step to take in determining the actual worth—or lack thereof—of the contents of her backpack. The conversation with Sandy and Gary couldn't have come at a better time, she decided. And after planning exactly what she wanted to say and checking her story for holes, she headed to her room to place a phone call.

"Diane, so nice to hear from you. I trust you're doing well?" Leon Haycock's refined tones brought forth image of a tall, impeccably dressed man with a thick head of snowy white hair that ended precisely one-quarter inch above the collar of his suit coat, thanks to weekly trips to a top men's hair salon.

"I am. Thanks for asking." Diane pictured the owner of Haycock Jewelers in the heart of the Ybor City shopping district. In addition to the anniversary gifts Tim had purchased from Leon over the years, the two couples belonged to the same golf club and attended the same church. "And you and Eleanor?" she asked. "Are you spoiling that new grandbaby rotten?"

"You know we are."

Leon's indulgent chuckle teased a smile from Diane. The man's son and daughter-in-law had presented the senior Haycocks with their first grandchild just over a year ago.

The jeweler cleared his throat. "But you didn't call in the middle of the week just to chat. What can I do for you? Tim's birthday is coming up. He's had his eye on a Rolex Explorer," he suggested.

"I'll keep that in mind," Diane said, tucking the gift idea away for future reference. "Today, though, I'd like to take advantage of your expertise on another matter."

"Go on."

"As I'm sure Tim has told you, I've been spending some time in Emerald Bay helping my aunt with the inn our family owns here."

"Yes, I heard. He also mentioned the second home you're buying there. I'm glad he'll be staying in Tampa for the time being. I'd hate to have to break in a new tennis partner." Leon and Tim frequently paired up for charity tournaments at the club. "But you were saying?"

"Yes," Diane said, thankful that Leon was helping her keep the conversation on track. "One of our guests found what he thinks might be an old coin at the beach this morning. A *real*, he called it. He wondered who he should see about getting it appraised, and I told him I would check with you."

"A Mexican coin? I'm not a numismatist, but there is a gentleman I've used whenever I've needed help appraising an estate. Do you have a pen and paper?" Now that he knew Diane hadn't called to make a purchase, he was all business.

"Yes," Diane assured him.

"You'll want to call Wyatt Porcher at the East Cove Trading Post. He is the only coin dealer I trust in the entire state. If you'll hold on a second, I'll get his number for you."

It was a good thing Leon couldn't see her face, Diane thought, because her jaw had come unhinged when he'd mentioned the same exact person Sandy had spoken of earlier. It took the full ten seconds while Leon looked up the number to gather her wits.

"Here you go." Leon rattled off ten digits. "Now, be sure to call first—Wyatt only sees people by appointment. And do think about that Rolex. It would make a very nice gift."

"I will," she assured him, though dropping a cool ten grand on a watch wasn't high on her list of things to do. Not when she'd just opened a business and bought a house.

What was at the top of her list, however, was getting in touch with Wyatt Porcher. A name that had come up twice in the same day. A man both people referred to as an expert. Which was exactly what she needed.

"Are you sure he knew we were coming?" Nat shifted impatiently from one sandaled foot to another.

"I confirmed our appointment with him this morning," Diane assured her niece. She checked her watch. They'd shown up right on time, but in the five minutes they'd been standing on the covered sidewalk outside the East Coast Trading Post, no one had answered the buzzer.

Might as well put the time while they waited to good use, she told herself.

"Remember," she reminded her niece, "we're only telling him about the two pieces we brought with us." They'd agreed to keep the bulk of their discovery under wraps on the off chance it had real value.

"Of course." Nat snorted. "One word about a treasure and we'll have lookie-loos crawling out of the woodwork."

To say nothing of the con artists who'd come calling with their greedy hands outstretched. She wasn't thinking specifically about Nat's father, but if the shoe fit...

"I just wish he'd answer the door so we can get on with this," Nat complained.

"Let's give him another minute," Diane suggested even as she dug in her purse for her phone. If Porcher didn't answer the door soon, she'd call him again. She hated to think they'd come all this way on a wild goose chase.

"Maybe the doorbell's broken." Nat rapped sharply on the door that had been painted to match the sea green awnings mounted on the otherwise white buildings that made up a U-shaped strip mall. Leaning to one side, she cupped her hands over her eyes and peered through the window. "Wait. Someone's coming,"

331

she hissed. She stepped away from the glass.

Thirty seconds later, a man's voice sounded through a hidden speaker. "May I help you?"

"It's Ms. Keenan. Diane Keenan," Diane answered. "My niece and I are here for an appointment with Mr. Porcher."

"Very well," the voice replied. "Hang on a sec."

Sure enough, a buzzer sounded. Diane pushed on the door, which swung wide. She and Nat stepped into what appeared to be a high-end jewelry store. Only, instead of diamond engagement rings and shiny earrings, the three rows of display cases held neatly arranged plastic sleeves filled with gold and silver coins that sparkled under the florescent lights. Shelves mounted on shiplap in the center of one wall held an old cutlass, a ship's wheel, what looked like a metal dinner plate and a few other antiques. Other than that, little broke the monotony of the stark white walls and gray carpet.

Diane hid her surprise when her gaze centered on a casually dressed senior citizen with the deeply lined skin of one who'd spent years basking beneath the bright Florida sun. Her mind shifted to her jeweler in Tampa. The two men couldn't be less alike. Leon was all bespoke suits and cultured refinement. Wyatt Porcher, with his thick shoulders and round belly straining at the buttons of a colorful Hawaiian shirt, was anything but. A bushy gray beard and a fringe of long, stringy hair surrounding a mostly bare scalp added to the impression that the man in front of them was nothing more than an aging beach bum.

Hoping that, despite Leon's recommendation, they hadn't made a huge mistake in coming all this way, Diane extended her hand. "Thank you for seeing us today, Mr. Porcher. I'm Diane Keenan, and this is my niece, Natalie."

"Sorry for the wait. I was working," he said shortly as he gripped her hand with surprisingly rough fingers. After giving Nat's a quick shake, he beckoned them toward the rear of the store with a gruff, "Follow me."

Wondering more and more if they'd come to the right place, Diane raised questioning eyebrows in Nat's direction. Her niece, however, didn't seem to share her reaction to the rough-around-the-edges numismatist. Like an eager young puppy dog, the younger woman immediately fell in step behind the store owner, leaving Diane no choice but to follow.

"On the phone, you said you found the coin and earring on your own property?" Porcher asked as Diane trailed him past a half wall into an open workroom, of sorts, at the back of the store.

"My family's," she corrected. "We have twenty acres on the outskirts of Emerald Bay." She purposefully didn't mention the inn by name. Though she'd never claim to be a world-class poker player, something told her this was not the time to lay all her cards on the table.

As if he sensed he might get more information from Natalie, Porcher addressed his next question in her direction. "And how, exactly, did you find these pieces?"

"On a treasure hunt, of course," Nat answered, as if it was perfectly normal for two fully grown women to search for buried treasure in their backyard. "The story I've been told was that my great-grandfather found a treasure map when he was clearing the land to build an..."

Diane coughed, and Nat's eyes flared slightly.

"A house," the girl said quickly. "For years, everyone thought that's all it was—a story. Various family members tried and failed to follow the map. But this week, my aunt and I—" pointing a finger, she indicated that Diane was the aunt in question "—we finally identified a key landmark. Once we had that, we traced the path to a pile of rocks. We started digging, and the rest is history."

"Uh-huh. Cute story." Porcher stroked his unkempt beard. Leaning with his back against a waist-high worktable, he faced them.

"Let's not waste each other's time here, okay? Ninety-nine out of a hundred people who visit me are absolutely convinced they've stumbled on the Queen's Jewels, which were supposedly on board the *Capitana* when it sank in 1715. I've had the unpleasant task of disabusing these treasure seekers of that notion. There are no Queen's Jewels. Oh, there were jewels aplenty on board the ships that were wrecked during that hurricane. But none bore that specific designation."

"No Queen's Jewels. Got it." Nat paired the thumbs-up sign with a wide grin.

Beneath his beard, the first hint of a smile tugged at the corners of Porcher's mouth.

Diane nodded in agreement. "I don't believe that's what we've found, either."

"Now that we've got that cleared up, let me tell you something else." Porcher picked up a pair of wire-rimmed glasses from the worktable and rubbed the lenses with his shirt tail. "There's never been a documented case of anyone in the entire state of Florida finding a cache of gold or jewels hidden by a survivor of the 1715 fleet disaster."

"Never?" Nat squeaked.

"Not one documented case," Porcher repeated gruffly. The glasses dangling from his fingertips, he folded beefy arms across his chest. "I believe all those stories about the sailors who managed to swim to shore carrying bags of gold are nothing but fairy tales. Pure hokum."

Diane gulped as bitter disappointment sank its claws deep into her chest. Though why she felt such a letdown was beyond her. Hadn't she been telling herself all along that her grandfather's treasure was nothing but bits of glass and flecks of paint? "I'm sorry, Nat," she whispered.

The girl, however, was not to be dissuaded so easily. "Just because no one has made such a discovery, or admitted to it, that doesn't mean it can't happen."

Porcher's smile widened into the kind an indulgent grandfather might train on a mischievous toddler. "Think about it. You go overboard in a raging hurricane. Your ship's sinking. You're trying your best not to go down with it. All around you, men—your friends—are dying. Are you really going to try to swim to shore weighted down with bags of gold?"

"Well, no." Nat scuffed her foot on the carpet. "But from what I read, the ones who did survive started salvage operations almost immediately. Who's to say one of them didn't sneak off and hide a coin or two for a rainy day?"

"Nothing much. Just officers with orders to shoot looters on sight. Clouds of mosquitoes so thick a body could choke on them. Wild animals—panthers and snakes. To say nothing of the Yemassee, the native inhabitants of the area who had very good reasons for killing every Spaniard they saw."

"But you have to admit, it could have happened," Nat wheedled.

Still holding his glasses, Porcher lifted his hands in surrender. Diane straightened when he appealed to her directly.

"You seem like nice people," he said. "You can leave now, and I won't charge you. I had to be here anyway today, and I got to hear a nice story, spend some time with a couple of charming ladies." Gray strands of hair brushed his shoulders when he tilted his head. "Or I can take your money and have a look at what you've brought with you. It's your call."

Diane's purse and the crisp stack of twenties she'd withdrawn from the ATM on their way out of Emerald Bay this morning weighed heavily from her shoulder. She glanced at Nat. At the girl's pleading look, she gave in with a long, slow exhale. Having come this far, they had to see it through. Otherwise, the possibility that they'd walked away from a gold mine would eat at them for the rest of their lives. A few hundred dollars seemed like a small price to pay to put an end to that uncertainty.

Retrieving the envelope of cash from her bag, she placed it in Porcher's meaty hand. "I know you think it's foolish, but I would like you to appraise the pieces we found."

Diane picked *fool* and *money* out of the words Porcher mumbled under his breath while he tucked her envelope out of sight. He settled the glasses on the bridge of his nose. From a drawer in a built-in wall unit, he withdrew a pair of thin rubber gloves and a square of black velvet, which he spread on the counter.

"If you could lay the pieces there," he said. Nodding toward the pad, he tugged the gloves over his wrists.

Diane shot Nat a look that she hoped held more encouragement and less doubt than she felt. Hesitantly, she pulled out the coin and earring they'd brought with them and placed them on the velvet. The yellow metal gleamed as bright as the sun against the black background.

"Hmmm," Porcher said.

Diane swore the tension in the room

increased ten-fold when the man bent low to study the pieces. Without taking his eyes off the coin, he flicked on a florescent desk lamp and adjusted the light until it shone directly on the metal. Porcher removed his glasses, rubbed his eyes, and re-settled the rims on the bridge of his nose.

"Hmmm," he repeated.

Retrieving a small brush, he ran it over the earring. "You say you found these buried in the ground?" he asked. Without waiting for an answer, he pointed to several tiny white dots on the black cloth. "See that? That's sand."

"I'm sorry. We cleaned everything off as well as we could," Diane offered, feeling a little like a housewife whose preacher had dropped in unexpectedly and found last night's dinner dishes still in the sink.

"No, no. It's all good. The sand supports your claim." Leaving the earring on the black cloth, Porcher turned the coin this way and that in his gloved fingers. Next, he withdrew a rectangular stone and scraped the coin across it.

"Stop!" Nat cried. "You'll ruin it."

Porcher chuckled. "Ruin my touchstone, more likely. This doesn't hurt the coin at all. I'm going to test the scratch with acid to determine purity. If the coin is made of any other metal besides gold, we'll see blue or green, or even white."

"And if it's gold?" Nat challenged.

Laughter rumbled in Porcher's chest. "If it's gold, there won't be any reaction at all."

"He's right," Diane interjected. She'd seen Leon step through the same process when he evaluated one of her bracelets for insurance purposes.

Porcher applied a drop of liquid from a tiny bottle to the surface of the touchstone. Leaning over the results, he grew serious. "Humph," he grumbled.

"What'd you find?" Nat tried to peer over his shoulder.

"Quiet, now," Porcher hushed. "I have to concentrate."

For the next hour, the burly man continued to make noncommittal sounds while he utilized a scale, microscope and several other pieces of equipment to examine the coin and then the earring. At last, he returned both pieces to the black cloth. For a long minute, he stared down at them with an expression Diane couldn't quite decipher.

"You say this map, this treasure map, has been in your family for a while? You still have it?" he asked without glancing up from his workbench.

Why the sudden interest in the map, Diane wondered. Perplexed, she said, "Yes. My grandparents moved to Florida in the early Sixties. Grampa said he found it when he was clearing the land for the house. That had to be before 1963, because that's when they moved in."

"Roughly sixty-two years, then. And you have it, the original?" he asked again.

"Yes. It's made of leather." Nat stepped a tiny bit closer to the coin expert. "My aunt recently had it framed. It's hanging in the library. Grampa found an old tricorne hat with the map. We have that, too."

"Good. Hang on to those. You may need them down the road."

Porcher seemed to have trouble wrenching his eyes away from the coin and the earring. Finally, he turned. Leaning against the counter again, he stared intently at Diane and Nat. "Now, one more question. You brought me these two pieces. Are there any more?"

Diane hesitated. Where was this conversation headed? She glanced at Nat.

"A lot," the girl blurted before Diane could stop her.

Porcher threaded his fingers through his beard. "Define *a lot.*"

Diane fought an urge to throttle the girl when

the man's no-nonsense order loosed a torrent of words from her niece.

"We have the other earring and a matching necklace," Nat babbled. "A long chain, a choker with, um, diamonds and emeralds, and one bar about an inch wide." She held her fingers eight inches apart to indicate the length.

Having lost the battle, Diane sighed. "There are another forty-five gold coins like that one." She pointed to the black cloth. "And two dozen other coins. We think they're silver, but they're badly tarnished. I was going to clean them when we got back this afternoon."

"No. Don't do that," Porcher said quickly. "You'll want a professional to handle that for you."

"Why is that?" Diane stared into Porcher's eyes. What she saw in them filled her with unease.

"Because the coin and the earring you brought me are…" Porcher stopped as if at a loss for words. "Impressive," he finished. "Assuming the silver coins are from the same time period, you'll want to preserve their integrity." He harrumphed, and a tiny flicker of humor danced across his face. "Just to be clear, that means you don't want to get the cheap commercial silver polish you picked up at the grocery store anywhere near them."

"And you'll do that for us—clean the silver

pieces, that is—for a price?" Diane hated the doubtful note in her tone, but she felt powerless against it.

"It won't cost you a dime." Confusion swam in Porcher's eyes. "I'll do it just for the privilege of handling such a unique find."

"You've called our discovery impressive. How exactly is it impressive? Is it historically unique?" So far, Diane hadn't heard one word about the value of what they'd found.

"I believe your pieces probably came from one of the Spanish treasure ships lost in 1715. Twelve ships set sail from Havana that July…"

"Twelve?" Diane had to interrupt the man. "I thought there were eleven."

"You know a little bit about that disaster, do you?" Porcher's eyebrows lifted. "Many people overlook the *Griffon*, a French warship, which was also part of the convoy. That brought the total number of vessels to twelve. Oddly enough, the *Griffon* was the only one that made it to Spain. The other eleven ships were destroyed in a hurricane."

Porcher paused long enough to glance over his shoulder at the coin and earring, as if he needed to make sure they were still where he'd left them. "It's most likely that these particular pieces are from the *Nuestra Señora del Carmen*.

Her wreckage is just off Vero Beach. We'll know for sure when we compare the jewelry you found to the *Carmen*'s manifest. But if what I suspect is true, it would make yours an important historical find."

"Historical," Nat echoed. Her posture slumped as disappointment bent her shoulders. "So, it'll end up in a museum somewhere?"

"Uh, no." Removing his glasses, Porcher rubbed his eyes. He took what seemed like a much-needed moment to gather himself before he said, "Follow me." In four short strides, he walked to a rolling cart that held a shelf of books. Running his finger over the spines, he chose a heavy tome, which he plunked down on top of a glass display case. He paged quickly through thin sheets of paper until he reached a spot near the middle of the book.

"This is the price an eight escudo coin made of eighteen carat gold brought at auction last year," Porcher announced. "The one you brought me is in better condition. Handled correctly, yours should fetch slightly more."

When the appraiser tapped his finger beneath a figure that made Diane's head spin, numbers with far too many zeros buzzed in her head like bees around a hive. That was the problem with being an accountant, she thought. She didn't need a calculator to do the math. Tears filled her eyes. "You're telling me…"

"What?" Nat demanded.

Diane swallowed. Swaying slightly, she whispered a barely audible, "Millions."

She watched as the expression on her niece's face morphed in quick succession from utter confusion to understanding.

"Oh, my Lord," Nat whispered. "We need to get to the inn right now!" she cried.

Porcher's head swung. A look of concern deepened the lines around his eyes. "Tell me you aren't keeping such an important find in a shoebox under your bed."

"Not exactly." Laughter that bordered on hysteria spilled from Diane's lips. She clamped one hand over her mouth. "A back…pack… stashed…in my…closet," she gasped.

Like an actor in an old TV show, Porcher grabbed his chest. "You two are going to give me a heart attack," he warned.

"Okay, before you do anything else," Porcher directed once they'd all taken a much-needed moment to regain control. He issued marching orders in short, staccato bursts. "Get the backpack. Take it to a bank. Any bank. Open up a safety deposit box, one big enough to hold the entire bag."

LEIGH DUNCAN

"Safe deposit box. Got it," Nat echoed.

"Do it now, before word gets out."

"No one knows," Diane assured him. "Just the three of us."

"Word always gets out." Porcher spoke with the voice of experience. "You haven't told your mother? Your husband?" He pinned Diane with a laser-sharp gaze.

"No one," she repeated. Who would she tell? Her mother was dead. Her husband was on the opposite side of the state. Besides, she and Nat had agreed to sit on their news for the time being.

"We didn't want to get anyone's hopes up before we knew for sure," her niece explained.

"I'd advise you to keep it that way for a while longer." Porcher stroked his beard. "You'll need to have the rest of the collection appraised, coin by coin, gem by gem. I can recommend someone if you…"

"You won't do it for us?" Diane asked.

"Yeah, we want you to do it," Nat insisted.

"I'd be honored." Porcher seemed to struggle to find the right words. He pressed a meaty fist to his chest. "I've dreamed of handling a discovery of this magnitude my entire life. It means a lot to me that you'd trust me. I'll do right by you. I swear I will."

346

Diane paused long enough to let the logical side of her brain kick in. Porcher could have lied to them. He could have said their discovery was worthless and offered to take the coin off their hands for mere pennies. Depending on his skills at sleight of hand, he could have stolen the earring or swapped it out for junk jewelry. He'd done none of those things. Instead, he'd given them sound advice and been more than aboveboard in his dealings with them. She stuck out her hand.

"We'll have a lot to discuss over the coming days. Agreements will have to be signed. For now, though, Mr. Porcher, welcome to the team."

"Thank you," he said, taking her hand in a firm grip. "This means more to me than you can ever know. And, if you wouldn't mind, I'd appreciate it if you called me Wyatt."

Eleven

Diane

"What's this big announcement?" Scott barged into the family quarters like an irritated bull who'd just been let out of the chute at the rodeo. "And why couldn't Fern come with me? You know she's pregnant, right?"

"Relax, Scott," Diane soothed. "Nat and I will explain everything when Belle and Aunt Margaret get here. In the meantime—"

"Nat?" Scott growled. "I thought this was just supposed to be the seven of us."

Diane's instructions had been firm—no one other than those on a list that excluded spouses and children could attend the mandatory family meeting on Saturday evening.

"If I'd known Nat was gonna be here, I'd

348

have brought Fern and the girls," he continued.

"I'm glad you didn't," Diane replied softly. "I love Fern and my nieces. But I have a very good reason for not including them tonight. And before you get your dander up, I didn't invite Tim, either. Now will you please open the wine? I think everyone could use a drink."

"I sure could," Kim said from her usual spot at one end of the couch. "If I have to give up a date with Craig for this meeting, a glass of wine is the least I deserve."

While Diane admitted that getting everyone together on a weekend night might put a crimp in their style, she refused to apologize. In this case, she was pretty sure the ends justified the means.

As for the wine, she could certainly use some. The last two weeks had passed in a blur of meetings with Wyatt, discreet inquiries into auction houses and so many hours of research she felt she could recite the manifests and bills of lading for all twelve ships in the 1715 fleet by memory. All that, along with handling the growing pains of a brand-new business and the needs of an active teenager, had worn her practically to a frazzle. But tonight, it would all come to a head, because this was the night she and Nat would share the results of their hard work with the rest of the family.

The rest of the immediate family, that was. There'd be enough debate between the seven of them about what to do with the windfall that was about to land in their lap. They didn't need to muddy the waters with the opinions of spouses, significant others or children.

"You didn't start without me, did you?" Amy asked. The baker breezed into the family suite carrying a cake box.

"Nope. You're right on time. We're still waiting on Jen. She's getting Caitlyn and her friend settled in the game room. The girls are manning the front desk while we talk." The two teenagers had been given strict instructions not to interrupt the adults unless the inn was on fire. "Belle's helping Aunt Margaret get ready. She wants to show off the new outfit she bought."

"Oh, good," Amy breathed. "I was afraid I was running late. The decorations you wanted for this cake took a minute. I hope you like it." Setting the box on the table, she began to open it.

"Let's leave that until later." Wanting to preserve the surprise as long as possible, Diane pressed lightly on the lid. "Could you help Scott with the glasses?"

"Uh, sure?" Reluctance showed in the glance she gave the unopened box, but Amy moved to the end of the table where her brother had plied the bottle opener with finesse. She lined up several glasses while he went through the usual motions of tasting the wine.

"Spice, blackberries, currants. Fruity," he pronounced. "I like it." He lifted the bottle and studied the label. "Expensive?" he asked.

"Not too bad," Diane hedged. In truth, she'd splurged on half a case of a top-rated domestic. After all, it wasn't every day her family had this much to celebrate.

The door to Margaret's room opened. Her aunt shuffled forward in a soft green tunic and flowing pants. The older woman struck a pose. "What do you think, girls?"

Kim eyed the new clothes. "That's nice. Where'd you get it?"

"I had to run to Vero to check out a venue for The Emeralds this morning. Mama rode with me. We passed a cute little boutique on our way to the church and just had to stop there on our way back." Belle, her makeup and hair flawless, offered her mother her arm.

"What's this all about, Diane?" Margaret asked as she sank into her favorite chair.

"We need to wait for Jen," Diane began.

"I'm here." The door to the family quarters closed with a snap behind the last member of the family to arrive. "The girls are all set. They're playing video games, but I made sure the pager is right where they can't miss it, in case one of our guests needs anything."

"Good." Diane waited until everyone had a glass of wine before she raised her own glass. "To family," she said, as tears pricked her eyes. "May we always be as close as we are tonight."

Truth be told, her wish was more a prayer than a toast. In the years she'd worked at Ybor City, she'd dealt with more than one lottery winner. People whose lives had been changed overnight by a sudden influx of wealth. Some hadn't been able to handle it; they'd spent every dime on a new, lavish lifestyle, blown through millions and ended up penniless in a matter of years. Divorce, squabbles with children, drugs and alcohol problems had plagued others. A few had dedicated their lives to preserving their wealth for future generations. She crossed her fingers and hoped her own family would make smart choices.

She took a breath and looked straight at Amy. "First off," she said, "no one is sick. No one is dying. I just wanted to get that off the table right from the get-go."

She'd known her sister would be worried. Sure enough, Amy pressed her palms together and whispered a silent, "Thanks."

"If it's not that, then why are we here?" an obviously irritated Scott demanded.

"I'm getting to it," Diane answered patiently. The discovery she and Nat had made was over three hundred years in the making. It deserved enough time to handle it correctly. With that in mind, she wouldn't be rushed. She was going to ease into this conversation her way, no matter what. Their news—as good as it was—signaled a major change, and change—good or bad—needed to be handled with kid gloves.

She cleared her throat. "Do you remember a couple of weeks ago when we were talking about the things we wanted to accomplish before Aunt Margaret sells the inn?"

"Our bucket lists." Kim nodded.

"Yeah. One of mine was to go on another treasure hunt using Grampa's map. Nat wanted to go, too." Her gaze sped over the room until it settled on her niece, who was standing against the wall. They'd decided earlier that Nat would handle this part. "You want to tell them about it, Nat?"

"I'd always heard that reading the map was the biggest problem." Nat's long strides took her to the center of the room, where she pulled a photocopy from a back pocket. "Aunt Diane and I solved that problem when we figured out that this tiny dot here was actually a compass." In short order, she led them through their adventure, stopping at the point where they'd pulled the first necklace out of the hole.

"If I hadn't been on my knees, trying to reach the bottom of a two-foot hole with a trowel, you could have knocked me over with a feather," Diane said.

"After all these years, you actually found something?" Margaret asked. "My goodness, that must have been exciting."

"Yes, ma'am," Diane said slowly. "More than one piece. There were three necklaces, a pair of earrings, a metal bar and some coins."

"A bunch of coins," Nat corrected.

"Where are they?" Belle looked around the room as if she expected to find the jewelry laid out on one of the coffee tables. "I'd like to see them."

"Yeah. Maybe we can divide them up so everybody has a memento," Kim suggested.

"It'd be cool if we could give everyone a piece at the reunion." Jen's voice filled with excitement. "We could make copies of the maps and use them like favors."

"I wouldn't mind having a piece of Grampa's treasure. You don't have it with you?" Amy's head tilted the way it did whenever she was trying to follow a complicated recipe. "Why not?"

Scott, who'd grown silent throughout the exchange, suddenly spoke. "Unless there's more you need to tell us?"

"Yes, there is." Diane motioned for silence. "The thing is, Nat and I were convinced the coins and jewelry were nothing more than cheap imitations. After all, everybody said Grampa drew the map himself. It stood to reason that whatever treasure he buried under those rocks, it wouldn't be worth anything."

"But we wanted to be sure," Nat interjected. "So we took a sample to a coin collector in Sebastian."

"What else did you think it could be?" Scott, ever the lawyer, asked the question that was on everyone else's minds.

Diane inhaled deeply. This was where things were going to get sticky. "Part of the 1715 fleet treasure?"

"Uh-huh."

Diane swore everyone in the room froze.

"And was it?" Scott probed at last.

"Yes." She let that sink in for a second before she added, "Forty-six of the coins are solid gold. Two dozen are silver. The necklaces are also gold. One doesn't have any stones—it's called a money chain. One has a pendant made up of emeralds and diamonds. The other one is a choker, decorated with more emeralds and diamonds. The earrings match the choker."

Scott slowly blinked. Softly, almost as if he didn't want to know the answer, he asked, "Total worth?"

"Ten point four million dollars…after taxes." Diane swallowed a burst of hysterical laughter. "Depending on which auction house handles the sale," she added lamely.

The silence that descended on the room was deafening. Not a sound, not a whisper broke the quiet. She didn't think anyone even breathed for a full thirty seconds.

Just when Diane was beginning to wonder if the shock was too much to bear, if she'd gone about telling everyone all wrong, Jen nudged Amy.

"Guess you don't have to worry about renovating Sweet Cakes Two," Jen said with a wild grin. "You can raze that building to the ground and build whatever you want."

Amy leaned forward to stare at Kim. "You can afford your own commercial kitchen. Or not. You never have to work again."

Belle draped her arm around her mother's shoulders. "You don't have to move to Emerald

Oaks, Mama. You can go anywhere you want. Or stay here if you want to."

Tears in her eyes, Margaret patted her daughter's hand.

Amy turned to her brother. "Just think—no more saving for college. You can pay off your house, your cars. Debt-free for the rest of your life."

"There's just one problem." Scott turned his formidable attention on Diane. "Where exactly did you find this buried treasure?

"Don't worry," she assured him. "It was on Dane property." As part of her due diligence, she'd traced the ownership of the land as far back as records existed. According to a survey taken when their next-door neighbors sold their home and moved up North, the property line ran just north of the big oak.

"According to Florida law, any treasure found on private property belongs solely to the owner of said property," Scott intoned as if he was quoting from one of the law books in his office.

"What's that mean?" Amy challenged.

"It means this treasure, this ten million dollars' worth of gold and jewels, belongs to Aunt Margaret. No one else is entitled to a dime. That includes you and Nat," he said, pinning

Diane with a no-nonsense look.

Air whooshed from several mouths as a different kind of silence gripped the room, a silence filled with dreams crushed as thoroughly as the coquina rock that lined the driveway. Diane's gaze fell on the box Amy had left on the table. Perhaps she'd been a wee bit hasty when she'd asked her sister to dust the cake with edible gold, she thought.

Across the room, Belle patted her mother's hand. The motion drew the attention of every single person in the room.

"What do you want to do with the money, Mama?" Belle asked in hushed tones.

Margaret sat motionless, her fingers gripping the arm of the yellow print Queen Anne chair that had been salvaged from a guest room ages ago. She stared straight ahead, her blue eyes focused on something no one else could see.

"Mama?" A hint of worry gathered in Belle's voice.

"Aunt Margaret?" Diane called.

Staring into space, Margaret sat in unblinking silence.

Thank you for reading
Treasure Coast Discovery!

Want to know what happens next in
Emerald Bay?

Sign up for Leigh's newsletter to get
the latest news about upcoming releases,
excerpts, and more!
https://leighduncan.com/newsletter/

Books by Leigh Duncan

EMERALD BAY SERIES

Treasure Coast Homecoming
Treasure Coast Promise
Treasure Coast Christmas
Treasure Coast Revival
Treasure Coast Discovery
Treasure Coast Legacy

SUGAR SAND BEACH SERIES

The Gift at Sugar Sand Inn
The Secret at Sugar Sand Inn
The Cafe at Sugar Sand Inn
The Reunion at Sugar Sand Inn
Christmas at Sugar Sand Inn

HEART'S LANDING SERIES

Cut The Cake
Save The Dance
Kiss The Bride

ORANGE BLOSSOM SERIES

Butterfly Kisses
Sweet Dreams

TREASURE COAST DISCOVERY

HOMETOWN HEROES SERIES

Mitch

Luke

Brett

Dan

Travis

Colt

Hank

Garrett

The Hometown Heroes Collection, Vol. 1 & Vol. 2

SINGLE TITLE BOOKS

A Country Wedding

Journey Back to Christmas

The Growing Season

Pattern of Deceit

NOVELLAS

The Billionaire's Convenient Secret

A Reason to Remember

Find all Leigh's books at:
leighduncan.com/books

Acknowledgements

Every book takes a team effort. I want to give special thanks to those who made *Treasure Coast Discovery* possible.

Cover design
Chris Kridler at
Sky Diary Productions

Editing Services
Chris Kridler at
Sky Diary Productions

Proofs
Raina Toomey

Interior formatting
Amy Atwell and Team
Author E.M.S.

About the Author

Leigh Duncan is the award-winning author of more than three dozen novels, novellas and short stories. She sold her very first novel to Harlequin American Romance and was selected as the company's lead author when Hallmark Publishing introduced its new line of romances and cozy mysteries. A National Readers' Choice Award winner and *Publisher's Weekly* National Best-Selling author, Leigh lives on Florida's East Coast where she writes heartwarming women's fiction with a dash of Southern sass. When she isn't busy writing, Leigh enjoys cooking, crocheting and spending time with family and friends.

Want to get in touch with Leigh? She loves to hear from readers and fans. Visit leighduncan.com to send her a note. Join Leigh on Facebook, and don't forget to sign up for her newsletter so you get the latest news about fun giveaways, special offers or her next book!

Made in United States
North Haven, CT
15 December 2024

62466713R00221